Men, Women, and Food

Ken Waldman

Men, Women, and Food

Ken Waldman

Ridgeway Press
Roseville, Michigan

Copyright©2025 Ken Waldman

ISBN: 978-1-56439-088-2

Ridgeway Press
P.O. Box 120, Roseville MI 48066

No part of this book may be reproduced or transmitted in any form or by any means electronic, mechanical, photocopying, or otherwise, without the express written consent of Ken Waldman.

Acknowledgments:

Grateful acknowledgment is made to the editors of the following anthologies and journals in which some of these stories, or versions of these stories, first appeared:

Anthologies
Movieworks: "Decisions"

Journals
Gargoyle: "Scientific Cuisine"
Heartland: "A Yen for the Sea"
Laurel Review: "Holden's Nursery Rhyme"
The MacGuffin: "Black Hair, Purple Lips" "My Grandfather's Story" "The Writer"
Octave: "Swampland"
Permafrost: "Not an Aztec Sundae" "Night and Rain and Stars and Everything Else"
Weber: The Contemporary West: "Mushrooms"
Wind: "Names"
Writer's Self: "Two Peas in a Pod"

"Black Hair, Purple Lips" was also previously published in *The Writing Party* from Mezcalita Press

Contents

Night and Rain and Stars and Everything Else 1
Decisions 3
Love, Sex, and Death 7
Not an Aztec Sundae 23
Swampland 26
Black Hair, Purple Lips 33
Five Spices Powder 37
Henry Speaks 42
Names 48
Two Peas in a Pod 54
Holden's Nursery Rhyme 57
A Yen for the Sea 64
The Writer 68
Mushrooms 78
The Legendary Nightclub 88
Oraño 93
Letters 102
Scientific Cuisine 115
Hagedorn Brothers 133
My Grandfather's Story 149
Whitemarsh 161
Tongue Talk 179
Sleep, Dreams, and Snow 194
More Decisions 205
The Ice Age 208

to my younger self

This collection is the direct result of a crowdfunding campaign. Every one of these backers helped make this print edition a reality: Paul Fericano, Rachael Fulbright & Charlie Carew, Elizabeth English, Hal & Lisa Tovin, Mark Tamsula, Barbara Rosner, Suzanne Todd, Stephanie Dickie, David Epley, Jennifer Spector, Sidney Myer, Alexis Knudsen, Jim Kruger, Sallie Mack & Jonathan Freese, Llysa Holland, Emily Pinkerton, Jamie Hascall, Jordan Wankoff, Jerry Hagins, Beth Chrisman, Eric Graves, Rich Russell, Cheryl Chrisman, Caitlin Warbelow, David McCormick, Maureen Kelly, Ellen Ferguson, Claire Holland LeClair, John Carnahan, Jay Best, Anne-Marie Holen, Susan Martin, Beth Nelson, Gabriel Furtado, Jeff Yeckel, Storm Walker, Perry Haaland, Hugh Robertson, Juan Romano, Bernard Ussher, Robert Daniel, David Volk, Jim Clark, Jeff Talmadge, Alison Moore, David Palmer, Emily Bunning, Joshua Kane, Chad Herzog, Jeff Corle, Kayla Oelhafen, Robert Baird, Tia Regan, Beth Nelson, Scott Sparling, John Freeman Jr., Michael Alexander, John Bunch, Stephanie Smith-Leckness, Hiren Amin. I deeply thank them!

Night and Rain and Stars and Everything Else

Once, there were two suns: a sun named Sun and a sun named Moon. The sun named Sun was a man. The sun named Moon was a woman. They lived together and were happy, and the world that was under them was a world that was happy too. Light was everywhere always. Flowers and grasses were everywhere always. Every inhabitant in the world below—from the largest, strongest animal beast to the smallest, weakest insect—respected each other everywhere always. Though no beings formally expressed their love to the two suns above, their every action expressed that love.

This world of two suns went along and along until The Sun arrived. The Sun was a sun from another world which had once had two suns: a sun named The Sun and a sun named The Moon. But that had not lasted, so The Sun had traveled, coming to this world where there were already two suns. Sun and Moon welcomed The Sun, and the three lived above the world that was under them, and shined more light than ever before.

This world of three suns went along and along and along. Sun loved Moon and Moon loved Sun. The Sun loved Moon and Moon loved The Sun. Sun loved The Sun and The Sun loved Sun. They loved each other equally.

But then, as The Sun loved Sun and Moon, The Sun remembered how once before he had loved The Moon. The Sun grew homesick then, and he began to spend more time with Moon. As time went on, as The Sun spent more and more time with Moon, The Sun began to love Moon more than Sun. Because Moon spent more and more time with The Sun, Moon began to love The Sun more than Sun. Because Sun noticed this happening, but didn't know what to do about it, he felt

angry, tricked, confused.
 Sun and Moon and The Sun stopped being comfortable around each other. Sun grew distant and stayed off by himself. Moon spent even more time with The Sun, and the two fell into a deep love that radiated fire. All the brightness hurt Sun's eyes. All the heat suffocated him. In the midst of great pain, Sun got the idea to travel. He wanted to find some dark place so he could forget about Moon and The Sun.
 Without Moon or The Sun knowing, Sun took off. He left silently. But before he got very far, he tripped and fell, first banging, then shattering into a million crazy, jagged pieces that took off in different directions into places where there was no light.
 Moon heard the noise, saw what happened, and though she knew she was already too late, chased and chased after the crazy, jagged pieces. She took half the earth to help her look.
 The Sun, who was no longer homesick, and considered his new home home, didn't want to leave. He stayed where he was.
 In the world below, the inhabitants have adjusted, not without complaints.

Decisions

"Five letters," the woman says as she stares at the crossword puzzle lying on her lap. "Starts with a D. Shepherd's flock."

"Drove," the man says as he rustles, then folds the movie page of the Sunday paper. "Like a drove of sheep or oxen. Like what we should have done a couple of minutes ago."

She scribbles the letters and furrows her brow. "I ought to just let you do this," she says.

The couple met almost a year ago at a party given by a mutual friend, a columnist for the weekly entertainment guide. At the time she was with another man, and he was with another woman. They talked briefly and found they worked within three blocks of each other: she as a technical writer, he as an assistant editor. That week they went to lunch. By Valentine's Day they had ended the old relationships and were sleeping together three or four times a week. In March they flew to Utah for a week of skiing. In May they found an apartment. The past month they have been talking about giving each other options. Last week he took an attractive writer to lunch, and she had an interview for an out-of-state job. This next week he is filling out applications to journalism school, and she is meeting one ex-lover for dinner on Monday and another ex-lover for drinks on Wednesday. For a second their eyes meet, and then she turns to the crossword puzzle.

"So," says the man after he drains the rest of his coffee. "The comedy, the drama, or the weird one? Or do you want to sit here all day and *not* see a movie? After all, brunch and a movie was *your* idea." He begins thumping the table with his knuckles.

"What time is it?" she asks, not looking up.

"Getting close to two," he says. "We're going to have to get moving no matter which we go to." He gives the tabletop one last thump before shifting his weight as if to get up. "So what'll it be? Honey?"
"Eight letters, third one's an R. Orange sphere." She begins drumming the table edge with the eraser end of the pencil.
"Some kind of ball. Fireball," he says. "Or else, I don't know, some kind of fruit. Now let's get going. Honey?"
"You're good at these, you know. It's got to be fireball." She jots the letters. "Now what were those movies again?"
"You mean you weren't listening?"
She shakes her head.
"The comedy's about a bunch of talking animals. It sounds stupid, but all the reviews say 'ironic, witty,' and stuff like that. It opened Friday. I haven't heard anything else about it. I'm not sure I want to see a bunch of talking animals for two hours, but I'll go if you want to."
"What else?"
"The drama stars Jack Nicholson as a psychopathic businessman. Sally and Clark said it was really bloody. The ads say 'surefire Academy award nominee,' 'a mature thriller,' 'Nicholson's superb—the performance of a lifetime.' It's called *Moneybones*. It's probably pretty good."
"Where's it playing?"
"Oh yeah, it's downtown. I don't want to drive downtown, but you like Jack Nicholson, right?"
"Did you say that was the weird one?"
"No, the weird one's low budget, all unknowns, a bunch of episodes three to twenty minutes long. It's playing by the university. Supposedly it's about getting into some character's head."
"Whose head?"
He shrugs. "I don't know. Some writer. Some unknown actor."
"What are the reviews like?"
"'Original, fascinating, worth seeing.' 'A strange, comic intelligence.' 'Unusual.'"

"Sounds weird, but interesting."
"That's what I was saying. The reviews aren't bad."
"You talk to anybody who's seen it?"
He shakes his head.
"What's it called?"
"*Men, Women, and Food.*"
"Well, I don't know," she says, looking down at the crossword puzzle. "They all sound the same to me. You choose."
"Me choose? You want me to choose? Last time I chose you hated the movie so much you said you'd never let me choose again."
"That was a while ago."
"That was three weeks ago.
She shrugs. "You know what your problem is? You're always so literal."
"We need to get going. What do you want to see? The comedy, the drama, or the weird one?"
"You choose," she says.
"You choose," he says.
"I need a ten-letter word," she says. "Gardener's midnight journey. Last three letters are A, P, E."
"Okay," he says as he goes to his wallet and removes a five-dollar bill. "We'll see the animal one. I got the tip. We've already paid the check. Put on your sweater and let's go."
"What about the weird one? I'm in that kind of mood."
"Okay," he says, "the weird one. Put on your sweater so we can go. I hate walking into movies late." He looks at the table. "Should I bring the paper with me?"
"Leave it," she says.
"What about the puzzle?"
"Leave it," she says. "Unless you want to bring it with you."
"Maybe I'll bring it," he says. "I can look at it while we drive there."
"I thought you'd drive," she says as they head for the door.
"You always drive."
"I don't always drive," he says. Then he goes back, grabs the newspaper, and runs to catch up with her.

"Why don't you drive," she says when he returns. "I'll drive to the theater if you drive home," he says.

"Let me think about that," she says, and pushing open the door, they have to shield their eyes from the autumn sun's glare.

"Killer sun," he says, squinting at her. "Should've brought some shades."

"You can say that again," she says, slipping her hand in his, her fingers squeezing.

Love, Sex, and Death

All he knew was this: the worst time of Saturday night, and he was walking up Tremont Street alone and cold. And to make matters worse, some drunk had punched the same song twice in a row right before he left the bar, so now the same eight jukebox words were spinning over and over, stupidly, in his head:

Slap Me
Slap Me
Pitiful
Oh Slap Me

He buried his hands further into his coat. It was no use. Either his gloves weren't warm enough, or his pockets weren't deep enough, because the chill penetrated, bullying him like he was nothing. It was *cold* out here. Too goddamned cold. Who the fuck ever convinced him that Boston was the answer?

Head down, body tight, he kept stepping on sidewalk cracks. It was a quarter to eleven. If he kept up the brisk pace, he'd be at work in ten minutes. Then he'd pour himself a mug of coffee and drink it down fast, even if it scalded his tongue.

Now his eyes watered from the whipping cold. He kept pace to the lyrics, eight steps at a time, and at the corner of Tremont and Boylston he took a left. The theater district, and up ahead groups of people were streaming out of wide-open doors. The marquees above were brightly lit. A NEW AND DELIGHTFUL EXPERIENCE, the bottom of one read. POSITIVELY WONDERFUL, declared another.

The sidewalks were full, but no one emerging took notice of the cold. The men all seemed overweight and hearty. They smiled like wolves. Their women were hidden under layers of make-up and clothes. Many wore furs. An aimless chatter hung over the length of the block.

He snaked his way through the crowds, trying to slip by as inconspicuously as possible. Up close, he could smell after-shave and perfume. These people were rich. Saturday night and this was their style, hopping from one entertainment to another, from dinner to theater to drinks. They traveled in big cars or taxis, and enjoyed a thick-skinned confidence. And him—he felt like a frostbite victim.

He was almost through them. He kicked at a pebble, aiming at a pair of black, shiny shoes. A few more blocks and he'd be at work.

"Dan? Danny Pearson, is that you? Over here."

It was a woman's voice, unexpected and warm. He stopped and turned. Two young women dressed in heavy camel's hair coats were standing and waiting for him. One he didn't recognize, but the other looked like Sandy Allen. It couldn't be; but yes, yes it was. The world was absurd. God only knew what Sandy Allen was doing running into him on a night like this. It had been at least two years since they had last seen each other.

"Danny Pearson. It *is* you. You have a beard! I didn't know you were in town!"

He watched them walk toward him, both in high heels, both taking measured steps. What could they want from him? Sandy was tall and pretty, and from Greenwich, Connecticut, the wealthiest town he had ever seen. For awhile at college she had gone out with a friend of his, Crazy Dick, the computer genius, the guy who spent his inheritance buying exotic drugs and throwing campus-wide parties. Crazy Dick was a character. And Sandy, he had forgotten all about Sandy. She stood in front of him now, reincarnated. Her friend was short and plain beside her. The two of them looked like they watched too much television.

"Danny, this is my roommate, Denise. She's in law school with me at BU. We came down to see the new musical. It was fun." Yeah, fun, he thought. He watched her smooth brown gloves wave and dart as she talked. "Denise, this is Danny Pearson, I think I told you about him once or twice. He's really a funny guy."

He looked down, not knowing what to do. It crossed his mind to start mumbling incoherently, to give them something to really laugh at. Instead he put his weight on one foot, then the other.

"No one even knew you were here in Boston," Sandy went on. "What are you doing up here? Are you in school?"

"Well, I'm not quite sure . . ." He heard himself trailing off and wanted to kick himself. If he didn't want to embarrass himself, he needed to act more sociably. "Say," he said. "Have you heard anything about Dick?"

"Haven't you heard? He's engaged to some hometown girl and working for his uncle in Pittsburgh. But that was a year ago."

Then she was quiet. And he was quiet. And Denise looked vacant and dumb, like she might never speak again. Gusts of wind were sticking into their faces. It was getting late. He stole a glance at his watch.

"Well listen," he said. "It was nice talking and running into you all, but I have to go. I'm working nights at the 7-Eleven on Charles Street. I'm running late. I need to go."

He was trying to be smooth, but knew he was speaking jerkily and fast, and with anger. Why? Was it from the cold? And he noticed Denise inching backwards, turning her head this way and that, like a scared, little muskrat. He didn't like that.

"Look, I'm doing okay," he said. Then he kicked at a sidewalk crack and looked up at Sandy. "Look, I work 50 hours a week and then come back to my room and write and think until I fall asleep. So what that I'm not in law school or working for my uncle. So what."

He caught his breath. Denise looked petrified. Poor, poor Denise; what was her problem? Suddenly he wanted to keep going and slap some sense into her pitiful muskrat mind. Ordinarily he would have. Tonight, though, it was too cold, and he was defeated before he could start. He stood there silently, for some reason not walking away.

"Danny, it was a pleasant surprise running into you." Sandy's gloves were now down by her side. She was stamping her feet to stay warm. "If you ever want to straighten yourself out and talk, or else just get together, give me a call. It's in the book. Or better, wait." She dug into her handbag for a pen and a card, wrote something on the back, and handed it to him. "That's my number. What's yours?"

"I don't have a phone."

"No phone? Not even in the building?"

"Yeah, in the building." He ripped the card in half, found his pen, and scrawled numbers. "Here," he said, and gave that half of the card to her. Then he stuck the half with Sandy's number in a pocket.

"Maybe you can come over for dinner some Friday or Saturday," she said. "I still remember how you love to eat."

He nodded, but their eyes didn't meet. They didn't touch good-bye. Then Sandy and Denise turned and walked away. He saw them begin to talk.

At once he turned in the other direction, and leaning forward, cut into the cold. The tempo quickened

Slap Me
Slap Me
Pitiful
Oh Slap Me

With long strides he rushed down Boylston, turning onto Charles. I'll fix you dinner, she had said. What a joke. He had absolutely no interest in law school or law students, and wasn't going to pretend that he did. Straighten yourself out, she had said. An even bigger joke. What did Sandy Allen know about Daniel Bart Pearson? She was good-looking, rich, self-righteous. All she saw was someone who wasn't dressed well, wasn't making much money, was barely getting by. A charity case. Well, he'd show her. Straighten yourself out, she had said. Why

don't you let yourself curve and soar, he should have answered.
He crossed the street, passed the hardware store, the plant store, the laundromat, and as he pulled open the door to the 7-Eleven, the song stopped singing in his head. The harsh fluorescent lights magnified everything: the shelves and shelves of candy bars and toiletries, the cooler windows full of juice, the dirty floor. Lines were long in front of both registers, and other customers were wandering the store's two aisles. Disco music pounded from the radio atop the Slurpee machine. At least it wasn't cold. He shook his head at Phillips and Dennis, the clerks working the 3-11 shift, and went straight to the coffee, and poured himself a cup. Phillips was big and broad and black. Dennis was forty and flamboyantly gay. And he, he fit in great: a tall, skinny, young white guy who wanted to write. Three sorry stereotypes: that was what they were. He shook his head once more as he hurried to take off his coat. Before Phillips and Dennis could leave, he had to do the accounting.

Coffee in hand, he began with the left register, the one that Dennis was using. 5, 10, 15, 18 pennies, 9 nickels, 22 dimes. He scrawled the figures.

"Daniel." The voice was aggressively gentle.

24 quarters. "Yeah, Dennis."

"He was here tonight, possibly the most enchanting young man ever. He was wearing a down coat, bulky stuff, but I could tell he had a body. The way he moved. And you know last night, Simon, you know Simon, well, Simon called me the sexiest, most together man in Boston. And he should know. That's one boy who's . . ."

$56.83. He left Dennis and moved to the right register. He counted quickly, without interruption. As soon as he was done he gave the register back to Phillips and stood for some moments. Watching Phillips work always made him smile. His square, black face was always sneering, always snarling. His every movement revealed anger and contempt. Phillips hated it here as much as he did, and there was so much to hate. The atmosphere. The pay. The . . .

But then he caught himself. How long had he stood there watching. Phillips wanted to go. Dennis wanted to go. He found the calculator on the back shelf, cleared a spot, and set to work. Every cent in the two registers and the safe had to match the amount transacted during the shift.
He filled the numbers and did the computations. Tonight he was lucky: first time through and the money balanced almost exactly, less than a dollar off. Good enough, he thought. He signed his name to the bottom of the cash control sheet. Then he poured himself a new cup of coffee and switched the radio from disco to jazz. As soon as he told Phillips and Dennis they could leave, their coats were on and they were pushing open the front door, disappearing in opposite directions.
11:25, the store was his, and as the jazz bounced, people kept coming and coming. Sometimes busy. Then busier. A parade of faces: boozed-up drunks, elderly insomniacs, one or two with their meaningless hellos.
"Hey fella, I'm in a hurry." He grabbed for Merits, Trues, Benson & Hedges. Then counterful after counterful of milk, eggs, detergent. Punch up the price. Tax non-food. Ask for money. Make change. Bag it. Again and again.
"I got a cab waitin' for me outside. Can you do me first?" He shrugged. An eye out for shoplifters. Drop the twenties in the safe. More people. More money. Faster and faster.
"Could you cut me a pound of bologna? And make it thin please?" A reedy, unpleasant voice, and he nodded with displeasure. The order was going to hold everything up. Slice the meat on the meat-cutter. Weigh it. Not enough. Cut three more slices. Too much. Stuff the third slice of bologna in his mouth. Chew and swallow while he wrapped the order, taped it, marked it. Then rewrap the meat and shove it back in the deli-case. Then a quick gulp of coffee before turning back to the customer. And more people waiting, impatient to leave.
No time to think, there was nothing to do but work. It was getting later, still more people, and imperceptibly the jazz had gone from a traditional energy to avant-garde soloing, the screeching saxophone first merging with bongo drums, then

veering off into electronics, the synthesizers like far-off galaxies of smoke, sizzle, suction, residue, all directed toward the dark prairie, the cratered savannah, the latitude that whirled: one part moon, one part Africa. He was not in the mood. At first chance he switched to a rock station. Across the street the lights outside the bar shut off and quit blinking. Finally the rushes in front of him became less frantic. Finally the lulls grew longer. It was like relearning how to breathe. Almost 3 A.M., and he was able to sip his coffee and relax. There was still a lot to do, but for the most part it was the kind of work he preferred: dull, menial tasks he could finish in solitude.

The store was empty now, the time to get things done. First, he wrapped the pastries and set them inside the pastry drawer. Then he began tearing open cartons of cigarettes, putting the loose packs on display. He worked on, his mind on the encounter with Sandy Allen. He couldn't understand why he had let himself be embarrassed earlier. Why hadn't he pointed his finger at her and said, Look Sandy, what do you want? Who are you to judge me and look at me like that? Who do you think you are?

The door opened, he turned his head. A shivering black transvestite. As soon as he warmed himself up, he fluttered his eyelids and gave him a smile. "Benson & Hedges Menthol, honey. How you doin' tonight?"

A smooth, cool voice, and every step was high-heeled and sexy. He often came in about this time.

He gave him his cigarettes and he stood at the counter, twirling his wig. Then he went into his handbag and dug up quarters, which he put in front of him.

"Can I have some matches now too, sweetie?"

He fished out a book and gave them to him. A wink. Then he watched him walk out, his ass wiggling under layers of clothes.

He shook his head and returned to putting up cigarettes. No doubt, there were bizarre characters walking the late-night Boston streets, and the transvestite was not atypical. He had no idea how they managed to get by. You couldn't tell by looking at them. There were old, raggedy ones. Mad ones. Others always high on drugs. Many came in night after night to steal bread or pester him. Depending on his mood, he sometimes offered them a cup of coffee or a sandwich. If he wanted to be alone, he chased them away.

But tonight was such a cold one that few people were walking in at this hour. It was fine with him. The rock and roll station played hits while he soaped and wiped the machines around the counter. A short break, and then he swept the floor and mopped it. Sandy Allen. What a coincidence. And what a waste, one more lawyer in a world filthy with them. He remembered her as a freshman, a tall blonde with a deep tan. It seemed like every upperclassman on campus was pursuing her because he always saw her in the center of a crowd around one or another of the fraternity benches. But spring of that year she fell for Crazy Dick, a guy down the hall who was only a freshman and shorter than her. He never could figure out the relationship. They went together for over two years, and it always looked like Sandy doted on Crazy Dick and Dick couldn't have cared less. When they broke up, Sandy dropped out of sight and Dick became celebrated for his drugs and his parties. That was when he really got to know Dick.

He finished mopping. It was 4:30, and Charles Street was motionless and dark. He sat on top of a counter and flipped through a magazine. Once the floor dried, he moved off of his seat and began straightening shelves. Up and down the aisles, section by section, from top to bottom, he carefully shifted cans and boxes. Peter, the store manager, relieved him on weekend mornings and he liked things neat.

Almost done, he moved down to the cookies. Once the papers came, he'd have to spend an hour putting them together. Peter usually came in by a quarter to seven. He couldn't wait. They'd talk a little, he'd say he could go, and then he'd shoot outside, run uphill the three blocks to his building on Pinckney Street, and take the stairs two at a time to the top floor. Once he opened that door he'd get right to work. Whatever else seeing Sandy Allen had done, it made him want to push on with his writing at twice the speed. Well, he'd show her. It would feel good to make a new start on that story he had quit on a week and a half ago.

He had not gotten far but he had plans to write something that would do justice to sex. He already had a title—"Love, Sex, and Death"—and the beginnings of an outline. Multi-leveled themes would run rampant, and through a mysterious, halfway-mad style he would re-enact the rhythms and swirls of his year dating Samantha, but compress the story into a single evening of lovemaking. He would tell all: the misunderstandings, the truths, the ultimate vision and emancipation. The potential was there. What he needed was the patience and discipline to sit down and execute.

Suddenly he put down the cookie boxes, hurried to the deli-case, took out a hunk of roast beef, and sliced himself three thick pieces. He was so hungry he couldn't eat fast enough, and as he chewed and swallowed and thought some more about his story, he moved to the coffee machine and started a fresh pot. Coffee was necessary. He'd load up on the stuff the next few hours while it was free for the taking. He had a long morning of writing ahead.

The roast beef wasn't bad, and a good portion of it remained, juices dripping. Just as he was debating whether to cut himself another slice, the door swung open.

"150 papers delivered. Mark it."

He turned but saw no one; that guy doing the *Sunday Globes* was fast. He left the roast beef and walked to the front door. Eight tied bundles, each of them waist-high, were lined-up outside.

As soon as he opened the door, he froze. It was no longer black, but a heavy gray. He dragged in the piles, two at a time, to a free area in front of the magazine stand. Once the papers were all in, he cut the cords. Then he went back to wrap the meat and return it to the deli-case.

Past 5:30, and it was getting lighter and patchier by the minute. Charles Street was spooky and deserted. He switched the radio back to jazz. A good choice. The music was languid and cool, an old Miles Davis standard, the sad, proud trumpet promising at any time to drive into something upbeat.

No one was in the store, and for almost an hour he worked steadily to the music, putting two, sometimes three papers together per minute. Peter would arrive in another twenty minutes, fifteen if he was early, so he slapped the papers together even faster, pausing occasionally to stretch his aching back as he skimmed the comics. He'd get to his desk by 7:15. He was sure he could write six or seven pages before he fell asleep.

Only a half dozen papers left, the last ones until next Sunday. He had to bend low. His back hurt. He didn't care. As he put the last one together, he glanced at his watch. 6:40. He looked around anxiously to see what else had to be done.

He remembered the cookies and rushed back to the far end of the far aisle to put the rest of the Oreo boxes in order. Then he quickly examined all the shelves: both sides, both aisles, the back cooler. Good—everything in the store looked untouched and somewhat appealing; even the floor was clean. Back behind the register, he wiped down the counter one last time and started a fresh pot of coffee. Then he switched the radio from jazz to the mainstream pop that Peter preferred. It was a quarter to seven.

Five minutes later it was ten to seven. He waited patiently at first, feeling more helpless by the minute as he stood at the counter and watched the second hand circle the clock face. 7 o'clock. Then 7:01. He began writing notes for his story, but it was impossible to concentrate between the customers trickling in, early risers out in the cold to buy essentials. He rang up the purchases curtly.

Twice he ran to the phone in back and called Peter's house. Twice there was no answer; he must be on his way. He leaned against the counter. He paced from the newspapers to the ice cream freezer. He tried to think about his story, but more people were strolling in all the time. Not many, but more; and they took up his attention. Bacon, eggs, orange juice, the Sunday paper: $6.18. It was past 7:20 now. Where the fuck was Peter?

The woman gave him a five and a couple of ones. $6.18—was that it? No quarters in the register, and as he broke open a new roll, the first chord of a song took him—it was that same pitiful jukebox song, he couldn't believe it, the same fucking song, and he didn't notice the customer rap her knuckles on the counter and demand her change. $6.18 out of $7.00? He handed her the coins. She took the money and picked up her bag of groceries.

Then he was alone.

For a minute he stood behind the counter nor really thinking, but then, as he listened to the lyrics, something clicked. Walking to work in the cold, seeing Sandy Allen, working this job, having Peter show up late—the whole situation seemed like someone else's problems. Now there was melody and irony. Now there was song. He smiled bitterly, and, funny, began to feel himself breathe more deeply and relax. *Pitiful, Oh Slap Me.* He was really listening, and, yes, it was true. He was pitiful. His life was a joke. Someday he would die. For the first time, it seemed, he was beginning to understand how everything related: how he was nobody yet somebody, how he needed to somehow go broke or get broken if he wanted to make it, how he didn't need pity. Just as he was making sense of it, Peter burst into the store and stalked the lengths of both aisles.

"D.P., looks good in here. Sorry I'm late, but nothing I could do. Damn Chevy of mine didn't want to start in the cold. Took forever. Say, it looks good in here. You must have been feeling good last night."

He mumbled something back. Peter was short and squatty. Must have been 5'9" and 200 pounds. Usually he amused him, but this morning the little tub was moving too fast.

"What did you say? Nothing to do? How about helping me out for a couple of hours. It'll add hours on the paycheck." Peter was already hunched over the left register, beginning to count the money.

He yawned twice, but Peter gave no indication of getting the hint. "Last night was busy as anything," he finally said. "Do you mind if I go?"

"You sure? Time and a half for staying." Peter finished with the dollar bills, made some notations, then closed the register and moved to the one he was tending. "D.P., give me a half hour and I'll pay you for the full hour. This weather means it'll be busy. We needs four crates of milk and another four of juice in the cooler. That'll do it. You can bring it in or let me. Either way."

There was no arguing unless he wanted to anger Peter. He thought about all the things he could have said, but, as usual, it was not worth the trouble. He turned, headed back to the stockroom, and brought in the crates. He realized the half hour made no difference, but this was one of those fine lines—it made no difference and all the difference—and he was being fucked over again. He threw the quarts of milk and orange juice into the cooler as fast as he could, filling it completely. When he was through, he lugged the extras back to the stockroom.

"Hey Peter," he called. "It's all in. Okay? I'm getting out of here."

"Hold on a second. We need a couple cases of Coke and one each of Diet Coke and Pepsi. Then go on home and get your rest. It's been a long one."

He brought it all in, and finished without saying a word. Then he put on his coat, grabbed a Sunday paper, and grunted good-bye. The clock on the wall had 8:30, and when he pushed open the front door, the cold hurt. The natural light seemed false and odd. His eyes didn't want to adjust, and he moved slowly down Charles Street looking at big, out-of-focus storefronts. At Pinckney Street he took a right.

He hated the walk up Pinckney in the morning after a night of work, and this morning the hill felt steeper than usual. He leaned forward with both hands in his pocket, the newspaper set in the crook of his arm. The wind was against him. Keeping his eyes on his feet, he walked the middle of the street until the slope finally leveled off. Then he looked up. His building was to the left, just past the realty office.

He fumbled with the key and pushed open the front door.

Sixty more steps and he'd be in his room. He knew those circular, winding steps well, and as he used the banister to help pull him up, he counted each step, twelve to a floor. As soon as he opened the door, he heaved the newspaper onto the bed across the room and stood dumbly in the doorway. For a minute or two he stood there until he remembered to take off his coat. Usually he liked to think of his room as cozy, but on a morning like this there was no getting around it: the twelve foot by ten foot space was a dump. Narrow bed, small bureau, desk, and chair. A clutter of papers and books. His only luxuries were a small refrigerator, which he kept stocked with beer, and an old AM-FM radio/cassette player. There was also the luxury of living by himself. But as he surveyed the room, he now took in the empty beer cans, the dirty clothes, the dinginess. As he stood there, he realized he hadn't swept the floor in months.

He wanted a beer, but he also wanted to wait. But if beer wasn't it, what should he do next? For awhile he stood there like that in the middle of the room, trying to remember what he'd been thinking about earlier. Then he bent over, untied his shoes, and slipped them off. Tiredly, he shook his head. Some energy returned. It was no use, he knew, but he found himself at his desk, shifting the chair into position. When he felt comfortable, he opened his notebook.

It felt better than he thought. First, he recopied the paragraphs already done to his liking, the beginning that two weeks ago he felt was foolproof. He wrote slowly and neatly. When he finished recopying, he stopped to reread it:

Love, Sex, and Death

```
                nddwwo
        ullaan      onnddeer
     rrffu      ddd       ard rgg
       ee       nn dd      noo oo
       dd        aa       ddudd ii
       nn               ddn    dud nn
       oo                    nuu   nn gg
       ww                        oorr  aa
```

20   Men, Women, and Food

> Starting here. No, there. Yes, everywhere, the story of love and sex, all emotions (except the blinking, streaming lights, and the scariest of all hallucinations—DEATH) compressed into 1/5 of a page. That's it, and it's a whirling, twirling skip of swirls into circles. Curls and hammers. No sense. No, actually a futile, inner, high-speed heightening of sense. An invasion of the deep reality coming every which way into a liquefied middle full of royalty and fun, fun and royalty, and royalty and fun and mud and mad and the meaning of men, women, and food and . . .
>
> . . . and I cursed God when it all finally stopped rolling around and left me alone to think and to be.
>
> The truth is I met somebody and at one point I thought I was dead. Dead. yes dead. That's it. I thought I was DEAD. It's all starting to come back now. Let's see. Tell me if these things really happened.

He stopped and stared. Reading it again, he couldn't quite believe it. He had forgotten what that page looked like.

For ten minutes or more he reread his beginning, unable to understand how he had gotten excited about the project in the first place. Not only was it terrible, it was something worse, something that had no name. It was terrible. Terrible. Everything was terrible. Without realizing it, he had begun drawing cartoon faces of men wearing glasses. Looking down at them, a half dozen frames and faces scrawled over the margins, the only thing he could think of was that he needed something to drink.

He pushed himself out of his chair, walked to the refrigerator, and reached for a can of Schaefer. He opened it and took a long gulp. It felt good to pace the room in small circles, beer in hand, and think. Finally, he took one more gulp and sat down at his desk. For a while he stared at the paper and drank.

As soon as he finished the beer, he grabbed another can, and this time, while he was up, he stuck a tape in the player. It was from an old concert, the Grateful Dead, and he cranked the volume. He didn't care who he woke. The first beer had tasted good, and he knew this one would taste better. When he sat back down at the desk he felt loose and eager. The music sounded great, and rereading the beginning, he decided it wasn't so bad. He quickly added a couple of lines that grew into a page. When he read it back, he saw that all he needed was to keep writing.

He worked and reworked sentences, trying for just the right fit, but he was grabbing for his beer, his beer was gone, and, besides, the last song of the side was almost over. He found another beer, and when the song ended, flipped the tape. Then he opened the bureau drawer in which he kept his pipe and bag of marijuana. He filled the bowl enough for three hits.

When he returned to his desk, he began writing Crazy Dick a letter. Quickly the letter stretched to five pages, complete with diagrams, and he even drew a map showing where on Boylston Street he had run into Sandy Allen. As long as Crazy Dick hadn't changed too much, he would read it and laugh. He folded the letter triumphantly and slid it into an envelope. He was confident he'd somehow find Crazy Dick's Pittsburgh address.

He returned to his story, but with three empty beer cans on his desk, he needed a full one. He got it, and while he was up changed the cassette tape. Jazz would do it. Then he sat back down at his desk and began to recopy his story, this time planning to incorporate the two new paragraphs.

Midway through the first curlicue, however, he stopped and riffled through his notebook. On a blank page he addressed another letter, this one to Samantha, his old girlfriend. He took a chug of beer. Then another. He wrote a few sentences, feeling hot and dizzy. Then he got an idea—he quickly walked over and shut off the cassette player.

The silence helped. How the fuck could anybody ever do any thinking listening to music like that? For a second he thought of digging through the mess for his copy of *The Catcher in the Rye*, a book that invariably inspired him when he felt like giving up. But then he thought better of it.

Instead he sat down on his bed, put the beer on the floor next to the Sunday paper, and dully took off his socks, his pants, and his shirt. Then he crawled under the covers. His could feel his throat as he swallowed, like it might be getting sore. He swallowed again, focusing. That was all he needed, he thought, as if he didn't already have enough problems. One thing he couldn't afford was to get sick and miss work. He glanced at the clock: 11:30. Work was less than twelve hours away. Just to be sure he didn't oversleep, he set the alarm for 10 P.M.

He picked up the paper and sucked on the beer, but he was getting too tired to either read or drink. He set down the beer, then the paper, and then shifted himself into a ball, curling tight beneath the sheets. He tried to shut his eyes, but they wouldn't stay shut. Instead he stared at the ceiling. There, above the bed, directly overhead, was a hairline crack about four inches long, the dirty paint peeling all around it. He kept staring at the crack, amazed he had never noticed it before. What else had he been missing? It took a long time, longer than he expected, and when it happened, he didn't feel himself fall into a vast, dreamy sleep.

Not an Aztec Sundae

"I'd like a scoop of vanilla ice cream, topped with tabasco sauce."

I eyed my date quizzically. That was supposedly an appetizer. I wondered what would pop into her head next.

"I'd also like a piece of black bottom pie and a turkey wing," she said. "That's all, thanks."

The waitress must not have thought it unusual. She took the order without question. I thought that black was not white. Meanwhile, I decided to order a shrimp cocktail and a charcoal broiled steak. That would show my date I was not going to sit still for nonsense, I thought. I also thought that Boston was not New York, and that bicycles were not jets.

The waitress left, taking the menus with her. I scratched the top of my forehead where my hairline receded. What was there to say to this woman I sought to impress, whose implausible veneer I wanted to crack? The trouble was she had already one-upped me. She had ordered a meal that was theoretically impossible. There was no black bottom pie, no turkey wing, on the menu.

"Do you always order ice cream before your entrée?" I asked. My manner was impeccable. My voice did not quiver and my gaze was straight.

"I always try putting a striped ball in first, if that's what you're getting at."

My expression must have shown I had not understood.

"Let me put it another way. I always sing north and flag a train before arriving at new fortune." And she sat in front of me safe and sunny, as if sure she had told me a wonderful truth.

I pretended to understand, but nodded uneasily. I thought

that fish were not fowl and air was not soil. I thought that cats were not dogs and dogs were not wolves. I thought that wolves were not sheep.

She smiled—I thought a bit condescendingly—and said, "Wolves can be sheep, but I eat meat only when the piano's swinging, and I'm drinking, almost spilling, some really wild news."

"Does that have anything to do with the turkey wing?" Did I catch her nod? Perhaps. But certainly I caught the radiance, the bright white teeth, the wide smile, the glowing cheeks. I felt trapped. My mind raced. I thought that birds were not bees and keys were not locks. I looked to the right and saw a couple holding hands as they talked. Their eyes sparkled. Their lips danced. When I turned to my date, I found her busy playing with our forks. I said nothing, but thought how the earth was not flat and cows could not jump, that slippers were not mittens and glass was not straw.

The waitress set down our appetizers. Immediately I dug into my shrimp cocktail, dunking the shrimp in tangy sauce. My date let her tabasco-vanilla ice cream melt to the consistency of pudding. Then she slurped as she ate. When a few drops fell on her blouse, I watched her put her index finger to the spot. Then she slid her finger into her mouth, first licking, then sucking.

She looked satisfied, but when she took her finger out, she pointed it at me and said, "You know, speaking of gray, cleaning windows is not my idea of a good time."

Her tone was blameful. I thought how sugar was not flannel and wool was not salt, how two was not eleven, and that three was unlikely. "What do you mean that cleaning windows is no fun?" I shot back. "And what are you talking about, 'speaking of gray?'"

"What I meant was I go on vacation when sparrows call. I meant that I like it slow. What I'd really like is to walk down Main Street with Fred Astaire and sit on a park bench with the foolish prince."

Fortunately the waitress returned, carrying our dinners. A

big, thick steak was set in front of me. My date received a piece of pie and a turkey wing, both on the same plate. I did not enjoy my food. Instead I thought how that farmers were not sailors and holy men were not thieves, that mirrors were not truth and beauty was not easy, that money was not important and beer was no help. I thought more thoughts, none of which comforted me. As I struggled with the steak, my date quickly ate the black bottom pie. Then she picked up the turkey wing and began gnawing. After watching her first few bites, I asked her how she liked it.

She put down the bone and wiped her fingers on the napkin. "There's no real hurry," she said, "when a bird can't fly. Or when a man can't swim."

"What?"

"It's all in the stroke," she said as she picked up the wing, then broke it at the joint.

Swampland

You're driving southeast on route 50 in Carolina. Your forehead is sloppy, hot. Your clothes stick like paste. Since getting in the car you've fiddled with the windows and vent, but nothing's helped. This feverish humidity. Air-conditioner? It stopped working last week. All you want is ocean, and that's where you're heading. But all this stretch of road reminds you of is the worst job you ever had: washing dishes in a hospital kitchen.

That gig had lasted a month. That same winter you participated in a starvation study. For two hundred and fifty dollars you spent a weekend without swallowing food or liquid, attached to a machine that fed you through your veins. Every four hours a team of doctors took blood samples, weighed you, stuck a thin plastic tube up your nose and down into your throat to suck out bronchial fluids. When you had to urinate, you pulled your feeding machine with you down the hall to the bathroom. The machine, which was taller than you, was set on wheels, and rolled like a dolly. You lost ten pounds that weekend and read *Crime and Punishment*.

The time had passed slowly. You shared your room with a middle-aged man dying of stomach cancer. He had many visitors; you had none. Sunday night, as you finished the book, you hallucinated that you were simultaneously awake and asleep, and you believed you discovered the heart of something profound. Monday morning, before you left, you wanted to talk about this to the cancer patient, but didn't.

Now it must be ninety degrees outside. It's moonless. You don't see a single star. Your high beams light the murk. You cough. The radio crackles and flares, a country-western station from Kinston. You hear Willie Nelson and Waylon Jennings wailing away, crying for love. You turn off the radio and cough again. Steamy air whips through the window. You glance at the gas gauge. It's edging toward empty. Up ahead there's an intersection, lights. You slow down. On the near right corner's a beer and barbecue joint, motorcycles and pickup trucks filling the lot. You wonder why all the business, but then remember it's Saturday night, and guess people must come from miles. You see a gas pump and feel lucky. You pull up, get out, remove the gas cap, and stick the nozzle in the hole. With your left hand you wipe sweaty hair off your brow. The numbers on the gauge go around. Men are shouting, their voices mixed with the heavy metal rock of the jukebox. You breathe in equal parts motor oil, beer, and burnt pork. You look around for a name or a sign to this place, but there is none.

The nozzle clicks, and you stick it back in the pump. You walk inside to pay the bartender, a woman. Her back is to you. She's wearing tight black leather and she's got long, straight black hair. She looks beautiful from behind and you keep your eyes on her, not wanting to look right or left, not wanting to act the gawking stranger in a rough place. Still, you're aware people are talking about you. You feel people staring. Then the woman turns to take your money. Her face is swollen red, a round welt of boils. You look away, and she knows why as she gives you the change.

You hurry to your car and drive off. Just past the intersection you see someone waving on the other side of the highway. You slow down past the figure and pull off to the dirt on the right. You don't know what to do so you stay in the car, keeping the lights on, the engine running. A half minute later you shut off the lights. Then you kill the motor. Hearing a harmonica now, you're out of the car and crossing the road, looking. Beneath a scraggly oak, a light-colored black man with deep creases in his forehead plays music. Seeing you approach, he takes the harmonica down from his lips and sings, "Don't, Don't, Don't, Don't. Don't you do it." Then he moans the lyrics twice more before raising the harmonica back up to play.

You watch him and listen close. His fingers curl around the instrument like he's eating a half an ear of corn. His cheeks puff. Every once in a while he bends a note this way and that as if it's a long green twig and he's testing how far he can go before he breaks it. With the lights of the bar behind him, you get a good look. He's wearing a seaman's cap propped high on his head. The hair underneath, charcoal-colored over flecks of pink scalp, remind you of a used-up Brillo pad. His nose is wide and freckled. A bull's nose, you think. He's wearing a sweater full of holes, no shirt, a ragged pair of blue jeans, greasy boots. At his feet are a small box and a sailor's duffel bag. You listen as he makes music that sounds first like a train whistle, then like a gospel number, then like a woman. You think: where have I seen this guy before.

"You like my music?" the black man says suddenly, palming the harmonica before putting it in a pocket.

You nod warily.

"Joe Jefferson," the black man says in a sing-songy voice. "I want to get up in the morning," he sings, "clear 'cross this state. And I want you to drive me, white man, clear 'cross this state."

You shake your head. You're going the opposite direction.

"Born on the Blue Ridge highway. Between Deep Gap place and Blowing Rock town." He takes the harmonica from his pocket, starts to blow it, and frowns. Then he bends, sticks the harmonica in the box, pulls out another, which he puts to his lips. Playing this one, he starts bobbing at his shoulders, the motion like a current rolling through him so his arms, then his chest, then his waist, then his legs wag and shake. Soon he's tap dancing in those greasy boots, his mouth still blowing in the holes. You think: you've seen an old man in Chapel Hill do this routine at a fair. But that was someone different: darker skin, glasses, a hat with a brim. You look from the feet to the face, and study the cracks in the forehead. They're dancing too. Where have you seen this guy?

"I'll be here now for a spell," he says, stopping for a moment.

Then you watch him begin playing something that starts bluesy, but then sounds like hillbilly music, something you might square dance to. Every few times through, he breaks it up by singing, "Old Joe Jeff's an old black man, Take me Take me home." Once, though, he changes the words to, "You go leave me, you go on. Take me Take home."

You begin to say something, but stop. You should, but shouldn't. You cross to your car, get in, start it, pull onto the road, and accelerate. You know the scene you've just experienced means something. But what? You ponder that question the next thirty miles, past Maple Hill, Holly Ridge, across the bridge to Surf City. You wonder if the answer has anything to do with the rank smell outside, or the mosquitoes that keep flying into your windshield, one after another, smashing their bug guts on the glass. You wonder if it has something to do with Angola Swamp, the awful spot you've driven past this muggy August night. You keep wondering as you enter Surf City, take a right onto highway 210, and drive a few miles toward Topsail Beach. Then you park your car and get out.

In bare feet you cross the asphalt, then skip over sand to the highest dune. You climb it and stand there for a minute, looking out, smelling saltwater, listening to the waves, feeling a cool, steady breeze. You want to own it, so you run off the mound, shed clothes, and sprint into the surf. The tide's high. The bottom's sandy. You run and run, still only knee-high in water until the shelf suddenly drops, and you're splashing around, swimming. For a long time you play near that spot, breaststroking, butterflying, backfloating, and somersaulting. When the clouds lift, the stars shoot brilliant holes. As the tideline ebbs closer, you let one big wave carry you most of the way to shore.

Atop the sand dune you put on your shorts. Then you return to your car. You find a flashlight, then scrape most of the bugs off the front window, using the shirt you're holding. Then you settle back in the car, start it, and make a u-turn so you're heading back to Surf City. As you drive north you look out the passenger side window, watching the first light as it barely grows. At Surf City you turn left, inland, back to the swampland. You keep glancing at the rear view mirror, stealing peeks at the lightening sky. In front of you there is still the blackness. Past Holly Ridge, you re-enter the stagnant mugginess. It's like opening the lid to a jar of creamed corn going bad, and taking a whiff. You're positive today's going to be hotter and stickier than yesterday. You press your foot on the pedal, making the air fly. The nighttime is dying in front of you, petering out. You feel a bead of sweat trickle down your armpit. Then you feel another.

You approach Maple Hill in the half-light. Your headlights shine, but you can see without them. A dark bug splats against your windshield. A pickup truck comes at you, no lights, a gray speck against gray sky. The truck gets bigger as it approaches, then backfires as it passes. You see the truck in your rear view and watch it disappear. Still looking in the mirror, you see the eastern sky's pink.

You plan your day. You'll reach your driveway before the midday heat, parking the car under the maple. Then you'll nap, read, bathe, eat, doing what you feel like in no particular order as long as you stay in the shade. And then you'll go to sleep, and when you wake it'll be Monday. Work. Past Maple Hill, you realize you're nearing the intersection with the beer and barbecue joint, kitty-corner to where you met the black man playing the harmonica.

The black man. Then you figure where you've seen him. He's the old man version of Vernon, the mulatto dishwasher. Vernon. All that time you were so goddamned miserable in that hospital kitchen, not saying a word about it, only talking about books to the goddamned mulatto, Vernon, who stood there running the machine and whistling. And when you told Vernon you were quitting the end of the week, there he was, Vernon, tears in his eyes, saying *you, white man*, you seemed so happy, and your talking about books made him listen, made him think of taking a night class. On your last day there, Vernon had given you that copy of *Crime and Punishment*, had told you to think of him as you read it.

Vernon. You wonder if the black man's still at the side of the road, playing. Then you think that's unlikely. Possibly he's already caught a ride home. Or more likely he's dozing somewhere nearby. You decide you'll offer him a ride if he waves you down again. This time you're going in the same direction, only he has twice as far to go. You can drop him off at the interstate.

As you approach the intersection and slow down, you see four or five small dogs jumping and yelping, trying to climb the scraggly oak. You stop your car, shine the lights, then look up and see the feet. You try not to puke as you push open the door and get out. Joe Jefferson is hanging, naked, from the lowest thick branch, a rope knotted securely around his neck. You stare at what someone's done to him: his forehead's been branded; his balls have been cut off. There's a coppery-black stain beneath the body. The smell of the dead man has put the dogs in such a frenzy.

You don't know why, but you stand for a minute, looking. Then you know what you need to do. You run to the beer and barbecue joint. It looks empty. It's locked. You scout all around it, looking for a phone. There isn't one. Then you run back to the car, open the trunk, grab a tire iron, and threaten the dogs. They scatter only after you hit one hard enough to injure it. Then, on your tiptoes, you stretch to touch Jefferson's lower leg. It's hardening.

You scramble up the trunk and pull yourself onto the branch which the noose is tied. Straddling the limb, you ease your way to the rope. Reaching it, you saw through it with a penknife. The body falls, thudding against the dirt. As it does, you avert your eyes and tears come. The crying does it. You feel flushed. For a few minutes you remain perched, looking up and down the highways in all four directions. To the southeast, the violet sky is turning blue. You breathe deeply and it smells like sex.

Then you look down at the body. If anybody saw you here, you'd be in trouble. You ease back toward the tree trunk, scramble down, hurry to your car, and spread a plastic tarp over the back seat. Then you grab Jefferson under his armpits, drag him to the car, lift him, lay him in the plastic, and wrap him. You go back beneath the tree to look and see if anything's left behind. Twenty feet to the right you see something metallic, shiny. You go to it: Joe Jefferson's harmonica. You pick it up, finger it, and put it in your pocket. You look further in the grass, and in a short time you find his sweater, an empty duffel bag, and his box of harmonicas, all the instruments gone. You set the box in the trunk of your car. The sweater and the duffel you stuff in the tarp with the body. As you do this you remember the black man singing to you, remember his harmonica playing, remember his dance. You think: last night the man still had a lot of life left in him.

As you get in your car you look at the bundle in the back seat. Then you study your map. In the middle of the Blue Ridge, you find the area between Deep Gap and Blowing Rock. Monday can wait. The whole world can wait.

You roll down all the windows all the way, start the car, and pull out on the road. The sun's behind you. The drive will be hell, but the mountains will be cool when you arrive. Somehow you'll find Joe Jefferson's family, and explain.

You'll help as you can, staying for the burial, and beyond.

Black Hair, Purple Lips

"Sylvia, a light?"

"Why thank you, my pet," Sylvia could have said, but instead she gave Alfred a look. Not a look actually, just the slightest curl of a mouth and the briefest flutter of a right eyelid. It said that she not only expected Alfred to light the cigarette, but that he better do it with flair.

Sylvia blew a smoke ring. Then another. The smoke rings had a frail grace to them. They floated across the table, breaking up into Alfred's eyes. Sylvia watched Alfred's eyes water. Silly man, thought Sylvia, as she watched him smile weakly at her. I'm not looking at your eyes. I'm looking at your eyes *water*.

The mirror directly behind Alfred more than doubled Sylvia's pleasure. Not only could she watch Alfred's eyes water, but she could watch herself blow smoke into Alfred's eyes. The scene was perfect.

Sylvia blew another smoke ring, shifted her eyes from the mirror, and watched the ring float and float, and then fade at just the right spot. Then she looked back into the mirror. Her black hair rose up in a wonderfully complex pile of activity on top of her head. She admired, too, how her cigarette fit in her mouth as she smoked. The lips did it, and it was an experiment, this lipstick. The color was the same as her shoes, a pair of expensive grape-colored high heels Alfred had bought for her last month. She smiled at her black dress with its provocative low cut. Her bracelets were fine, but now she felt her earrings and necklace needed more flash, more something.

Sylvia blew one more smoke ring before setting the cigarette in the ashtray. She sipped from her glass of Chardonnay. She looked at Alfred, then the mirror. She saw herself, then beyond herself. She began to stare at what must have been a mistake. Behind her, one table away, a man wearing a golf visor was pulling out a chair and sitting down. His companion, a woman with waist-length blonde hair, wearing a teeshirt and blue jeans, was pulling out the chair directly behind Sylvia. Looking in the mirror, Sylvia watched her chair get knocked by the woman.

"Sorry," said the woman, who then sat down and maneuvered up to the table.

Sylvia turned in her seat, and gave the back of the woman's head an ugly look. When Sylvia saw that the man wearing the visor was staring at her, she smirked. The man wearing the visor looked at Sylvia's lips for a moment, shook his head, and then looked downward to where her left breast pushed against her black dress. Immediately, Sylvia turned to Alfred, picked up her cigarette, took a furious drag, and blew a thick, low-flying smoke ring that sailed across the table. Sylvia crushed the cigarette in the ashtray. Alfred fished around his vest pocket for a handkerchief, and when he found it, he gently dabbed the moisture from around his eyes.

"The nerve," Sylvia said.

"Nerve?" said Alfred. "What?" He began folding his handkerchief, making sharp, exact creases.

"The nerve," Sylvia repeated. "New money means no class as far as I'm concerned. Put a few dollars in their hands and every place is a pizzeria."

Alfred put the handkerchief back in his vest and stared at his drink. Then he picked it up and sipped. "Sylvia," he said as he swirled the drink in the glass. "Are you saying we should go out for pizza tonight? I thought you decided you wanted to come here for dinner." He nodded to her and smiled thinly as he set down the drink.

Sylvia took out a cigarette and gestured for Alfred to light it. "New money means you come into a nice place like this dressed in the latest of picnic attire. Alfred, this is no picnic ground. A look at the menu and the decor will tell you that." She leaned over and whispered to him. "Let me tell you some-

thing, Alfred doll. The man I used to see last summer took me on a picnic. In ninety degree weather we sweltered in a field drinking warm coca-cola and eating soggy tuna fish sandwiches. That's what he called food. And then he put his arm around my shoulder and said we would be each other's dessert. You can imagine how I felt. I was going to vomit and I told him so. And he thought his little picnic was so romantic. Well, I had my own secret treat after he took me home. And I'll tell you, it was no picnic." As Sylvia giggled, she could almost overhear the conversation at the table behind her. She strained to listen, and thought she overhead the word "bitch." She blew a smoke ring.
 "What do you mean, no picnic?" asked Alfred, his eyes watering.
 "You know, a picnic," said Sylvia, raising her voice so the table behind her could hear. "That informal time for ants and dirt." Sylvia looked into the mirror where she saw the man wearing the visor drinking from a bottle of beer. Sylvia sipped her wine. The man took another gulp of beer. Alfred flecked a particle of dirt off his dinner jacket.
 "Yes, dirt," Sylvia said, and as she spoke, she thought she overheard the man wearing the visor say, "whore." She blew a smoke ring. "Going on picnics, drinking kegs of beer, frolicking men and their whores, dancing in mud, studying worms. By god, where does it end? You get dressed for a night out and you find yourself in a middle of a picnic. Alfred, doesn't that bother you?"
 "Me?" he shook his head.
 "Just look in front of you with your own two eyes." Sylvia took a deep drag and blew. Then she looked into the mirror. There was nothing wrong with the way she looked, and for a second she smiled and saw herself smile. Then she looked farther to see what the man wearing the visor was doing. He was staring at her body, and nodding.
 "Alfred, let's go," said Sylvia. "I won't stand for it a minute longer." She crushed the cigarette in the ashtray, rubbing the gray and blackened tobacco on every surface of the glass.

"Go?" asked Alfred.

"Go," said Sylvia. "To dinner. We've had a drink. Take me somewhere nice for a change. Take me to The Club."

"The Club? But Sylvia, I thought you didn't like the food there."

"We'll try it again," she said. "Maybe they've hired a new chef." As she pushed back to get up from her chair, she thought she overheard the man in the visor say "poodle" and then "leash." She turned to look at him. He was talking to his woman friend. But when he noticed Sylvia staring at him, he stopped talking. His eyes went from Sylvia's shoes, to her hair, to her lips, to her breasts.

His woman friend turned so she could look too.

Five Spices Powder

I met Tanya a week ago Friday at a happy hour. After a few drinks I suggested dinner at my place. She declined. However, one thing led to another, and there she was sitting patiently at the kitchen table as I stood at the stove preparing a broccoli stir-fry with five spices powder. Now, if I get it in mind to seduce a woman, I sprinkle five spices powder in my wok, add vegetables, stir, and allow nature to take it course. Tanya was easy. Our shoes and socks were off even before we got to the fortune cookies. Then she practically forced me to feed her Chinese food all weekend. When she staggered out the front door Sunday afternoon, even her crooked grin wobbled. I walked her to her car where she gave me an unsteady kiss. We made a date for Friday at the bar where we had first met.

At work on Monday I realized that though I knew most everything intimate about Tanya, I really didn't know her at all. For instance, though I knew she'd get flushed and prickly if I wet my pinkie and made crazy eights around her chin and throat, I didn't know if she had any brothers or sisters. Though I knew her voice would take on a certain huskiness and her tongue would go absolutely wild once I got her aroused, I didn't know what kind of job she held or where she worked. Though I knew she'd pant "Godzilla" and make monkey sounds if she came more than twice, I didn't know how to contact her if she didn't show up on Friday. Tanya, Tanya. I realized she had no last name, no address. How had I been so stupid?

All week her lovely, thin body grew lovelier and thinner as I tried to re-create her. I fantasized that on Friday we'd walk into the bar at the exact moment and sit at the same bar stools as the week before. I'd start off polite and ask her who cut her hair, what bank she used, how she liked the past week's weather. She'd tell me to quit acting coy, and to try some new Asian recipes on her. The more I thought about her, the more I knew she was the woman for me—if only she showed up as planned.

Friday, I took off work early and went jogging. I ran along the lakefront dreaming of Tanya. It saddened me that I hadn't yet asked about her father or grandfathers. I didn't know if she had ever been married or engaged. I didn't even know who her last lover was, or who the lover before that one was. I wanted her to tell me when and with whom she had lost her virginity. Watching couples paddle around the lake in kayaks made me that much more desirous.

After jogging for almost an hour, I returned home. Then I showered and dressed, putting on the exact clothes I had worn the previous Friday. As I drove crosstown to the bar, I hoped I could arrange it so that we'd spend the night at her place, and that before going to bed she'd show me her scrapbooks. Saturday, we'd go for a drive and a long walk. It would be wonderful, I knew, to hold hands and listen to her tell me about herself as we walked. Then I would tell her about myself. The more I thought, the more I knew I'd be crushed if she had forgotten our date. I pressed my foot on the accelerator to make sure I'd be on time.

In fact, I arrived ten minutes early. I parked my car, and strolled the few blocks to the bar. There was Tanya, wearing jogging shorts and a halter top, waiting outside the front door. When she saw me come around the corner, she ran down the sidewalk to greet me. She put a hand on my arm and kissed me lightly on the lips. "I've been starving myself all week," she said, and her voice was already husky. "Take me prisoner. Drive me home with you." Then she slid her tongue into my mouth. "Are you hungry?" she whispered after the kiss.

"Now?"

She nodded and grinned.

"You don't want to sit inside and have a drink?" It's not even 5:00."

She shook her head.
"Now? Chinese food? My place?"
Tanya kept nodding. I felt her lean against me and I held her close. I knew I wanted a drink, but Tanya was rubbing her breasts against me.
"Okay," I said. "You win. But if you want Chinese food, I need to pick up a thing or two. You sure you don't mind being in Mr. Grocer fighting the crowds?"
Tanya put her hands on my shoulders and looked up at me. "I love going food shopping," she said. "And this will be a first, going in with you. Besides, maybe we can pick up some other fun foods."
"Now that's an idea," I said. Then we kissed briefly. "So, do you want to come with me, or follow?" And as soon as I asked, I knew I wanted her to come with me in my car.
"I better follow," she said.
"You sure?" I tried saying it in such a way that she'd understand what I wanted, but she didn't seem to get the hint. "If you do decide to follow," I said after we kissed again, "just make sure we don't get separated on the way."
"Don't worry," she said. Then she gave me a funny look. "You're not a worrier, are you? I've always given those types a hard time."
As I watched through the rear view mirror, Tanya followed closely, expertly weaving and speeding through the rush hour traffic. That part was fine. But when we got to Mr. Grocer, the scene there was even worse than I anticipated. The huge parking lot was full, and I pulled in next to a red, dented Pinto, hundreds of yards from the store. Tanya parked a few rows away. Even from a distance, it was obvious that inside was about what you would expect at Mr. Grocer on a late Friday afternoon. There were too many people, that was all there was to it. Tanya hurried across the parking lot while I lagged behind. As soon as I entered the store, I found myself a basket. Tanya was waiting for me, pushing a cart.
"Tanya," I said. "Let's make it quick."
"Okay," she said. "You go get your Chinese food. I'll find

you there, or you can find me in the produce section. See you soon." She gave me a tiny wave and blew me a kiss.

I knew exactly where to go, and a couple of minutes later had my jar of five spices powder. Since there were so many people in the store—the lines at every check-out looked long and slow—I decided not to buy another thing. Peanut oil and pineapple juice weren't essential; I could improvise there. And we could make do without a fancy dessert. If Tanya wanted produce, that was okay; but she needed to make it quick. I needed to get out of this place.

When I found Tanya, she was painstakingly checking over the cucumbers, seemingly unaware that her outfit was distracting every man who passed. I saw them looking, and as I hurried to her side, I noticed that her cart was empty except for a small cactus plant, a loaf of French bread, and a salami. I tapped her on the shoulder. "Let's go," I said.

"You get your Chinese food?"

"Yeah," I said, showing her the jar. "Let's go, Tanya."

"That's all you got? Wait, I want a salad."

I looked at the cart, then back at Tanya. She saw what I was looking at. "Yeah, I got sidetracked," she said. "As soon as you walked away I saw this stuff. Now I can make a quick sandwich while you're cooking. And I wanted to get you a house plant."

"Well, let's go."

"Wait, I want a salad."

"Tanya," I said, and as I glanced around, it seemed like people were pouring into the store from all directions, filling every aisle. "Tanya," I said. "Let's go."

"If you can't wait, why don't you buy more Chinese food or something."

"Tanya, I don't want anything else; I've already thought of it. Besides, I want to go home and cook you dinner. You're the one who was real hungry. Remember?"

"Just wait for me outside in your car then. I'll be by real soon. Promise." Then she blew me a kiss and sent me on my way.

Even the express line that looked the shortest took ten minutes. I paid for my five spices powder and put the jar in my pocket. Then I walked out the door and across the parking lot to my car. It felt good being outside, and after I opened the door and climbed in, I rolled down the windows, leaned back against the upholstery, and made myself comfortable. I would wait for Tanya, I thought, and fantasized myself waiting for her, forever, in the Mr. Grocer parking lot.

It was then that I began noticing the cars circling in search of parking spaces that didn't exist. I noticed one pointy-eared woman working herself into a slow frenzy because I was sitting behind the wheel of my vehicle, evidently not intending to move. At the right moment I glared at her. She drove off. A few minutes more and I remembered a Friday afternoon traffic jam I once got stuck in back in Pittsburgh, a painful memory having to do with a long, complicated story involving two women and a sleeping bag. Because of that traffic jam I had literally gone nuts, had lost both a job and a fiancée, and had ended up in therapy for almost two years. The depression and worry associated with that time was something I never wanted to live through again.

I looked at my watch and then over to Tanya's car, a sporty Nissan. It had been more than twenty minutes since I had opened my car door and begun waiting. Don't ask me how, but at that moment I knew Tanya was still at the produce section, perhaps weighing bananas, but, more likely, still checking and rechecking every cucumber on display, all those men watching her. Tanya, I thought, at this moment I hate you.

So I started my car, felt my pocket to make sure I had my five spices powder, and maneuvered out of the space and into the parking lot traffic.

Henry Speaks

I am sitting in the sauna when Ronald comes in, a newspaper in his hand. He sees me, and though it is crowded where I'm sitting, he squeezes in next to me, making everyone move and grumble. It is odd. I do not take saunas often—once a week is my average and there is no regularity to my schedule—but invariably I run into Ronald when I do. Though we act like friends, we never see each other outside of the sauna and the locker room. Today I look at Ronald and wonder why he has brought in a newspaper. I've never seen him bring one before.

"Hey Hank," Ronald says to me once he's gotten comfortable. He pats my knee with his hand. "Plenty hot, huh."

"Over 180," I say. "Almost too hot." A couple of men nod in agreement. There are wet spots from our sweat all over the wooden benches. Arms, bellies, and faces are shiny and glistening. Even though I just got in, I'm beginning to drip. We all watch Ronald spread his newspaper and begin reading. "What's with the newspaper?" I ask.

"You want the sports?" he says.

"Sure," I say.

The man on my left, prematurely bald, probably still in his twenties, reads over my shoulder. In the corner, on the floor, an undergraduate in a sweatsuit grunts as he does push-ups. Ronald speeds through the first section and asks for the sports page. We trade. I am reading the editorials, the bald-headed man on the left still reading over my shoulder, when Ronald says, "Hey, look at your namesake today."

"My namesake?"

"Henry. The comic strip character. You know. Henry."

When I shake my head, Ronald spreads the comics over both of our laps and points to the strip entitled, "Henry."

"Is that Henry?" I ask, pointing to a boy with a bubble head who despite wearing a scarf and earmuffs also has on a pair of shorts and short-sleeve shirt. The three panels of today's strip show him plugging in a vacuum cleaner to remove snow from a sidewalk.
"Sure is," Ronald says proudly.
"He looks brain damaged," I say.
"He's mute," Ronald says. "Henry never grows up and never speaks. I mean look at him." Ronald points with an index finger as a big drop of sweat falls from my nose to the bottom of the page, narrowly missing Beetle Bailey. "I mean who wears shorts in the snow? Who would ever think of shoveling snow with a vacuum cleaner? Only Henry, that's who. And you know what's really mysterious? The character has a tongue but no mouth. Look."
I look at Henry's tongue hanging out of his little boy's bubble face. I see no mouth.
"Do you realize the implications?" Ronald asks, and pats my knee with his hand. "There's something very inscrutable about this Henry who never speaks. Something very inscrutable."
I quickly look around the sauna. Everybody is looking at us and edging away as if we might be contagious. Even the young man doing the push-ups has stopped exercising and is eyeing us coolly as he breathes deeply and flexes his biceps. "Enough heat," I suddenly say, and stand up. I feel my toes touching the tile floor and wiggle them. I realize I am light-headed. "See you, Ronald," I say, and walk right out. I shower and dress more quickly than usual. Outside it is snowing. When I find myself noticing that people people are dressed in pants and are wearing coats, I shake my head. When I see the snow accumulating on the sidewalk, I begin trotting to my car, thinking of vacuum cleaners.

Two weeks later I take my next sauna. I have gotten up early, driven to campus and run a three-mile loop through nearby woods. It is still before 10 A.M., the locker room is empty, and I figure I'll have the sauna to myself. When I push open the door, there is Ronald, both sections of the morning paper spread out in front of him.

"Morning, Hank," he says pleasantly. "What are you doing bright and early?"

"Just ran three miles," I say, taking a seat halfway down the bench from him. "Warming up out there."

"Plenty hot in here," he says.

"The heat feels good, I say." We sit silently for a bit. I can feel drops of sweat forming on my forehead as I slide over to skim the front page headlines. "Henry doing anything spectacular lately?" I ask. "You know, my namesake."

"You'll never believe what's going on with Henry."

"What? Is he growing a beard?"

"You ever hear of Mark Trail?" Ronald asks.

I shake my head.

"Well, Mark Trail is a comic strip character who lives a double life. Monday through Saturday he's this mysterious park ranger who has continuing adventures with poachers and scoundrels. In the Sunday paper he turns into an educator. I mean he just talks about wildlife, no story or anything."

I look at Ronald to let him know I have no idea what he's talking about.

"Anyway," Ronald says, "Mark Trail always smoked a pipe and a few years back there was an article in the paper how the creator of Mark Trail was going to have Mark quit smoking, and that starting Sunday, Mark Trail would be without his pipe. I mean there was an article in the newspaper all about it."

I keep looking at Ronald. He is perspiring everywhere. I wipe my forehead clear of sweat with my hand.

"Anyway, look at this." Ronald points to a small print article on page 17. I read it. Don Trachte, the cartoonist of "Henry," is quoted saying that in response to the many letters he has received from readers, Henry will speak his first words this coming Sunday.

"You know what it all means, don't you," I say as I finish reading it.

"You know what it means?" Ronald asks.
"Of course. Henry's going down the tubes. The cartoonist Trachte's probably losing syndication and he's pulling a cheap stunt. The first words will be something unintelligible or stupid. I'll prove it to you. Let's see what Henry's up to today. What page is he on?" I look up the index, and then grab the back section of the paper and turn to page 29. "I guarantee you, Ronald, something idiotic will be going on."

I find the page and we study the comic strip. We see Henry going to a friend's house and getting scratched by a cat. Then he goes home and draws a sign that reads "BeWaRe oF KaT." Then he returns to the friend's house to stick the sign in the front yard. We look at the three panels for a minute. "The strip's a loser," I say.

"Wait a second," says Ronald. "I liked Henry today. I mean there's wordplay with the vowels and consonants. And just the fact that he made a sign. I mean the guy can't talk and he's dyslexic, but there he is writing away, getting things done. And on Sunday he'll talk. What an inspiration. I wouldn't be surprised if his first words are $E=MC^2$ or something."

I look at Ronald.

"Seriously," he says. And then he begins scratching his groin.

"It's too hot for me in this sauna. I'm taking a shower," I say.

"Me too," he says.

Ronald leaves the newspaper in the sauna and follows me out the door. I find a shower and Ronald chooses the one next to mine. As he soaps himself up, he keeps talking about what a genius Henry is. "How about a bet?" Ronald says suddenly.

"A bet?"

"Sure. Here's what I'm thinking. Henry speaks on Sunday. We'll have ourselves a fancy brunch at someplace like Riverrun. I say Henry says something smart; you say Henry says something stupid. Let's say loser buys the meals and winner pays for the newspaper. In case of ties the maître d' decides if Henry is smart or stupid."

I look at Ronald. He is lathered from head to toe and is doing a little jig. I can't believe it, but I agree to the bet. We shake hands and then I rinse myself off. I am already dressed and ready to leave before Ronald gets out of the shower. Before I go we make a date for noon at Riverrun.

On Sunday I arrive fifteen minutes early, but Ronald is earlier. He is sitting at a window table, sipping a Bloody Mary. I notice the Sunday paper is a neat, thick bundle on the floor. "Well," I say. "Smart or stupid?"

"Hank," Ronald says. "Manners. We'll have ourselves a leisurely brunch with Henry for dessert. A Bloody Mary?"

I look at his drink. "Sure," I say. When it comes, Ronald toasts the occasion. "To Henry," he says, clinking glasses. Then he waves to our waiter and orders another round of drinks.

As we sit and talk, Riverrun fills with people, most of them dressed as if they have just come from church. Tables get moved together to accommodate their large parties. Some couples sit reading *The New York Times*, barely talking. There are one or two single people. Eventually we order melon wedges and Mexican omelets. I begin drinking coffee and decide to dig into my wallet to show Ronald a picture of my wife and son. They live in Ohio and will join me in May, I explain. Ronald gives me a strange, strange look, and drains half his drink. I quickly put the photo back in its place. The restaurant has a line out the door, I notice. Our local paper remains on the ground as we are served our food.

It is past 1:30 when we order dessert. I have had three cups of coffee. Ronald, who has had four Bloody Marys, finally switches to coffee also. We share an order of chocolate cake, and when it arrives, Ronald brings the newspaper up to the table. "May I have the honors?" he asks. I nod.

Ronald separates the comics from the rest of the paper and opens it over the table, covering the steaming coffees and the chocolate cake. We both look at the six color panels. In the first, the bubblehead, Henry, is dressed in black shorts and a red shirt. A yellow sun is out and Henry is walking down the street, his hands in his pockets, a drugstore in the background.

I notice a cleft in Henry's chin that may well be a mouth. There is no tongue, however. In the second panel an older boy wearing a cap runs into Henry and says, "Henry, there's a fire down the street." In the next panel Henry runs after the older boy who has taken off so fast that his cap has left his head and remains hanging in the air. In the fourth panel Henry runs as fast as his knobby knees will let him. The fifth panel shows them after they have arrived at the fire. The older boy is pointing to the house that is going down in flames as he says to Henry, "The firemen should be here soon." "Good," says Henry, in the last panel, as the two boys watch the house burn.

Ronald's shoulders slump so dramatically that at first I think he's joking with me. "You win," he says. "Don Trachte has made Henry into a blabbering imbecile, a goddamned blathering fool." Then he shakes his head once, furrows his brow, leans toward me, and shoots a look. "And you, you sit there like it doesn't mean a thing. You, the big winner. What do you have to say for yourself, champ?"

I study Ronald's bloodshot eyes. He seems so angry and hurt I want to give him a hug. "Put away the paper," I say, and I reach over and pat him once on the shoulder. "Have some coffee. It'll do you good."

"Henry's an idiot," he says, dropping back in his seat.

"Maybe he is," I say. "Maybe he is."

Names

Faith considered herself a doubter and a questioner, but when Richard scratched her scalp and jokingly dubbed her Faith/No Faith a quarter hour after meeting her, she neither doubted nor questioned: she allowed him to seduce her later that night. In their intimacy he shortened the name to No. "No," Richard said in bed the following morning, his fingers making corkscrews of her hair. "You better watch out. I might fall in love with you, and if I do, something's going to happen." No soon discovered Richard often talked like that in the mornings. But instead of letting him continue, No would put an index finger to his lips to let Richard kiss it, lick it, suck it, bite it.

The table was by a screened window. As No looked outside past the patio, the herb garden, the oak tree, Richard watched the waiter set down their Bloody Marys, their basket of bread and crackers, their plate of pâté, cheese, and raw vegetables, and then walk toward the other table in the room to check whether the couple there needed anything.

"No," Richard said. "Drinks."

For a few seconds she acted as if she hadn't heard him. Then her fingers crept along the table until they found the glass, and without looking she picked it up, brought it to her lips, drank from it, and set it down. Richard cut a slab of pâté, spread it thickly onto a slice of bread, and set the knife on the plate. Hearing silverware touch china, No turned from the window and watched him eat. Then she watched him pick up his drink and sip it. She watched him watch her break a thin stalk of celery into two, put the larger piece back on the plate, break the smaller piece into two, put the larger piece back on the plate, and begin nibbling.

"Ophelia," she said after she chewed the celery down and swallowed.

"Ophelia?"

"Ophelia," she nodded. "Or Odetta. Or Nola even. Especially Nola even." She repeated it a third time. "NO—la."

"NO—la," he said, the long, round O sound making his lips pucker into a small, round o which he held until his tongue dropped and rolled, his mouth loosening and widening. He pronounced the name once more, leaning over to kiss her as he did. After the kiss, he leaned back. They sipped their drinks. They ate hors d'oeuvres. She looked at him closely for a moment, her right hand closing around her glass. He answered her look. Then she looked outside past the patio, the plants, the big tree, the twilighting sky.

"Lola's a good one," she said, her nose pressed against the screen. "Or Lois. Or maybe Antonia or Toni." No turned to Richard, slyly picked an olive from the plate, and reached over. "Open," she said. "O-livia," she said, and she let him tickle and caress her fingers with his tongue and teeth as she gently let the olive go on the tip of his tongue. Then Richard picked up an olive, pushed her fingers out of his mouth with his tongue, and said, "O-livia," so he could do the same for her and she could do the same for him. But No trapped Richard's thumb and index finger with her teeth, and slowly bit down. Richard surrendered the olive and returned to his drink. The ice cubes were melting and he swallowed them. No swallowed her olive and took a sip from her drink.

"Mona?" Richard asked hopefully as she put her glass down.

"Mona? Mona's a good one. And so is Hope in a way."

"And No Hope is better, and Hope/No Hope is even better, right?" Richard made a nervous sound like a giggle, and when No made the same sound back, he understood that she understood that he probably understood about half of what was going on. Richard then spread most of the remaining pâté on a cracker, and with a mouth full of food said "What about Sophie? Sophia?"

"Yes."

"Or Josephine or just plain Jo. You know, like Mary Jo or Becky Jo or Bobbie Jo or Jo Jo. Or Koko," he added after pausing to drink the rest of his Bloody Mary.

"Naomi," No said.

"Rosalie. Or Rose anything. Rosemarie. Rosetta. You know that song, Rosetta? I . . ."

No put a finger to Richard's lips. "Clove," she said.

"Clove," Richard nodded in agreement, and closed his eyes. Yes, Clove is a good one. Let me think for a second. Let me think. Okay. No, you ready? You ready for this one?" Richard opened his eyes and waited for No to nod her head. "Thelonia."

No picked up the larger piece of celery and threw it at him. Though Richard turned his head fast and ducked in his chair, the celery hit him just below the ear. "I got an even better one," he said. "What do you think of Bo-linda?"

No just shook her head back and forth, back and forth, and said he was too silly for words.

A minute later the waiter came, removed the drink glasses and the appetizer plate, set a candle on the table, lit it, and presented the wine. After opening the bottle, he placed the cork by Richard's spoon and poured a small amount of the wine first into Richard's glass, then into No's. Richard tasted the wine, and when he nodded that it would do, the waiter poured more so that their glasses were a little more than half full.

"Feels nice getting waited on for a change," Richard said half to himself after the waiter left the table. He picked up the cork, put his nose to it, sniffed, and then offered it to No. She took it, put it to her nose, and breathed in. "Oak," she said. She smelled it again. "Oak," she said.

"Well, take a taste then. It tastes oaky too."

No kept twirling the cork around in her fingers. She sniffed it one more time as Richard kept talking about the wine was a good buy for the price, how it would go well with the seafood they'd ordered, how maybe they'd order a second bottle if they felt like it.

"Richard," she said. "Okay if I tell you something?" She moved the bottle of wine and the candle to the right, the basket of bread and crackers to the left, and rested her elbows on the table so her hands and forearms fell to where the wine, the candle, and the basket had been before she moved them.

"Here," she said. Richard put his elbows on the table, took her hands, and looked at her.

"You see that tree out there, the oak?" No said. Richard turned his head and nodded. In the dusk it had darkened into a silhouette. Richard nodded again so No would explain.

"Where I grew up we had a front porch, and a tree just like that one off to the side. Other trees too, but the big old oak tree off to the side was the biggest." No squeezed Richard's hands, and let Richard squeeze hers back.

"Anyway, one summer my dad and little brother got on the roof, and from there they got on the tree, and they had ropes, and they climbed down a couple branches to the thickest branch. I remember my mom had the camera out and was taking pictures.

"Anyway, they made knots and tied the two ropes tight. Then they were back on the roof. When they came down to the yard they cut the ropes right and fastened the boards to the dangling ends so we had a swing. My dad tried it first, then mom, then me, then my brother. We all took a long turn, and being new, and homemade, and with that branch real high, even higher actually because the ground sloped downward near the tree, it was really fun. You could really get going sometimes. Sort of like this." No began swinging Richard's hands in ever-widening, ever-higher arcs, threatening to topple the basket of food on the one side, and the bottle of wine and the candle on the other. Richard guided their four swinging hands back onto the table, letting No understand that he understood how swings worked, and to continue the story.

"That whole summer almost the swing was so much fun. Friends would come over, and we'd get going medium-high and jump and roll downhill, or else we'd just swing, one pushing the other. My brother used to get almost as high as the second floor windows. Sometimes all we liked to do was sit and drag our toes in the dirt, hardly even moving.

"One night after dinner, the fireflies were out now, god, I'm really remembering, and my dad was pushing me on the swing, and he could really push if he wanted to, and I just went higher and higher, kicking to go even higher, and I was shouting like I sometimes did on the swing, when suddenly I really meant it. I mean I meant I was scared and I wanted to stop, and I kept shouting, and my dad thought I was kidding or joking, and he kept pushing me harder, and then I started to howl. What a mess. My mom ran outside and yelled at my dad, and he yelled back, and my brother rode his bike from down the block up to the driveway to see what the yelling was about because he heard it all the way down the street. And all the time I was up in the air screaming and crying. Even when I stopped swinging, I couldn't stop."

No began staring at the wine bottle. "Richard," she said, "I don't know why I'm telling you all this. Let's name names or something."

But Richard just held her hands tighter, rubbed the backs of them firmly with his thumbs, and then lifted them a bit to kiss the knuckles. Then he went back to holding her hands as before, knowing she knew he was letting her continue her story. But since she didn't continue, they sat in silence, the evening darkening, the candle flickering, the two of them holding hands. When the waiter approached a few minutes later to see if everything was fine and whether they were ready for their main course, they both nodded and said it was and they were.

Then No let go of Richard's hands, picked up the cork, smelled it, and put it down. Then she raised the wine glass, swirled the wine, and tasted. "You're right, Richard, it's a lot like oak. Oak," she repeated, emphasizing the O sound. Then she took another sip, put the wine glass down, and put her hands back in Richard's.

"Willow?" asked Richard.

"No," she said. "Try Daisy May, or Sadie, or Grace Baby."

Then she laughed as she pulled her hands out of Richard's, lifted her wine glass, and drank.

Observing her curiously, Richard also raised his wine glass and drank.

The waiter entered the room carrying a tray of food.

Two Peas in a Pod

It was Saturday night. She was standing there pretty as a picture and I was drunk as a skunk and hot to trot. Yessirree, Joe Smith and the Hawks were playing the rockin' rhythm and blues—you had to see them to believe them. The drummer pounded away like a maniac. The bass player looked crazy as a loon. The guy playing lead guitar, Joe Smith, well, his fingers moved fast as lightning, and the sounds coming out of that thing hit you where it hurts. All in all, though, the harmonica player was the one who really turned me on—the guy knew his business. You could really tell he had a rock-and-roll heart.

Anyway, she was standing by the bar cute as a button, and, by the way she was moving, it was plain as day she wanted to dance. Like I say, I was higher than a kite, so, sharp as a knife I made my way across the room. Quick as a wink I said, "Hey, baby, you wanna dance?" Light as a feather she took my hand. Then we looked into each other's eyes.

She was gentler than a lamb, I thought.

It was like Christmas come early, I thought.

I must be in heaven, I thought.

I felt like I was floating on a cloud while we danced. I looked around and for a split second I thought I heard wedding bells. I'll never forget that moment for as long as I live. Everyone else looked stiff as boards while me and my partner moved smooth as silk. I felt as happy as a lark. This was my lucky day. If anybody I knew had seen me, they'd have thought yours truly was looking like a million dollars out on that dance floor.

The fast song ended and a slow, gut-bucket blues began. I held her tight, like I'd never let her go. I was proud as a peacock, feeling her leaning against me—all warm as toast. For a minute we danced like that, our souls as one. I began to whis-

per sweet nothings into her ear.
But then—from warm as toast, to cool as a cucumber, to cold as ice. What? What??? Had the bubble burst??? A guy bigger than a house was running across the dance floor.
"Elmo!" she shrieked.
I knew it! Her boyfriend!! I knew I had smelled trouble!!! The guy looked mad as a hornet and strong as an ox. The band stopped playing, and the bar grew as quiet as a grave. You could have heard a pin drop.
I could see what was about to happen as clear as glass. His right fist met my left temple like a ton of bricks. The room went dark as a dungeon, then black as night, then I saw stars.
I woke with a crowd surrounding me.
"Is there a doctor in the house?" someone yelled.
"Doctor, my ass," I said. "Get me a beer and I'll be as good as new." I got up and wiped the blood from my lip. Then I spit out a tooth. "Get me a beer," I shouted, and banged the bar with my fist. "I'm dry as a bone."
I tossed down the beer and ordered one more. Elmo must have knocked some sense in my because I could feel something special as the band started playing Johnny B. Goode. I just had to dance, and as I checked the scene, wouldn't you know it but a foxy blonde came and stood by me at the bar. I chugged my beer, licked my chops, then looked her in the eye.
"Don't I know you from somewhere?" I said.
"You do now, lover boy."
As she led me to the dance floor, she wriggled her butt like there was no tomorrow. The earth shook. The seas parted. Joe Smith got down and dirty, playing licks that made his guitar smoke. As we danced we moved closer and closer.
"Oh baby," I said. "I'm a dancing fool."
"Oh baby," she said. "You speak my language."
"Oh baby," I said. "Do anything you want with me."
"Oh baby," she said. "The way you move."
When the song ended, we hugged so tight it was like we were glued together. Then we kissed as we headed to the bar.

"So, what'll it be?" I asked. "My place or yours?"
"Oh baby," she said. "You keep taking the words right out of my mouth."
"What did you expect, sweetie pie? You and me, we're two peas in a pod. We're made for each other. So, let's get this show on the road. What's that great line: Isn't this the first day of the rest of our lives?"

Holden's Nursery Rhyme

The ridiculous situation made him very, very tired. For more than thirty-five years he had been saying good-bye to the same old man, the grippe-stricken and smelly history teacher, Spencer. Back in the living room, Mrs. Spencer had treated him kindly; but here in the bedroom, well, Spencer was lecturing him again, grippe or no grippe. The truth was he had been kicked out of a prep school, yet again, and sitting here, having to listen to Spencer, was making him more and more depressed by the minute. The worst, most ridiculous part of all was having his name stuck in *capital letters* on the middle of page 12. And absolute worst of all, that name of his was signed to the bottom of a ridiculous note of apology he had written. It was embarrassing was what it was. Not to mention tiring. God.

Indeed, the five Holdens were very, very tired of it. The apology letter, the situation in Spencer's bedroom, the countless other mishaps lived through for 214 pages—all weighed on each of them equally. And the apology letter was the worst. It was so bad that one night, sometime between 11 P.M. and midnight,they decided to leave page 12, simultaneously popping themselves out of their books onto the Strand Bookstore's linoleum floor. On page 12, the fifteen letters after "Respectfully yours" vanished. On the bookstore floor, the quintuplets eyed one another cynically. They were dressed identically in scuffed brown loafers, gray corduroys, and blue button-down oxford shirts, a pack of Lucky Strikes bulging in the breast pocket. All five had gray hair clipped in a neat crew cut. Although they were all nearly fifty years old, they looked somewhat younger.

No Holden spoke. Then, as the other four waited, one Holden wended his way out of the paperback fiction section, detoured through an aisle of biographies and autobiographies, circled past a display of new hardcovers, and headed toward the main cash register. Slipping behind the counter, the Holden rummaged through the drawers until he found a key with a tag marked *Duplicate Broadway Entrance*. He grabbed the key, unlocked the door that opened on Broadway, and walked onto the street. The other Holdens followed him outside. The Holden carrying the key locked the door and stuck the key in his pocket. Then, at the corner of Broadway and East 12th, the five Holdens separated, their movements precise, like robots, each leaving the others without a word or sign.

The first Holden, the one with the Strand's front door key in his pocket, walked with a cigarette in his mouth from the corner of Broadway and East 12th to a Greek coffeeshop on Greenwich Avenue where he ordered a beer, a hamburger, and french fries. At the next table, two men were drinking wine and talking about their roles in the upcoming production of "Lesbian Vampires of Sodom." Holden watched and listened to the men as he ate and drank. He was not quite sure, but it looked like the two men were holding hands and stroking each other on the wrist. After the meal, he took out a cigarette, went outside, and started to smoke.

"You look familiar, sort of like an older James Dean," one of the actors told Holden when he returned. Holden coughed several times. Then one of the men winked at him. Though Holden pretended not to noticed, he grimaced when the same man laughingly blew him a kiss. Holden stared down at his beer until the actors left.

Holden stayed at the coffeeshop, drinking beer and smoking until past 3 o'clock. Then he strolled back to 6th Avenue, walked down steps under a sign marked "Trains to Brooklyn," and waited for the B to Coney Island. He waited for almost an hour. Once the train arrived, the ride went quickly, and at Coney Island Holden ambled up and down the empty boardwalk, smoking Lucky Strikes, looking out over the ocean as the sky lightened. For a while Holden sat in a booth in a delicatessen where he ate two bagels with cream cheese and drank coffee. Occasionally he went outside to smoke. In the middle of the morning, he left the delicatessen and sat on a bench on the boardwalk. He noticed two young lovers walk hand-in-hand into a fortune teller's stand, and emerge a half hour later arguing. Soon afterward, Holden went for a walk on the beach. Though it was sunny, it was not very warm. After reaching the pier, Holden took off all his clothes, waded into the water with his mouth wide open, and kept wading until the water covered him. Then he swam away.

The second Holden walked twenty-five blocks up Broadway from the Strand. Along the way he took deep breaths of the cool, humid night air. It smelled of taxi fumes and of dog shit. It smelled of urine. The longer he walked, the worse the smell.

Holden walked with his hands in his pockets. Though he knew he was somewhere near Times Square, he felt somehow disoriented. He thought of going to Schrafft's, but he realized it wouldn't be open. Besides, he doubted he could even find the place. As he wandered further uptown, a yellow woman over six feet tall come out of the shadows, and asked him for a light. Her perfume nauseated him. Holden shook his head, and as he did, he saw a short, stout black man with a silver tooth come at his with something that looked like a baseball bat.

"Commie Honky," the man muttered, and then clubbed him.

As Holden fell, he thought he saw the man and woman run off together. When he came to, the only things he was sure of were that his wallet was gone and his cigarettes were crushed and useless in his shirt. He took a mangled cigarette out of his shirt pocket and lit it anyway. When he got up, he tossed it aside.

Holden walked toward 6th Avenue. When he felt the back of his scalp with his right hand, his fingers came back bloody. He noticed his left and wrist were badly scraped and his pants were torn. His head began to throb. Soon he felt dizzy, like he might vomit. The city smelled like an open sewer. At 6th Avenue, he crossed the street and then turned left, heading in the direction of the park. He thought he might want to sit by the lagoon for a while, perhaps lay his head on the fragrant grass. Somewhere along the way, just inside the park entrance, Holden put his right hand to the back of his head, felt the blood now gushing out, sniffed suspiciously, and sneezed. Black stuff poured out his nose.

The third Holden strolled from the corner of Broadway and East 12th to Washington Square Park. He stood on grass on the periphery and watched a pair of Russian-speaking old men play a game of chess no more than ten yards away from where several teenagers drank from bottles and performed skateboard tricks. Two young men from the group, their white and purple hair sticking out like spikes, offered him his choice of coke, smack, hash, weed, blue valium, and goofballs. Holden refused. He walked up to the fountain, and then around it. He offered a cigarette to a woman who had been juggling four cans of Schaefer beer. She refused. Eventually, Holden found a bench where no one was sitting, fell asleep, and dreamed of the past.

In the morning, Holden, sauntered up 5th Avenue. It took him more than fours to walk thirty blocks. He read every sign and studied every store window. He watched the women in high heels on their way to work. He watched men carrying briefcases. He saw messengers on bicycles moving faster than taxi drivers in cars. He smiled at people, and one or two smiled back. He looked up and up at the buildings until he got a headache.

When Holden reached the big public library, he raced up the steps. The doors were not yet open, so Holden sat on a vast, concrete step, smoked a cigarette, and waited. An old white-haired woman, who Holden imagined was ninety years old, sat and waited too. When the library finally opened, Holden dashed in ahead of the old woman, followed signs, and ran upstairs to the stacks of contemporary American fiction. When he found the book he was looking for, he plucked it from the shelf, cradled it in his hands, shut his eyes, and made a wish.

The fourth Holden walked uptown from the corner of Broadway and East 12th to Penn Station, where he bought a ticket to Boston. Holden fingered the ticket, picked up a schedule, and looked at the board over the ticket seller's window. The Night Owl, the next northbound train, was about to leave, so he hurried down the stairs, barely getting on the platform in time to board the nearly empty train. With so much space available, Holden let his lanky body sprawl carelessly across the length of the seat. As the train journeyed north, Holden briefly looked back at the lights of New York. Then he slept, even sleeping through stops in New Haven and Providence en route to South Station, Boston.

Arriving in Boston, Holden considered taking a cab, but instead walked up Tremont Street through the South End to Park Square. The early morning walk was a fine one. In the first hundred yards he knelt twice to pick up shiny pennies lying on the sidewalk. Both times, as he put them in his pocket and resumed walking, he was aware just how purposeful and wide-awake he felt, how wonderful it was to feel his loafers rhythmically hitting the pavement. Though it was cool, the spring sun seemed to soften his bristly hair, and though it may have been his imagination, he thought he could smell the salt water as a light breeze blew from the east.

It was just past 8 A.M. When Holden reached the bus terminal at Park Square. At the counter he bought a ticket to Hanover, New Hampshire. The bus was scheduled to leave at noon, and while he waited, he closed his eyes and meditated, letting thoughts come and go as they wished. When Holden boarded the empty bus at a quarter to noon, he chose a window seat in the back. With his nose pressed to the glass, Holden thrilled as the bus aimed north out of the web of the city and into the New England countryside. Even when the bus broke down, leaving him stranded, it didn't change his mood. Another bus came to pick him up. That one traveled north, then west into the sunset, and after a lengthy stop in Manchester, arrived in Hanover close to midnight. A full moon shone over the college town.

As soon as Holden stepped off the bus, he walked down a hill, and no more than a half mile off the road he found a pond.

Though it was chilly and he wished he had a coat, he took off his clothes and dived into the water. He swam, splashing noisily. After he got out and dried himself, he slept for a few hours among tufts of reeds. Just before daybreak, as he walked along the road toward town, a woman driving a pickup truck, her two huskies leaning in lookout on top of the bed, offered him a ride. The woman drove by the university, took a right turn, and sped into the landscape, the dogs barking in the wind.

The fifth Holden remained at the corner of Broadway and East 12th where he stood, shivering from time to time, in front of the locked doors of the bookstore. When the clerk opened the doors for business the following morning, Holden was the first inside. Immediately he marched to the paperback fiction section, The five maroon books with the yellow lettering were still there. Quickly he turned to the page 12 apology note. "Respectfully yours,   " they all read. Holden put his left ear, then his right ear, to the page. He heard nothing. Holden shut the books, jiggled them, and put his ears to them again. Still he heard nothing. When he noticed the bookstore clerk staring at him, Holden shook one of the books he was holding, then opened it and began to skim. For the rest of the day, Holden watched the five books as the clerk watched Holden. At closing time, the five books remained on the shelf.

Holden spent the night outside the Broadway entrance of the Strand, next to a window, his ear pressed to the glass. When the same clerk opened the doors for business the following morning, Holden was again the first one in the store. Throughout the day, he again kept vigil over the books as the clerk kept vigil over Holden. When Holden felt no one was watching, he would quickly pick up one of the maroon books and hold it to his ear.

On the third day, a tourist from California bought a copy of the book. Two days later an NYU freshman from Long Island bought a copy. The other three books disappeared one by one over the next week. Holden watched them go. After the last copy was sold, he asked a clerk whether there had been any complaints, or, more specifically, whether any of the books had been returned because something was missing. The clerk looked at Holden and asked him what he was talking about.

Holden shrugged his shoulders once, walked out the door onto Broadway, and headed up to 14th. When he reached the steps leading down to the subways, he stood there, waiting. As soon as he heard the roar of the trains below, he began his descent.

A Yen for the Sea

I woke up in the morning with a yen for the sea. How odd, I thought, because for years and years now, ever since that time my parents took me on a ferry ride, and I vomited on my father on the ride back across, I've wanted nothing to do with the sea—it's made me feel queasy and ill. But this morning I didn't feel queasy and ill, and it was odd because I kept thinking of the sea as I limbered and stretched my way across my tiny studio into my even tinier bathroom, a joke of a room with a bathtub only a dwarf could relax in, a toilet that often clogged when flushed, and a mirror the size of a postcard.

This morning my toilet worked perfectly. But when I washed my hands, rust-colored water dribbled from the spigot. After drying my hands, I looked in the mirror. Nothing on my face was where it should be. My blue eyes were brown, and they shone with a nasty glint. My long, thin nose had flattened into an ugly pug. The small scar on my forehead had quadrupled in length, and ran a tight zigzag down my left cheek. I was wearing an earring. Though I had shaved yesterday morning, a three-day black stubble sprouted from sideburn to sideburn.

I shaved, and as I ran the blade down and around my chin, I hoped my feeling for the sea would pass before I did something uncharacteristic. My hot shower felt good, but didn't wash away the sea. The steamy fog inside the bathroom almost reminded me of something. I decided to go out for breakfast.

I dressed without thinking, putting on my oldest, most beat-up clothes. After locking the door to my apartment, I walked down two flights of stairs, pushed open a door, pushed open one more, and I was out on the sidewalk. Olympic Avenue. It was warm, pleasant, and sunny outside. A perfect Saturday. A breeze blew from the west—a sea breeze, I could smell it—and I could feel a swimming inside me. My walk felt different. Now my shoulders swum more. Now my hips felt loose and wavy. I felt like wriggling and jumping. Across the street I saw an acquaintance, Hunter, sitting on a bench. I waved and shouted a greeting. Either he didn't recognize me or was not himself this morning. I let it pass. Then I took a deep breath, held the sea air in, and slowly breathed out the rest. A man and a woman walked by me, and the man said hi. He had dark hair, a stubble of a beard, an earring, and he was wearing a tank top that said *Newport*. I said hi back. As they passed I heard the woman ask the man who I was. That guy is Phil, the man said. Though my name wasn't Phil, I let it pass.

All around me the shops and stores of Olympic were opening. There was a line waiting outside Daniels and Son Deli, so I walked into Heron Books. At the front register was a girl from the nearby college who worked in the bookstore on the weekends. I nodded to her as I walked in, and her face flushed as red as her hair. I spent a half hour walking the wooden aisles. I thumbed through a guide to turtles. On my way out, I talked to the clerk and asked for her phone number. We made a date for that evening which I knew I wouldn't keep.

Next door to the bookstore was Popeye's Sporting Goods. As soon as I walked in, I fingered some scuba gear and fishing equipment. Then I tried on a sailor's cap and admired my reflection in the mirror. Choppy, wavy curls twisted out over my ears, and with my left hand I rubbed the thick stubble that had returned to my face. I smiled crookedly into the mirror. Then I started whistling. When I left the store, the cap still on my head, no one asked my to pay.

I walked down Olympic. This time as I passed the deli, I noticed a single seat open at the counter, so I went inside and grabbed it. My waitress was a woman named Marie whom I had once been involved with. When she stood in front of me to take my order, I touched the bill of my cap, pulled on my face,

and whistled a tune.
"Whodoyouthinkyouare andwhatdoyouthinkyouwant? I'mbusysoifyoudon'tordernowit'llbeawhile."

"Phil," I said and soon as I did, I started laughing hard, slapping my hand on the counter. It was one of those high moments. Marie had always been too busy, had always talked too fast, and here I was calling myself Phil. When I ordered an omelet filled with shrimp and pineapple, she looked at me funny. When she asked about coffee, I yelled that it better be black. Everybody in the restaurant turned to stare at me, but I didn't care. I studied myself in the mirror behind the breakfast counter, and, when my omelet came, watched myself eat. Afterward, I ordered a bowl of cereal and extra toast. Marie stopped in front of me two or three times and asked me questions like where I lived, what kind of job I had, what other songs I liked to whistle. I asked her out for that evening, and we made a date that I knew I wouldn't keep. I left her a two dollar bill for a tip.

Back outside, I walked up and down Olympic Avenue, then up Eighth and down Ninth. No one I recognized recognized me. People I didn't know called me names like Pete, Phil, and Denny. For a while I sat on a bench and whistled.

Early in the afternoon I returned to my building, and climbed the two flights of stairs. In the hallway, just outside my door, I noticed a navy blue duffel bag identical to the one I used for my dirty laundry. I loosened the drawstring. The inside of the bag was filled to the top with things like my flute, my toolbox, my favorite wool sweater. I hoisted the bag over my left shoulder. Then I took out my key chain, and tried fitting the apartment key into the lock. It didn't work—it wasn't even close—and as I kept jiggling the key frantically, the door cracked.

"Cassandra, look who's here. It's Phil." A tall pleasant-looking man, just my height, with watery blue eyes, a long, thin nose, a small scar on his forehead, a silver whistle in his mouth, greeted me as he opened the door wider. His tank top said *Newport*, and his broad shoulders sloped to sinewy biceps. He looked like a lifeguard, I thought, and I stood there, steady and erect, feeling my brown eyes turn. Then I put out my hand.

"Make yourself at home," he said as he gripped me and shook, his right hand big, like a paddle. "Water's in the kitchen."

I dropped my bag, then gave the man a hug, squeezing him tight before heading past.

The Writer

The writer was born in a zoo. His mother, a tiger. His father, a wolf. Early on, both parents abandoned him, and a zookeeper brought him home as a pet. For two winters the arrangement worked. The second spring, the writer chewed through his collar and leapt the fence. Sun and sky welcomed the writer. Then the lake took him to her shore.

* * *

The writer discovered television: first cartoons, then sports. One day Wild Kingdom was on the air. Look, the writer said. Look.

At what, a bunch of zebras? the father said as he flipped the channel before settling on To Tell the Truth. Go get your mother. Her favorite show's on.

* * *

The writer learned to read: first newspapers, comic books, biographies, then literature, music, a glance.

* * *

The writer stood before the mirror. Behind him, his mother advised. If you don't have anything positive to say, don't say anything.

Fifteen years later, the writer answered.

* * *

When he was twenty-one, the writer journeyed to Taos, New Mexico. The three-day stopover lasted three months. The writer found his first lover, a silver-haired jewelry-maker who owned a ranch. They met at a Thanksgiving dinner, the writer's second night in town. My pet, she said, taking his hand, touching him where he had never been touched before.

* * *

The writer visited a friend, a carpenter who lived near a military base. One morning they went downtown. It was just like a college town, the writer thought: homey little storefronts, a post office. But instead of bookstores, tattoo parlors. Instead of gift shops, pawnshops. Instead of taverns, topless bars. The friends had a drink, then walked two doors down where the writer bought a fiddle, the carpenter a banjo. They met a tattoo artist, who offered a deal. The writer left town with a horseshoe on his shoulder.

* * *

The writer's parents divorced. His father remarried. His mother moved to Arizona, where occasionally the writer visited.
Any new men friends? the writer once asked.
Men? Who needs them? his mother answered.
Any new women friends? the writer asked.
Men? Women? They're all nothing, his mother answered.
It sure is hot down here, the writer commented.
The sun's wicked, his mother said, eagerly.

* * *

When the writer saw this certain woman enter the room, he thought: I've always wanted a woman like this. A few minutes later she was standing beside him and saying: As soon as I walked in here I knew I'd talk to you.

That night the writer dreamed of the woman twice. In one dream the woman was sixty-six years old. In the other dream the woman was five years old. In both dreams he could see into her eyes.

The writer and the woman went out, first to a party, then dancing. I like being with you, the woman said later as they stood at her front door.

I like *you*, the writer said. Then he hugged and kissed her. They made a date for the following week.

Two nights later the woman called. I can't make it, she said. I've met someone else. I think he loves me.

No, said the writer. I love you.

You don't even know me, the woman said.

This new guy can't possibly know you, said the writer.

Look at you — you're jealous, the woman said. It can't work. Good-bye.

The writer lit a candle. When it burned out, he drove to the woman's house. He went to the window. She was lying on the couch, reading. The writer went to the door and knocked.

You, she said, opening the door. I don't know you.

Then she shut the door.

* * *

The writer had fallen in love. But in August his girlfriend left him. In September he lost his job. In October his apartment was broken into. His back ached. He went for a massage. You need to see a therapist, the masseur said.

I do not, said the writer.

That night the writer drank tea and read Henry James. The next morning he started his car and drove into a tree. A month later the writer entered therapy.

One day, after a year of therapy, the writer suddenly burned his ex-lover's pictures and letters. One day, a year later, as he lay in bed, he felt his mother spiral out of his belly. Another day, one more year later, napping, he dreamed he had vomited up his father.

This was the writer in his twenties.

* * *

For five years the writer didn't write. For part of the time, the writer waited tables. Writer, waiter—only a letter separated. But the writer couldn't write that letter. Instead, every night he took home sixty, seventy, eight-five dollars.
One Valentine's Day night he made well over a hundred dollars. At midnight he was still celebrating at the bar. The phone rang. For you, said the bartender.
You waited on me tonight, a man was saying over the phone. I was sitting with an attractive dark-haired girl. A window table. We left you fifteen bucks.
I remember, said the waiter.
Let's meet for drinks some time, said the man.
Who? Me, you, and your friend?
Just me and you.
Me and you?
Yeah. Me and you. We'll have drinks.
I can't, said the writer, hanging up. I just can't.

* * *

Once or twice a year, the writer liked to treat a girlfriend to dinner at a good restaurant. They'd sip Bloody Marys, share three appetizers, drink wine, try unusual entrées, split desserts, and order coffee laced with frangelico or amaretto. If the coffee did the trick, the sex was fantastic.

* * *

It became a joke, the writer's bad luck with women. The ones who he wanted didn't want him. The ones who wanted him, he didn't want. He bought an answering machine and a mannequin. The answering machine took care of the phone. The dummy greeted people at the door. No one knew the difference. The writer wrote in the back room.

* * *

To earn money, the writer substituted at a day care center. At recess, the little ones crowded the writer. Tell us the piggy story, they'd scream.
One little piggy goes to market, and one little piggy stays home. One little piggy spills orange juice, and one little piggy slides down the sliding board.
NOOOOOOOOOO!! screamed the children.
And one little piggy goes wee, wee, wee, all the way, all the way home.
YAAAAAAAAY!!! they screamed.

* * *

For five summers the writer taught tennis at a camp just outside Boston. Sometimes after finishing the afternoon lessons, a few of the instructors rode to Cambridge, the Plough and Stars bar, and drank pints of Guinness for dinner. Grumbling about having to go back to work, they'd return to camp for the evening lessons. Afterward, in the twilight, the writer would stay on the court with one of his drinking buddies. Trading underspin crosscourt backhands, they'd only need one ball, and they hit perfectly, even after it was too dark to see.

* * *

Just as the writer was about to make a left turn, a pickup truck, passing on the left, smashed into him. Though both vehicles were badly damaged, the drivers were unhurt. When the trooper arrived, both drivers were ticketed: the driver of the pickup for passing in a no passing zone; the writer for an improper turn signal.
When the driver of the pickup contested the ticket, the case went to court. First, the driver of the pickup testified. Passing

around photographs of the accident scene, the driver of the pickup explained that the writer was so far off the road to the right that the pickup had room to pass inside the double yellow lines.

The writer answered: Ever since the accident, I've tried to be aware of turn signals. But no matter how hard I concentrate, I forget. What I'm trying to say is that putting on my turn signal is an ingrained habit, as automatic as zipping my pants after I use the bathroom. The fella in the pickup truck is saying my zipper was down. I'm saying my zipper was up (here the writer touched his fly). To tell you the honest truth, I have no idea whether I put on my right or left turn signal just before the accident took place. But I do know I was about to make a left turn.

After studying the writer's crotch, the judge ruled in his behalf.

* * *

One cold, foggy March day the writer biked to the bay, then walked along the shore. I have to change, the writer said to himself, then repeated it over and over as a mantra. After returning to his bike, he rode as fast as he could to where his girlfriend worked.

Give me your best hug, he told her. I'm about to disappear.

* * *

Planning a potluck for his thirty-third birthday, the writer invited everybody he knew. All day he cooked, preparing for it. The party was called for 6 o'clock. By 8, no one had arrived. Depressed, the writer took out the story he was working on and toyed a while. When no one had showed up by 10, the writer went to bed.

Two hours later, the heroine of his story crawled off the page and slid beside him under the sheet.

* * *

The writer grew up believing applesauce was a vegetable. Junior year of college, having moved off campus, the writer had to learn to shop and cook. For a while it was hamburgers, hot dogs, and applesauce. The big discovery: the produce section of the supermarket. The bonus: alcohol and drugs. That was what the writer learned in college.

* * *

When the writer passed through New York, he rode the subways. It was the only thing he trusted in the city.

* * *

Thanks to a friend, the writer began writing poetry. Poetry. The writer had never heard of such a thing. Then people started to die, millions of them.

* * *

At a party, the writer met an autograph collector with a collection so valuable it was insured for a half million dollars. How much is your Marilyn Monroe worth? the writer wanted to know. How much your Al Capone? Your Willie Mays?
The autograph collector rattled off prices.
How much your Dan Pearson? Your Earl Hagedorn?

* * *

Almost everyday those three months the writer lived in San Francisco, he rode the buses from one end of the city to the other. In the evenings he worked as a security guard for Goodwill Industries. That was the period he read Henry Miller and Charles Bukowski.
The writer was making $140 per week. On paydays the

writer went to a bar on Pine Street where hustlers sometimes hung out. There he drank double whiskeys, shot pool, and played the Billie Holiday numbers on the jukebox. The writer was learning how.

* * *

When the writer lost his passport, he didn't report it because he wasn't going anywhere. This went on for years. The writer grew old, then sick.
What have I done? the writer asked his wife. We've never traveled.
You have such a big head, she said tenderly.

* * *

The writer encountered a beautiful activist.
If you get in my way, she told the writer their first night together, I'll make it so hot that after you boil, I'll feed you to the chickens.
So this is politics, the writer thought, his fingers reaching for hers.

* * *

The writer had a dream.
A cop car pulled him to the side of the road. From out of the car popped a clown, who pointed a gun at him. Out, out, out of your car, and dance, the cop/clown shouted, singing it to the writer.

* * *

For twenty years the writer lived in Alaska. The winters were like death: frozen, long, white. There was nothing to do but write. Summers, the writer lumbered like a bear.

* * *

In Seattle, the writer met a ghost. At first the ghost was so powerful that the writer kept respectful distance. After five years the ghost let the writer hold its hand. The seventh year the writer proposed, and was accepted. What would the children look like, he wondered.

* * *

The Valentine's Day his grandfather died, the writer went to a bar. A three-piece jazz band had started up—bass, piano, violin—and the writer was the only one listening. Blue Monk, My Funny Valentine, Lullaby of Birdland, the writer requested. The trio played them all. For Green Dolphin Street the writer sat in on drums.

* * *

The writer was waltzing. The way his partner was looking at him, he could tell she wanted to be kissed. Then he did it, lips and tongue, and waltzed her through the door.

* * *

The writer grew up juggling. Two he could do with either hand. Using both hands, three was easy. Four was tougher. After learning, he quit to become first a sword swallower, then a high wire artist. When he broke his back in a fall, he was through for the season—and lucky to live. It took a while, but with practice he learned to juggle again, starting where he left off: five, six, seven, eight.

* * *

The writer stood with a camera in front of the mirror and posed. Through the viewfinder, the writer saw himself viewing himself through a viewfinder. He checked the light one more time, then shot. Three weeks later, the writer picked up the film. The photo in question? There was no writer, only a camera suspended six feet in the air, and, in the background, a bathroom wall.

* * *

The writer married an eagle. The oldest child was a giraffe, the younger a moose. They had a cow for a pet. This made for a difficult living situation in New York City so the family moved to Europe.

When the writer died, one part of him was reincarnated as horsefly, one part as oak seedling, one part as October wind that heralded winter.

Mushrooms

It is midday Sunday. Rod is back in the greenhouse tending to the roses. I am out foraging for mushrooms with his wife, Valerie, and their llama, Rex. Valerie is a maddeningly pretty blonde with grayish green eyes and the most wonderful shoulders I've ever seen. How I admire those shoulders. She and Rod own a nursery on Whidbey Island, and for awhile yesterday morning I watched from a window as Valerie shoveled manure and wheelbarrowed it uphill to where they were planting garlic. It looked to be strenuous labor. After lunch I had grabbed a spare shovel and worked alongside her for most of the afternoon. It had been all I could do to keep up.

Today my muscles are a bit sore from yesterday's effort. The sun shines through the cedar and alder as we walk down a rutted path about to enter the woods. Since it is October, there are as many leaves off the trees as are on them. Valerie walks Rex by gently tugging the leash that is tied loosely around his neck.

"You know," Valerie tells me. "Rex is a handsome llama. All llamas are smart, but only some are handsome."

"Hey Rex," I say. The llama's ears perk and he nuzzles my face. Then we stare at each other right in the eye.

"He really likes you," Valerie tells me as Rex breaks off our staring contest and goes for a mouthful of apple off an apple tree.

I pat Rex on the head and say, "Good llama, smart llama, attallama."

Humoring llamas is easy here. Whidbey Island's been that kind of place. I arrived two nights ago as a complete stranger, looking Rod and Valerie up partly because we had this mutual friend in Minneapolis, but mainly because I needed a shower.

As a cabinetmaker with a truck full of tools, I understand this couple who work seventy hour weeks to run their small business. And I know they understand me. From the beginning, I felt as ease, and even before showering I quickly told them the background of my visit: that I had left St. Paul to escape a long-term, dead-end relationship; that I had meandered south, then northwest, fishing and camping; that I planned to see more of the Northwest and then California once I left Whidbey; and, most of all, that I was confused about my life, and was using this trip to gauge possibilities. When I told them that I was considering moving to towns in New Mexico, Colorado, and Montana, I mentioned that from what I had seen of Whidbey Island, I was going to have to add it to the list.

Meanwhile, Rex, the llama, steps down into a shallow creek and prances for a minute, his hind legs making small splashes. Now he's off and pulling us along. The woods are wet underfoot as we trample leaves and dirt. We scan the ground for mushrooms but there are none. I breathe in the damp, sweet air.

This mushroom expedition was Valerie's idea. After I showered on Friday night, the three of us drank beer at the kitchen table and talked. When I mentioned how much I enjoyed spotting mushrooms everywhere I hiked, Valerie immediately suggested I stay through the weekend and go mushrooming with her on Sunday. Then she said I better be prepared, and hurried into the living room where she fetched several of her mushroom identification books. She put one on my lap, and the rest by my bed in the guest room. She told me that because work kept her so busy, she hadn't gone out foraging for months, but luckily for us this was the best time of the year to go. I told her I couldn't wait until Sunday.

While Valerie and I talked, Rod sat smiling at the table, moving only to get more beers or find another jazz CD. He was a big, handsome guy with a light brown beard. Muscular but supple, he reminded me of a friend, Tony Murphy, a contractor back in St. Paul.

On Friday night, Rod kept lighting joints and I kept smoking, something I rarely did. We talked about their work, but I kept forgetting what exactly we were talking about. I was higher than I had been in years. At one point Rod and Valerie excused themselves. I thought about getting up but was too stoned to move. A few minutes later they returned clad in robes, and carrying towels. They motioned me to follow them to the hot tub in the back yard. I felt brilliant for suddenly remembering that they had said something about a hot tub earlier in the evening.

    Outside it was cold. When I looked around, Rod and Valerie were already in the tub. Quickly I shed my clothes and eased into an empty corner. We talked, the words floating from my lips. The water felt wonderful. A dog bark echoed. Valerie said something about stars so I looked up and saw a nearly full moon. Then Rod pressed a button and the water turned into churning jets of energy. On the other side of the tub I heard Rod, then Valerie, moan softly. Again I looked to the moon. Then the jets stopped. We all looked at one another, then shyly looked away. Before I knew it, Rod and Valerie were getting out of the tub and slipping into their robes. I waved them inside while I stayed in the water. Scissoring my legs, I began playing with the jets, for an instant even wishing I had Karen, my ex-St. Paul love, with me. The water pulsated around and around. When I finally felt as if I'd had enough, I shut off the jets, climbed out of the tub, and covered it with boards. The air was cold and bracing. I shivered as I dried my hair. Then I scurried inside.

    I slept deeply and dreamlessly. It was late the next morning before I opened my eyes, and even then I was too exhausted to move. I lay in the bed for an hour more, thumbing one of the mushroom books Valerie left for me, reading the introduction, then skipping to the chapter on poisonous mushrooms. I tried memorizing their Latin names, but didn't have the patience. For a while I looked out the window, occasionally seeing Valerie push the wheelbarrow uphill.

    Finally at noon I got up, though felt thoroughly worn out. I groaned at my reflection in the mirror. Valerie and Rod laughed when they saw me at lunch dragging myself without a trace of energy. The hot tub syndrome, they called it, and said it happened to everybody. They said when they first got the tub installed it made them fall so far behind on their work, they had to empty it so they wouldn't be tempted until they caught up. I nodded that I understood. It wasn't until I helped Valerie shovel manure that afternoon that I felt like myself again. Now we walk deeper in the woods, our eyes peeled for mushrooms. With Rex it is slow going. He doesn't maneuver well through the knee-high brush and heavy vines. Valerie tugs at him, then jerks his rope. He's sniffing at some shrubs, and then he eats. Valerie decides to let him continue. I look down to the side, and spy a miniature army of mushrooms, fragile-looking things with narrow stems and tiny, round helmets. They're milky-colored. I point them out to Valerie. She tells me they're too common to bother with, but then decides to take one anyway.

I grab Rex by the leash. Valerie kneels, and equipped with a knife and tweezers she scrapes the dirt from the bulb of the mushroom and very carefully digs it out from the ground. Using the tweezers, she drops the mushroom into a plastic bag which she then ties up. In the meantime I see large, pulpy-looking mushrooms growing out of the tops of decaying logs. The mushrooms look like swollen ears. When I point them out to Valerie, she unsheathes her knife, expertly separates the fungus from the wood, and puts the sample in a new plastic bag. I ask her why she needs a new bag. She explains that if two kinds of mushrooms share the same airtight space they can take on each other's taste, smell, even poison.

I reflect on what she's said. It's something I haven't read yet in any of the mushroom books. I ask a few questions, and then I am quiet, my eyes darting from tree root to tree root, sometimes down to my shoes. I am enjoying it out here. When we speak, it's about mushrooms, and the mushrooms are plentiful. Then Valerie gets excited. "Look," she says. "Chanterelles."

To the right I see a patch of mature yellowish mushrooms,

their caps jauntily flared like sombreros. There are so many we pick two dozen, leaving five or six intact, Valerie telling me never to pick all the mushrooms from any group. I watch as Valerie rinses one of the chanterelles with saliva and then puts it in her mouth, chewing off a bit of one end. "Boy, this is delicious," she says. "Wait 'til Rod sees these. Is he going to love us. We'll put a few in our dinner salad and then have chanterelle omelets for breakfast tomorrow. Boy oh boy."

Valerie breaks off a piece of one of the chanterelles and offers it to me. I have never eaten a wild mushroom before and I think twice before putting it in my mouth. I notice though that Valerie hasn't keeled over so I eat it, working my way through it in tiny, mincing bites, just in case. It is like no other mushroom I've ever eaten, so lemony and pungent. I tell her how I'd like to sauté them in butter and pile them in a baked potato. "I knew you'd understand mushrooms," she tells me.

Sometimes it's Rex leading us. Sometimes we lead Rex. The woods are full of mushrooms. Valerie collects several more samples. One she doesn't collect she laughingly calls a Space Needle. She points it out to me. It is by itself, tall and slender, vaguely futuristic-looking. "Wait 'til you see the Space Needle in Seattle," she says. "Craziest thing you'll ever see. Almost looks a little like this mushroom. I'd pick this mushroom up," she continues, "except you never ever disturb a lone mushroom. It's bad manners."

The thick brush of trees filters the diminishing sunlight. It's getting cooler. We decide to head back to the house. The gluttonous but handsome Rex has been eating all day, and still he nips at anything remotely edible. At one point he sticks his nose in Valerie's backpack. "No you don't, Rexy," she says, and cuffs the llama tenderly on the nose. "If you so much as touch a chanterelle we'll make *you* into an omelet tomorrow morning."

I watch as Rex backs off from the backpack and takes a renewed interest in the scenery. "Smart llama," I say.

It is past four o'clock when we make it to the top of the driveway. We call out to Rod who is digging a ditch off to the side of the house. He gets excited when Valerie tells him about the chanterelles. He tells us he has another hour of work before he can quit for the day. The plan is to buy salmon and have a feast.

Valerie showers first. After I shower, Valerie is already set up at the kitchen table with a magnifying glass, her mushroom books, the tweezers, the scissors, some sheets of white paper, and the plastic bags of mushrooms. "I'm all ready if you are," she says.

Identifying mushrooms is fun, but not as much fun as I hoped. We pick a mushroom, consult the books, and then run through a battery of yes-or-no questions. Then we compare our mushroom to the picture in the book. As a final test, Valerie separates the stem from the cap and places the cap on top of the white paper. In time, the cap emits spores which show up on the paper in a distinctive color.

I am the assistant, watching over Valerie's shoulder. I help out where I can, sometimes with good, sometimes with absurd guesses. For some reason, I am preoccupied with the poisonous mushroom group. Every time Valerie keys a mushroom, I ask if it's poisonous. I can't help myself. At first she's amused, but then she gets annoyed. Finally she accuses me of not taking the identifications seriously. After the reproach I go off to the other side of the room, sit on the couch, and bury my head in one of the mushroom books to show her how serious I am. She doesn't notice.

By now, Rod is showered. When he comes to the kitchen table he takes a chanterelle, eats it in two bites, and washes it down with a beer. I accompany him into town to pick up the salmon at the grocery store.

We buy the salmon, grab beer, bring back a few other odds and ends. I tell him I love his wife's shoulders. He tells me that when they met she used to be a scrawny thing. I tell him I can't believe it. When we return, Valerie is still hunched over the table, keying mushrooms. "Hey," she calls to us as soon as we step inside the front door. She's holding up a mushroom for us to see. "Look at this. I knew I'd never seen one of these before.

It's quite rare and mildly poisonous." She looks my way with a special look. "You hear that? Mildly poisonous. You happy now?"

I go over and examine the mushroom. "Happy," I say.

Rod and I let Valerie finish with the mushrooms as we prepare dinner. First, I fix the chanterelle salad, and then use the blender to whip up a batch of avocado salad dressing. Then I wash the carrots and begin steaming them. After that, Rod has me chop two whole bulbs of garlic to use as a topping for both the steamed carrots and the potatoes Rod has baking in the oven. On the patio Rod grills the salmon over glowing coals. We all sip Mexican beer.

During the meal, Rod and Valerie both rave over my avocado dressing. I pay homage to garlic and tell them that from now on I will consider a baked potato naked without it. The silver salmon is moist and buttery; the steamed carrots are just the right touch. For dessert, Rod produces a joint from his shirt pocket, and sipping on beers, we pass it around. For a few minutes we giggle. Then Rod rolls another and Valerie changes the music. I clear the dinner table and start on the dishes. When I turn around, Rod and Valerie are dressed for the hot tub. We head that way, passing the joint between us as we walk.

We take off our clothes and ease into the tub's warmth. The night is clear. The moon is full. The darkness is both wide-open and womb-like. I feel absurdly good and compare myself to the moon. I am that high, I think. I am that full.

Then Rod puts on those jets again. As I play in the corner with the hot, churning streams, I get a crazy idea. Leaving the tub, I go into the cold air, find the garden hose, and wet myself down with icy-cold water. I shake involuntarily as I howl at the moon. Valerie and Rod soon join me. We point the hose at one another, shriek at the coldness, and howl and howl. Toward the far end of the driveway, I notice a silhouette running in circles in an awkward gallop. I begin doing the same.

Then Valerie and Rod pull me back into the hot tub. We hug and kiss one another as the hot water caresses us. We touch each other everywhere. Rod's cheeks are like mushrooms,

I think. So are Valerie's lips. So are her breasts, especially the nipples. So am I. The water runs over us until the three of us, smiling, leave the tub and enter the house together. Valerie and Rod go to their room and motion for me to join them. I think about it, and as soon as I think, I know I shouldn't. I wave them good-night before I continue to my room. Then I turn off the light and soon fall asleep.

Not much later I am awakened by a strangely vivid dream, nothing more than an image of a plastic bag with four mushrooms in it, the Latin words *amanitas phalloides* spelled underneath the bag. Immediately I flip on the light and look up the name in the index of one of Valerie's mushroom books. It's the death cap mushroom, the most poisonous mushroom of all.

I close the book, turn off the light, and ponder my dream. Somehow the spooky puzzle pleases me, and I keep picturing the dream image, trying to juggle significant facts. I can't stop thinking of the four places I'm considering moving to: Taos, Boulder, Missoula, and now Whidbey Island. As I continue thinking, I begin believing that one of these places is lethal to me, and the poison of one has made the others equally dangerous. It's a crazy interpretation, but I love it. Before falling back asleep I decide to leave Whidbey Island in the morning and resume traveling.

I wake early Monday morning feeling clear, momentous even. When I remember my dream, I grin. When I recall our antics in the hot tub, I laugh. I dress and go to the kitchen. Perfect timing. Valerie is sautéing the chanterelle mushrooms. Rod is cracking the eggs. They put me in charge of making the orange juice. The omelets turn out to be every bit as good as promised. We help ourselves to more coffee. Doing the dishes, I tell them about leaving.

"You know," Rod says. "Me and Valerie were just talking earlier. You could stay here for a month or two, no rent, help us around with this and that. We'll pay you a bit, feed you, hot tub you," he smiles, "and introduce you around town. In no time you'll be set." He sips on his coffee. "You want maybe to stick around and think about it?"

It's the first real offer I've had since leaving St. Paul. With tears in my eyes I thank them, but tell them there are a few more places I need to see, and if things don't work I'll be sure to return.

It is before 8 A.M. and I am packed up. We all squeeze each other and kiss good-bye. I honk at Rex as I drive along the fenced pasture. The llama is nipping at a tree. When he hears my horn his ears perk for an instant, and then he's back to munching.

I leave Whidbey Island and get on I-5 heading south. My plans are vague. Though the day is overcast, I feel great, and think of driving to San Francisco in a single leap. Or maybe I'll detour into downtown Seattle and board a ferry for the Olympic Peninsula. I have heard Port Townsend is worth visiting. I have heard I ought to explore the rain forests near the coast.

Without realizing it, I am already past Everett and fast approaching Seattle. I keep passing hills, and speed closer. Suddenly the Seattle skyline opens, and is is like no other. Of course there are the tall building, but to the right, apart from everything else, I see this curious, funny-looking tower with a long, thin, buttressed stem and a mushroom-like cap. It's obviously the Space Needle that Valerie mentioned in the woods.

Irresistibly I am drawn to this weird, metallic fungus, this mycological skyscraper. I am no stranger to the unusual, but this is the craziest thing I have ever seen. To study it up-close, I exit the interstate, park my truck, and walk toward it, entering a sterile downtown park. As I walk, I am staring up at its gills, the silvery underside of its cap. Above, the sky is a thickening gray.

For an hour or more I stand in front of it, awed by the insane technology, the ungodly shape. I try to guess about the architects who designed it, the workers who built it, the people who live in a city where such a monument exists. When someone walks right beside me, the spell is broken, but not for long. I begin walking back to my car. Though I know no one here in Seattle, I am ready to begin looking for an apartment. Just then a woman whizzes toward me on her bicycle. Even though she's wearing a helmet, I can see she's pretty. As she flies past me, I twist my neck to follow her path.

I am still watching as she briefly turns her head and flashes me a smile.

The Legendary Nightclub

After a scattering of hand claps, Cinderella's off scatting the blues. Rumpelstiltskin's on piano. A stoop-backed Frankenstein bends over his stand-up bass. In the front of the room, fitting around a tiny table, Snow White, Shirley Temple, Lois Lane, and The Three Stooges crack jokes and drink champagne. Shirley Temple is making Curly jealous by flirting with Donald Duck, who is smoking cigars and drinking scotch with Charlie Chan and Napoleon. Aesop and William Shakespeare sit nearby, eyes closed, heads nodding to the music.

Onstage, Cinderella snaps her fingers to Rumpelstiltskin's romping and riffing. Then Frankenstein solos. Aesop hoots. Shakespeare hollers. Tarzan swings through the front door. Paul Bunyan strides to the bar wanting three beers. God draws them. Bunyan grips all three with a fleshy hand, and stumbles, spilling beer on his shoes. A waiter, Fats Waller, hands a pack of Marlboros to Karl Marx, who tells Fats to keep the change. Across the room, Oedipus Rex is making out with his lover, Jocasta.

"Yo Oeddie," a genie taps Oedipus on the shoulder.

"What?"

"Shoot some eight ball?"

Oedipus turns to his woman, who flashes a 'you better not' look. "But I'm in the mood for love," Oedipus croons, making like Al Jolson. Rising, he plants a kiss on the woman's forehead.

"Be back soon, sweetheart. And watch out." He points a finger at Napoleon. "I see how he's looking at you."

Oedipus hiccups as the genie tugs at his sleeve, and a moment later they're cutting through the crowd, Oedipus, still hiccuping, tagging behind. After elbowing past Marilyn Monroe and Madame Butterfly, they're pressed against the bar. The genie flags down God, then turns to Oedipus. "What'll it be, Oeddie?"

Oedipus shrugs.

"We'll have a couple of Jack Daniels then," the genie tells God. "Make 'em doubles." God pours halfway to the top of two highball glasses. Grabbing them, the genie hands one to Oedipus, then leaves a twenty dollar bill on the counter.

Sipping the drink, Oedipus follows the genie down a short hall and into the poolroom. The jukebox is blasting Elvis. Near it, couples are jitterbugging. Diners, seated in booths, are enjoying late meals. At one table, Rembrandt is lining up a shot as King Tut kibitzes. At another, Jerry Garcia is teasing Cleopatra, who has just knocked in the eight ball by mistake. The middle table is free. Oedipus and the genie set down their drinks and choose cue sticks. They lag. The genie has to rack; Oedipus gets to break.

Oedipus places the cue ball just left of dead center, chalks the tip, and as soon as the genie removes the rack, rifles his shot and sinks the eleven.

"Nice break, Oed," the genie admits.

Oedipus circles the table once, twice, then abruptly assumes his stance and shoots, dropping both the thirteen and the nine. The cue ball stops rolling beside the seven. Oedipus curses under his breath: no clear shot next. Going for the fifteen, having to bank almost the length of the table, Oedipus misses.

"You had me worried, Oeddie," the genie says, and then tips Oedipus's knuckles with his cue stick.

"What?"

The genie points the stick to the dance floor. "Get a load of that one. Wouldn't you like to get in her pants?"

"I thought she was married," Oedipus says.

"What Dagwood doesn't know won't hurt him," the genie says, shaking his head. "Look at her dance." Then the genie sips his whiskey as he studies the table. "Oed, Oed, what am I going to do with you? For a second there I thought you were Minnesota Fats." The genie sets down his drink, makes the three, then the four. Next, trying a combination into the side pocket, he misses.

The first game is perfectly even. At the end, both players have to make the eight ball. Oedipus misses twice on difficult long-distance shots, the genie flubs an easy one, and then the genie wins, the black ball falling in the side pocket, the cue ball coming to rest against a cushion. Immediately Oedipus racks for a second game, and the genie breaks. Oedipus easily takes this contest, only missing once, running his last five balls to win.

"What do you say we call it even?" the genie says after Oedipus sinks the eight. "Joan of Arc just came in. She's giving me the eye. And I'm supposed to hook up with Queen Elizabeth sometime tonight."

Oedipus shakes his head, laughing. "Fuck Joan of Arc. Fuck the queen. Rack 'em. We're playing best of three, and it's my break, motherfucker."

"Easy for you to say."

"What?"

"Forget it," says the genie. "Just break. And what do you say we put a small wager on the game. You win, I grant you any wish in the world. If I win, I give you a riddle."

"Big deal, a riddle."

"Death is a riddle."

"What are you saying?"

"I'm saying the riddle can be a very big deal."

Oedipus looks at the genie, who is smiling mysteriously. Oedipus tries imitating the smile. "You're on," Oedipus says.

Oedipus chalks the cue stick, puts the cue ball just left of center, sets up, and strikes the cue ball more powerfully than he has all night. A clean crack, and fifteen balls scatter. But no balls drop. The two ball hangs on the lip of one pocket, the seven on the lip of another.

First, the genie sinks the two as part of the combination with the four. Then he sinks the seven. The four's next. Then the one ball in the corner, the five in the side. He knocks in the three. Trying to bank the six, the genie misses, but leaves the green ball so it's almost completely blocking the corner pocket. It's an easy shot from anywhere on the table. The only other solid, the eight ball, is close to a cushion on the far end of the table. The stripes are a clutter.

"Your turn," the genie says, smiling. "I'll wish you luck now, Oeddie. It'll be your only chance."

Oedipus quickly drops the nine, ten, and thirteen. Three easy shots. Then he has a choice. The fifteen is the obvious. It's kissing the cushion and now's the time. If he spins it just right and hits it hard enough, he can squeeze it in the corner behind the six, and from there be in good position to run the table. If he doesn't go for it now, he may not have the chance again. But there are two problems with the fifteen. First, he may plain miss. Second, if he doesn't hit it just right, he may sink his ball, but knock the six. Either of those, it's the genie's shot and the game will be as good as over.

Oedipus circles the table, stops, circles again. The fifteen it is, the maroon striped ball. Oedipus shuts his eyes. It's geometry he's up against. After the fifteen, he'll come back this way for the fourteen, then the twelve in the side, the nine in the corner, and then the eleven, same corner. That'll leave him with the eight and he'll be in position. He opens his eyes, blinks. The fifteen is a bitch, but it has to be done now. He'll need to hit the upper right corner of the cue ball with just so much wrist.

"Thinking away hard, Oed," the genie says then.

"Thinking just right," Oedipus says as he leans over the table, lining up his shot. The fifteen's as good as in as long as he follows through. He takes one more breath. The fingers of his left hand are spread wide, a strong bridge. His eyes on the cue ball, he feels the cue stick slide. Textbook perfect.

The fifteen's there, then rebounds out from the corner pocket like a basketball. Oedipus bangs the fat end of the stick on the floor. "No! No! No!" he shouts. "No, goddamnit! I hit it perfect."

"Shut up, pool player," Albert Einstein shouts from the dance floor, then puts Miss America in a pretzel, spins her, draws her in tight.

"Too bad," says the genie, smiling. "You would have had me. And you hit it so perfect too." Chuckling, he nonchalantly sinks the six, then the eight. "Good game, Oeddie," he says, offering his hand.

"Fuck you."

"Now, now," says the genie. "Your riddle. What creature has horns like a goat, wings like an eagle, has the heart of a lion, and must die for the knowledge?"

"Fuck your riddle," says Oedipus. "I'm getting out of here."

"But you can't," says the genie, blocking the way with a cue stick.

"You can't," says Satan, who suddenly pops from behind the jukebox. "Not until you answer."

"I can," says Oedipus, wriggling free.

In the front room, Cinderella begins singing 'Round Midnight a cappella. Frankenstein sips on a brandy and lights a cigarette. Rumpelstiltskin turns sideways and leers at Snow White. Jocasta lets Napoleon feel her thigh. At the bar, Sinbad and Noah try cheering up a very depressed Davy Crockett. A few stools down, the tortoise and the hare arm wrestle. Next to them, Florence Nightingale is passing out, drunk. At the end of the bar, Sigmund Freud takes notes as he sips coffee.

Then, above the din, Oedipus screams and screams. Sirens blare. Aesop and Shakespeare stick fingers in their ears. God follows their lead.

Oraño

Who has not heard of Oraño, the poet? His works have been translated into seventeen languages. Followers revere him. It is hard to understand. Five years ago this man, Oraño, did not exist. Now he is legend. Only a handful call him huckster or fraud.

Once, under another name, he had been a professor. He taught classical literature, and his classes were the most popular at a prestigious university. There was never enough room, even in the largest lecture halls, to hold all the students who wanted to attend.

His scholarly works had been notable. His interpretations of Homer and Dante brought the ancients to life. He published prolifically and received numerous fellowships. He was awarded tenure at age thirty-two.

And his wife had loved him. In the early years of their marriage she had been a nurse, and had supported them both while he attended graduate school. Later she cared for the house, and raised the two children. She was a woman to depend on. The children were special and bright.

Then, the day after his fortieth birthday, he disappeared, suddenly leaving his family and quitting the university to travel southwest with a woman half his age. Her parents were wealthy. They lived off her money.

They spent the that first summer in Mesilla, New Mexico. It was a hot, dusty place, not far from the border, and they lived in a one-room adobe dwelling at the edge of town. During the day, it was easiest to stay inside, drink, and play sex games.

At night they walked up and down the streets. Often they would stop at the Peacock Lounge. There they drank, and got loud and boisterous with the locals. When the bar closed, they went back to their room for sweaty sex mixed with uneven sleep.

When the weather changed, they headed north. They settled in Grand Forks, a prairie town where there was a school. The winter was cold, and they did little but stay indoors and drink. When one or the other ventured out, the other would tag along. They usually ended up in the bar around the corner, the Jackknife. A whiskey and water was two dollars. They drank silently, eyes fixed on the mahogany counter.

When the ice thawed and the grass appeared, they migrated west, to Seattle. They moved into a small room in the International District. Rent was only three hundred dollars, which was good. Without income they barely had money to last the month.

When he told her to go find work, she acquired a job waiting tables at a Mexican restaurant. She earned money while he stayed home and drank.

He became very distant. He no longer talked to her; they no longer had sex. Instead, he sat in an easy chair that was about to fall apart. All day he drank whiskey out of the bottle and stared at the wall above the refrigerator.

Occasionally, he would get up and pace, sometimes writing a few words in a notebook. He would smile sardonically as he read what he had written. Then he would sit back down in the chair and put the whiskey bottle to his lips.

At night he would pass out, sitting in the same chair, facing the same bit of wall he always stared at. Sleep would be restless and dumb, broken by the first morning light. Even before rising, he would gargle with whiskey to remove the taste of sleep from his mouth.

One night when she returned home from work, she looked at him closely. When they met, he had been a big man physically, a strong man. Now he was soft and fat, and it looked as if the buttons might pop off his shirt. An unkempt beard hid most of a watery, bloated face. His hair had thinned. A stranger would have mistaken him for an ageless, stupid drifter.

She packed quietly, careful not to wake him. Before she left she placed five twenty-dollar bills under the bottle of whiskey. Then she was gone.

When he awoke the next morning, he understood what had happened. As he drank, he felt strangely content. A funny word came to mind: Oraño. He said it to himself over and over. Oraño. Oraño. Oraño. He rolled it on his tongue. He repeated it fast. Oraño. From then on, it would be his name.

The next day he moved several blocks into a tiny furnished room. His new home was in a neighborhood known as the Market, an area that each night was overrun by drunks, pimps, and prostitutes. His building was on the roughest corner.

When he needed money, he would rummage trash bins, hoping to find something of value that he could carry away and sell. Sometimes he begged. He drank even more, cheap whiskey that sometimes made him sick. He made friends with a street preacher who was addicted to drugs. They saw each other almost every night. They spent many hours sitting together, rarely talking.

Inside his furnished room there was a rickety desk set by a window that looked to an alley. He sat in this chair as he drank. He drank steadily and forgot more and more about what surrounded him. One day he began to write.

The first attempts failed. After a few words he would trail off, drop his pen, then stare onto the alley until the evening darkness set in. Then, if he did not leave the room to poke through trash, he would sit, drink, and wait for his friend. If his friend did not come, he would sit alone and drink himself to sleep.

As time went on, he picked up the pen more and more. Day after day he wrote for hours, filling paper. Just as the sound of his new name had touched him, so did these words, Every night, before he passed out, he would reread what he had written that day. The pages filled him with gladness.

He did not know how, but it was all there, out in front of him. It meandered, darted, soothed. There were strange, abrupt projectiles, made complete by pauses that exploded. God and

Truth, Hope and Beauty, Faith and Death: all writhed, punctuated. Ah yes, Homer, Dante, and Oraño: poets of a kind.

One night he showed some writing to his friend. The street preacher read slowly. Even when it was obvious he had finished, he kept his head down, eyes fixed on the paper. *"Burn this stuff,"* he finally said. *"Burn this stuff and make believe you ain't ever heard of the fella who wrote it."* Then the preacher, his skin suddenly gone milky, looked at Oraño. "Burn it, because if you don't, *you'll wish you had.*"

Oraño did not consider the advice. Instead he spent more and more time poring over what he had written. He shook his head. These words were proof.

One winter morning Oraño gathered his manuscript and crammed it in a small suitcase. It was an uphill walk to his destination, the office of the well-known poet-publisher. When he entered the reception area, he immediately approached the young man who was typing at a front desk.

"I've come to the see the owner," said Oraño.

The young man looked at the immense older man standing before him. First he saw the suitcase, a few sheets of paper half sticking out of it. Then he saw the beard, its long curly strands a nest of gray. Then he noticed the visitor's eyes: they were half-closed, glazed with a farway look; they were rimmed on the bottom with pouches of fat. The young man did not know how best to send the older man away.

"I've come to see the owner," said Oraño. *"I want to see him now."* Oraño opened his eyes wide and glared.

Now the young man knew what to do. "He's upstairs," he said, and pointed to steps blocked by a chain. "Up those stairs and it's the door on the left. But I'm warning you. When the chain's up, he doesn't like to be disturbed."

Oraño unhooked the chain and climbed the steps. When he found the door, he knocked once, then opened it. The publisher sat at his desk. Oraño handed him the suitcase.

The publisher studied Oraño, smiled faintly, then unsnapped the latch and took the top page. He read it. Then he lit a cigarette, took out the next page, and skimmed it quickly. He shuffled through the rest. Then he looked once more at Oraño, examining first his face, then his body, before returning to the writing. "There's no name on this," he finally said.

"My name is Oraño."

"Don't play around with me. Who are are? Where are you from?"

"Just Oraño."

The publisher coughed once, coughed again, then stubbed the cigarette in an ashtray. "Okay," he said. "Oraño, then. So you've come up with something different. I'll tell you what. There's a poetry reading tomorrow night here on Capitol Hill, eight o'clock, a bar called Singers. It ends with an open mike. Come and read something and we'll talk afterward. Say you'll come."

"Of course I'll come," said Oraño. When the publisher extended his hand, Oraño reached and shook it.

Late the following afternoon Oraño walked to Singers, a high-ceilinged tavern that smelled of tobacco. Oraño sat at the bar, ordered a beer, and surveyed the space. Two women, corncob pipes in their mouths, played chess in one of the far booths. The next booth, their dogs slept. On the other side of the room, a tall redheaded man sat on the pool table and blew into a pennywhistle. According to a poster tacked to a wall, most nights blues musicians sang in the bar for tips, and once a week a local poetry group showcased talent.

Oraño drank as the sun set and the bar grew shadowy. By seven the room was half-filled. When the publisher walked in and saw Oraño sandwiched between strangers and staring at his beer, he approached, lit a cigarette, and started talking. Oraño ignored the publisher except to nod when asked if he was still prepared to read. Then the publisher joined a table of friends and motioned Oraño over. Oraño did not move. As the reading began, Oraño sat at the bar, his eyes still focused on his beer.

After an intermission, the publisher himself took the microphone to introduce the newcomer. Hearing his name, Oraño slowly rose out of his stool and shuffled across the room. In one hand was a sheaf of papers; in the other, a bottle. When the publisher finished, Oraño set the beer and the papers on the makeshift podium. As he looked out to the audience, Oraño pulled twice on the beard that hung to his chest. Then Oraño took a swallow from the bottle, and pulled on his beard once more. Several people applauded. A few hooted. Oraño heard them all, grabbed the papers he had brought onstage, raised them overhead, and then started to rip. Then, roaring, roaring, he hurled the pieces up and out like a cretinous monster-boy flinging sticks at the sun.

Oraño shut his eyes. The papers fluttered down, one piece landing on his shoulder. He stood like a statue for thirty seconds, a minute, a few moments longer, his eyes closed.

"There," he suddenly snorted, and he was off. A loose flappy tongue filled the air, heating it, a lightning rod flaring. Then a huge bear hug and a wet sloppy kiss, on and on, one on top of another, a patchwork pyramid that smoked. He jumped. He danced. He clasped his hands, a moneyed grip, his eyes opening like dimes. And words, always words. Strange words, cool words, words that froze.

Oraño stopped and applauded himself. A clap-along commenced. Then he took a drink, shut his eyes, and there, right there: the repossessed oddball-man reciting secrets. Sloping up, veering, a merry-go-round of sounds, a staccato burst.

Then he cradled the rhythm with both hands before smashing it into three. He growled. He sweated. From Mississippi now, he grovelled with a shovelful of manure, and howled. He dug deeper. He scraped the midst. He made it smooth. He sharecropped.

And later, much later, when he wound it down, slowing gradually, there was no skid. The ovation was long. Other poets came forward to meet him.

The publisher stayed by Oraño's side after the others had gone. He told Oraño that he wanted to bring out a book as soon as possible. He could set up reading dates. They worked out a deal that evening.

The next six Thursday and Sunday evenings Oraño read at

Singers. It was poetry, but not. It was mime and stage, dance and sport, joke-telling and trivia. Oraño quickly attracted followers who attended every appearance.

Within a month of that first public reading, the publisher released a chapbook of Oraño's work. Within two weeks, another edition had to printed. And then another. Even before there was formal publicity, booksellers in other areas of the country placed orders.

Despite the recognition, Oraño kept to his routine. He had grown comfortable in the Market, so stayed there. He continued to spend many hours with his friend, the street preacher. They often drank until dawn, favoring the cheap whiskey that made their heads pound.

But the street preacher was curious why Oraño had chosen to become a public figure, and during their nightlong sessions he asked about it often. For many weeks Oraño made no attempt to answer. One night, though, Oraño responded, talking in a kind of code, the phrases rolling like balls down a hill. "Call it what you want – it comes to – you should know – you plead – I write – they read – I come – you come – we come – they come – animal worship – sacrifice – art – and then what – and then what – this is service – there is the void."

The street preacher nodded and frowned. Then they drank.

Oraño's popularity spiraled. Inside the small halls where his poetry readings were now held, the scene would be hot and uncomfortable, people crowding to find standing room. Outside, the sidewalks would be jammed with people scheming to make their way in. Sometimes the impatient mob grew disorderly. Occasionally, police had to be called.

Before long, Oraño read semimonthly at a seven hundred seat music hall. He was the lone poet scheduled, and the readings were marathon affairs, sometimes lasting as long as three hours. These would end with the audience applauding wildly, clamoring for more.

Over the next season, as Oraño read in the hall, he experimented with light and sound. He'd read, his skin changing from a smooth blue to a rough red to a scaly gold. He made up his face white so it glowed in the dark as he knelt and looked rapturously upward, elegant flute quartets seguing to honking saxophone solos and barking dog recordings. He hired actors to sit in the audience and heckle models who posed nude on stage as the poet stood behind an easel and painted. One night a circus entertained, its chief attraction a crew of jugglers dressed in tuxedos who used Oraño's poetry to cue their antics. Oraño changed venue once more, moving his readings to a two thousand seat opera house.

The publisher brought out a full-length volume of Oraño's poetry. Then another. And then another. Each volume sold more than the last. The demand for a tour was overwhelming.

An entourage from the Seattle poetry community traveled with Oraño, and the tour sold out from Los Angeles to Boston. Onstage, Oraño introduced himself by teasing out poems as if whispery dreams. He sank to the floor, then popped up, dollar bills dropping from his back pocket while a wind machine blew the currency—the poet's face pasted on the front—all over the hall. He guzzled liquor, tore off his shirt, and punched his fat belly while a horn man blew and the lights dimmed. He held yellow balloons filled with gas, and then let them go and watched them rise as sparklers shot pink.

"Drink!" he'd bellow.

"Be good!" he'd exhort.

"Now bleed!" he'd demand, departing, as a big sign unfurled with the message: SHOUT ORAÑO, ORAÑO, ORAÑO. And if the shouting was loud enough, Oraño returned for an encore.

To end the tour, Oraño had promised something special for the Seattle homecoming show.

"Shhhhhhhhhhhhhhhhh," a sharp whisper, and he trailed off into nothing. The arena quieted except for breathing.

"I SAID 'SHHHHHHHHHHHHHHHHHH.'"

Except for a white light that shone on Oraño, the hall was dark.

"Shhhhhhhhhhhhhhhhhhhh." Like jets of gas, a soothing

hiss, and the command ceased. Audience members leaned forward for a better view. Nothing . . . Nothing . . . and then Oraño quickly squinted. When the shrieks died, everybody held their breath. The squint remained, and as it remained, implanted, it became dull and heavy. Dull and heavy. So dull and heavy. People fidgeted. Five minutes passed, five minutes of fidgeting and squirming, the discomfort growing. Then, suddenly, the sounds of wind rushing, a car horn honking, someone cursing, two cars smashing, a windshield shattering, someone crying,

From somewhere in the dark, a drummer started to play exactly sixty beats a minute, minute after minute. As the drummer drummed, Oraño's eyes loosened. Under the single beam of light he stood chanting, arms outstretched, a holy smile spread wide.

The drummer kept beating for one hundred minutes. The audience sat transfixed, breathing in time to the drumbeat. There was a deepening, then a steadying, then a thrusting. And then there was a WHOOOOOOOOOOOOOOOOOOSH. A super-long breath, loud like a train, burst and kept bursting. The drummer stopped and red lights flashed. Oraño spread his arms, flapped once, and was gone. As soon as he disappeared the stage blackened.

At first, nothing. Then a few murmurs as the lights turned purple. A shout. Someone pointed to Oraño hanging from a rafter. A man in the front row rose to applaud. So did the woman next to him. And then one by one, row by row, all those attending stood and cheered.

Oraño.

Who by now has not heard his name?

Letters

Dear Ira,
6/22
Since you're a writer now, I wrote you a story:

THE PIE

Thursday night began like any other at the Pie. I (that's you) was waiting tables with R, N, E, S, and my best friend, U (that's me). X was behind the bar, filling in for J, who usually bartended Thursday nights, but tonight was sick with the flu. Since it was early, we stood around the kitchen, waiting for it to get busy. E was talking to K, the new dishwasher, who was furiously scrubbing a big pan that had scraps of semi-burnt lasagna noodles stuck to the sides. E was telling K that if the pan had been let soak longer, it would have been easier to clean. K told E to help wash dishes or fuck off. E wandered off in the direction of the fry cook, Z.

Meanwhile, R and N sat on boxes in a corner sharing a linguine with clam sauce that Q, the sauté cook, had quickly fixed for them. R and N were a couple, and had been living together for several months. The week before U had told me they were thinking of getting married. This was the first time I had seen them since I heard the news. I watched R stick a forkful of pasta into N's mouth, whisper something in N's ear, and point in the direction of U, who was circling aimlessly around the wait station repeating $A=\Pi r^2$. N started to laugh, almost choking on the food.

S and X stood near R and N, and they were sharing a Greek Salad. Like R and N, S and X lived together, but, according to U, they were on the verge of breaking up because S had been chasing after M. That was an almost unbelievable piece of gossip. S and X had been together for almost three years, and everybody considered them the perfect couple. Meanwhile, M had moved here the year before from Milwaukee, hoping to make a go of it with an ex-lover, Y, who was in law school at the university. Two weeks after moving here, M got hired at The Pie as a lunch cook. The following week, W, the owner of The Pie, took M out to dinner, and within days M moved out of Y's apartment and into W's house, a two-story Colonial on the lakefront. M and W remained together for six months, until just past Christmas when one night they dined at The Pie and sat in U's section. Although U would never admit it, it was rumored something U said that night triggered the big argument, a nasty and very public name-calling session that ended with M throwing a half of a baked red snapper at W. In the aftermath, W spent a month in Italy, then Greece, while M quit The Pie and got hired at Bea's, a natural foods cafe two blocks up the street.

U must have told others about S and M because a few nights earlier, O, a dishwasher who was working on a master's in Political Science, told me there were important Marxist/Feminist considerations in the quadrangular relationship of M, W, S, and X, and to understand these considerations in their entirety would mean getting to the root of society's most pervasive spiritual ills. O was obsessed with both community politics and spiritual growth, and though everyone was sympathetic, no one listened seriously to such outlandish, overly philosophic theories. If anything, they were funny, like good parody, and U and I learned we could savor them best by repeating them late at night over shots of tequila. Over the past weeks, U and I had taken to spending more and more time egging O on.

I was the last person to take O seriously, but it unnerved me to be thinking of quadrangles at the exact moment O walked in, nodded to me, said, "hi, I," rolled up shirt sleeves, and took a position next to K at the dishwashers' sinks. I studied O for a minute. Tall. Thin. Ragged clothes. Small hands. Coarse, curly hair. Oversized glasses which covered a pretty face. Androgynous. It bothered me that O worked so hard and talked so much about psychic phenomena, especially in conjunction with money.

I looked around the rest of the kitchen. Z, P, A, Q were cooking. G and D were running around doing their prep work for bussing tables. V, the new baker, was back near the spice counter, kneading a big ball of dough. U's circles, not surprisingly, had trailed off in that direction, and U stood there, hanging around, talking to V. As U grew more and more animated, V turned full attention to the dough.

Suddenly U said, "Get away? Why you *vamp*? Get away? Why I *work* here. This is where I make my dough. Get it? I need you and you need me. But the question is, will you let me knead you?" I saw U put both hands on V's shoulders. "You're my money, honey. You're my bread, baby." And U began massaging V's neck in the exact rhythm that V kneaded the bread dough.

Then V elbowed U hard in the stomach. U smiled queerly, backed off, and wandered out past me in the direction of the bar. "What nerve," I heard O say, and I had to chuckle myself. I couldn't decide to attend to U, go talk with O and exchange viewpoints, or go check my section.

I decided to see what was happening in the dining room. It was still early, but the restaurant was much slower than usual. Instead of three or four tables, I still had only my first, a family with two kids, a boy and girl who were throwing pieces of lettuce at each other with what looked like their parents' approval. I didn't want to intrude on this happy family. However, I noticed that C, the host, had sat two tables, a pair of couples, in U's section, section one, and had neglected to tell U. The couple by the window were sniffing about in their seats, noses in the air, waiting for the show to begin. I brought both new tables their glasses of water, recited our dinner specials, took their drink orders, and assured them their waitperson would be with them presently. I hurried back to the kitchen where I found U massaging V's neck, this time to V's seeming compliance.

"U, you got two tables. I took their drink orders. The ones by the window ordered gin and tonics. The others want a pitcher of Molson."

"I, my imp, my incurable implement. Thanks. And as for you, V, my vixen, I'll victimize you later." U blew V a kiss before rushing to the bar to put up the drink orders."

"Pretty crazy, that U, but a real sweetheart deep down," I said.

"Pretty crazy," V nodded.

Seeing V nod, then, blush, I could see the resemblance: U and V—it made perfect sense. Somehow, U, as always, knew. Who knew how long it might last, but there was V, smiling and reddening, ready for U's next move. I'd bet the night's tips that U and V would be pressed together at the bar after work, and I even thought there was a good chance they'd go home together. I could tell. I hadn't been employed at The Pie the past eighteen months for nothing. Thinking about this got me thinking about O and the love quadrangle, and that got me thinking about a theory of my own. I hadn't told anyone about it, not even U, who was the key link. It was just something I didn't want to share, how U was the collective unconscious of The Pie. This was something I'd been mulling for several months, ever since U had started work here.

From U's first night at The Pie, it was obvious that U and I already understood one another in unusually intimate ways. When we were introduced by our manager, T, U said, "I, huh? Well, *I'm U*, and *I'm* hot tonight," and winked at me lewdly.

"You are, are you?" I answered right back, deadpan, and our friendship had begun. That first night was a busy Friday. U had it easy, watching us, following us around, learning how the restaurant operated, helping us when we fell behind. U began the teasing, calling me an irrelevance, an icicle, an itch. I'd take a second from my work and call U my unctuous urchin, my ubiquitous uncle, my uppity undertaker. It began with silly stuff like that, a game we could play with infinite variations. Later in the shift, as I rushed around panicked because a table of nine had just sat down and ordered everything difficult and time-consuming to do, U's lingo momentarily distracted me so I felt less pressure. I was thankful.

After work that first night, I let U buy me a couple of beers and we talked about ourselves. Though I learned U spoke three languages and had been abroad twice on art fellowships, what I found most interesting was that several times U would say exactly what I had just been thinking. Late in the night, when we were the last ones at the bar, I admitted what was happening.

"Friend," U said, "the same thing's been happening vice-versa. Let's shake."

We shook.

Then U said, "I, keep your *eyes* open. Tomorrow you're about to receive a very important letter. Or should I say letters?" And then U began laughing so hard that J, the bartender that night, asked us what was going on.

"Nothing," we both answered simultaneously, and that got me laughing too, and we both laughed so hard we slipped off our stools, and before I knew it we were slithering on the carpet, belly down, like snakes. The next instant, J jumped up, rushed around the bar, and fell to the floor to join us, and as the three of us slid drunkenly into the dining room, twisting our bodies like overfed pythons, we continued laughing so hard that whenever one of us stopped, just looking at the others set us off again. At last J calmed enough to stand up, close the bar, and order us across the street to Tijuana's Cat, the Mexican place, where we drank tequila and lime juice until two in the morning.

The next day I received mail from my mother, a bulging manila envelope, and enclosed were a number of letters, keepsakes she had missed the first time she rummaged my dad's closet. She wrote that she thought I might want to save the letters because from the return address they were the ones I had written when I was away at college. I immediately wrote my mother back to thank her. I wanted those letters very much. Included were the only personal thoughts I had ever shared with my father, thoughts I had been coming back to over the past several months. It felt good to spend the early afternoon rereading the letters and thumbing through my photo albums. That night, as soon as I saw U at The Pie, I said, "I got my letter today. So what's next?" "Never underestimate the value of letters in the mail. Or male in the female." Seeing me cringe at the awful pun, U clapped me on the back. "I, I need to whip you into shape, you irrepressible inkling. Stay open, my impala." And then I had to quickly sidestep as U grabbed for my crotch.

The next few months I didn't so much stay open, as observe, and that was where my theory of U as the collective unconscious of The Pie took hold. I saw the place change. When I began work there, the restaurant did an average business. Though the food and atmosphere were good, the place just slid by, serving reasonably priced Greek and Italian dishes, one more restaurant in a university town full of restaurants. The staff would have been excellent, but we were unbelievably bored. I was a twenty-five-year-old college graduate who listened to a lot of jazz and felt depressed about my father's death. Z, the cook, was trying to save money to travel to New Zealand, but was spending it on cocaine. H, the day busser, couldn't decide whether to be straight or go gay. Every other day I heard the rumor that W, the owner, was selling the restaurant.

However, once U got hired, things began happening. I received the letters from home, which indirectly got me started writing. Z decided to forget New Zealand, began dealing cocaine, and made lots of money. H walked into the restaurant one day and announced that bisexuality would improve everybody's love life. W sank money into the restaurant. Almost immediately most of the staff began hanging around the bar after work. When word got around, most of the town folks did too. The dinner business picked up. So did lunch. F, a cook who was married, got involved with Q, who was also married. R and N fell in love. M get hired on and soon after got involved with W, who was now making almost as much money as Z. U flirted with everybody, both staff members and customers. I had a one-night affair with B, a substitute bartender and cashier who took me tree climbing after we both drank too much brandy at The Pie's Halloween party.

U and I had plenty to talk about when we sat at the bar after work. U was the unknown artist; I was the irreverent writer. Both of us were cult figures who had corresponded for years; our collected letters would be worth millions. We were a pair of internationally unrecognized celebrities who had decided to hide out and wait tables at The Pie, a cover that allowed us to earn money as we worked inwardly, urgently by day, and drank and flirted uninhibitedly by night. When our fun stalled, U and I would walk down the street to the Indian restaurant, Sahib Sahib, where we'd drink gin and speak in ridiculous British accents.

Not only did U and I have our own language, which kept our friendship intact, but I noticed that U had a different code going with everyone, whether individual or group. It was as if T had hired U for the express purpose of saying aloud or acting out what everyone had been thinking, so that when U said it or did it, we all shook our heads, laughed, felt better, and went back to work refreshed. It was U who'd run around the kitchen and tell about having the urge to spill blue cheese dressing over an old lady because "the biddy wanted another spoonful of 'that exquisite dressing for my last little bit of salad,' and I gave it to her all right: right on those thin gray hairs sprouting from her oh so delicate scalp." And it was U who'd tell us about the mother, breast-feeding in section seven, who was sipping a Bloody Mary through a plastic straw. "Reminds me of my own mama. But, Jesus, there are some things you just shouldn't do. That poor little drunken nipper—having to suck titty in public like there's no tomorrow."

But if you didn't count U's behind-the-scene value in boosting staff morale, it was obvious U was a horrible waitperson. Because U spoke languages, had studied art, and knew more about food and wine than the people paying for the meals, U felt little need to serve tables with the customary grace. If someone told U they wanted a glass of water, U would smile mischievously, and answer, "I'll get your water *please*, thank you," then stroll from the table, perhaps to fetch the water, perhaps not.

Inevitably, customers complained about U's service. But while W wanted U fired, T would argue that since U had begun working, The Pie's business had improved. Every month or two T would talk W into giving U one more chance, and W would agree, shaking a head because according to the computer, the restaurant had never been so profitable. Knowing the situation, it was always amusing to see W and U interact. There was W, the owner of The Pie, the wealthy and conservative wine connoisseur and bon vivant; and there was U, the collective unconscious, the undisciplined and reckless underling. At parties they kept a distance, an eye out sizing up the other. W paid us. U distracted us and gave us reason to work as well as we could, which meant, among other duties, covering for U's shortcomings.

Thus it was all in the course of things that I had delivered glasses of water and taken drink orders for U's two tables while U had massaged V's neck. Nothing exceptional had happened. Yet there was a sweet, inner harmony at work. The restaurant continued to operate in its fashion, and we all felt good, especially V, whose neck now looked as long and supple as a swan's.

I watched V return to the ball of dough. By the side stove Q and Z nibbled on shrimp. P stood nearby, chopping broccoli. A, meanwhile, was casually assembling a salad. For this time of night the pace *was* slower than usual. I walked over to the dishwashers' station where O was running a load of glasses through the machine and K was still scrubbing pots.

"What's up, O?" I said.

"Not much, except the new baker, V, hammered U in the belly, and the next minute they're all lovey-dovey. Your pal U's a strange bird, and by the looks of it V's a perfect match. T's been hiring them these days, that's all I can say. Just looking at U operate makes me want to get the degree and get the hell out of this town."

"I need to check my section," I said, and left O, now grumbling to K, waiting for the rack of glasses. On my way out of the kitchen, I passed U, who said, "Don't even bother, Ironfeet, unless you're bringing out the food. You still got the one table. And I got a couple of assholes out there." Then U took my hands and waltzed me for a minute, leading forward one step, then backward two, gracefully maneuvering past the dishwashers to V's spot in the kitchen.

"The next dance is yours," U said to V, and then let go my hands and shoved me slightly aside. "My itinerant friend here has a prior engagement this evening, a table of four in the dining room that needs attention. So, my ad*venturer*, do you *valtz*?"

Most of the night went like that. The Pie never got particularly crowded, and at every opportunity U would hurry to the baker's corner to flirt with V. R and N left early, as did the early busser, G, and for a while it looked like one or two more of us would also be able to leave. But at eight o'clock a few tables walked in at once, enough business to keep S, E, U, and I busy waiting until past 10:00.

During a lull, I was standing in section three when U gave the bill to a table in section one, the window table that had sat drinking gin and tonics for almost two hours before ordering and eating. After dinner the couple had lingered over coffee and brandy until they were one of the last tables in the restaurant.

When U gave the couple the bill, one of them said to U real gruffly, "You'll take this," and handed U a Mastercard.

U's eyes widened, and then U smiled, gave a little salute, and said, "I sure will, chief. I always wanted one of these." U took the card, put it in an apron pocket, and began walking off.

"You wait a minute," said the customer. "That's to pay for the meal. It's a card to pay for the meal."

"Oh, is that what that card is," said U, turning back, talking slowly, and enunciating every syllable just loud enough so the few other diners still seated in the restaurant could hear. "Well, I sure will *wait*. That's my job. And as for you, I say make up your mind. First you say I'm to take the card and now you say I can't. If you wanted to give me the card to pay for the meal you've eaten, you should have told me that to begin with. Your initial request was something altogether different, something very, very different." From the end of section one, U marched to the cashier B, and gave B the card to pay for the bill. Meanwhile the owner of the card had followed U to the cashier, signed the bill at the front register, made a big deal about leaving no tip, stuck the card in a pocket, and complained loudly to the manager on duty, C, the host. Then the couple left.

For a minute The Pie was silent. Then everybody who witnessed the incident starting laughing. U ran to the kitchen and told the cooks what they had missed. Later, the staff that worked that night congregated at the bar. When C left, X, the bartender, locked the front door, turned the stereo up, and announced anyone drinking tequila wouldn't have to pay.

We stayed late getting drunk on tequila and lime juice. Z divvied up enough cocaine so we all snorted a line. Q and P did their comedy routine where they wore their clothes backwards, smeared their faces with black bottom pie, and threw the king-sized pepper grinders back and forth, juggling them like bowling pins as they exchanged quips. B, the cashier, did a striptease. A did another. O ogled from a couch on the opposite side of the room. K killed the first bottle of tequila, and we began a second. U was in top form, a hand in and on everything, tongue flapping fast and funny.

But it was V who U touched and talked to the most. They sat at the middle of the bar, their barstools pulled close, the two of them looking both sweet and tough, a pair of baby eagles who had not yet flown. When the party broke up, just U,V, S, X, and I remained there drinking. Every so often U and V would kiss, and when they did you could tell they were far away from The Pie bar, and it wasn't the tequila that was taking them.

That Thursday night was the last shift U worked at The Pie. The customer whom U had waited on, and who had paid with the credit card, was L, the president of the local Chamber of Commerce. L called W on Friday morning, complained about the service, and threatened a boycott of The Pie unless W got rid of U. Although a boycott by the Chamber of Commerce would have scarcely affected business, as T was quick to point out, W was only too happy to use L's complaint as an excuse to finally fire U. This time T was unable to save U's job. So U was fired, and a few weeks later left for Spain, taking V along.

Things went on at The Pie, but without U. In the next months, many of the staff quit, new people got hired, and with each change I felt more and more disengaged from the day-to-day activities of The Pie. I quit in September exactly one year to the day I was first introduced to U.

U and I still correspond, but not as often as I'd like. The last I heard, U is in Morocco, still married to V. They have two or three children, and U's done well as a painter and a photographer, and has learned yet another language. I live in the Northwest where I make a living as a writer. I think I'll write U a letter to see what's new. It's been more than a year, too long a time.

THE END

Anyway, my inkberry, me, Viv, and the two kids are fine (yes, sometimes it does seem like three). No, we don't live in Morocco, but I'd sure like to. We're still in Spain, same address. Also I'm picking up not one, but two new languages: Arabic and Hebrew. Viv's maternal grandfather was Jewish. I've been listening to a lot of North African music. I know. You're about to say that doesn't explain anything. Maybe you're right.

I'm selling a few paintings and photos, but I'm also depressed. It really worries Viv because I keep talking about death. It's a wonder it hardly showed up in the story. You remember me telling you how my mother drank herself to death? Now I'm drinking quite a bit myself. Usually when I'm feeling my worst I'll shoot pictures or paint, but this last time I decided to write a story. So, what do you think? Too clever for its own good? Let me know. I may try another one. It was rather fun. My best to you, my impudent insect.

—Up

And P.S. Have your written that complicated story about your father's funeral. It wasn't in the collection you sent. Myself, I'm putting it in my will to have one of those New Orleans funerals—music and tequila as I soar like a hawk.

* * *

Dear Upton,
9/15

    I'm getting to it. It's a story I'll write someday when I get the nerve. My own writing's going well, but it's much different than yours. A few comments and questions:
    How'd you remember the people? A pretty accurate rendering of the Pie scene with a few thoughtful changes. Good work.
    By the way, *did* you have anything to do with Marcy and Walter splitting up? I'd like to hear more.
    I liked a lot of the story, but, yeah, you *are* too tricky for your own good. You're just dancing around being smart when you could have done more with I and the father, U and the mother, and most especially U and I. You talk about this great friendship and I hardly see it, just the outline. That could have been the best part. I thought O was well-done, a nice invention, but needed more there. Don't you think you need to do more with U and V. And what about the end? My question to you: what do you think the story's about? Answer and expand from there.
    I'd write more, but my life's busy as usual. Still single, still teaching, and still hoping my big break's around the corner. It was good hearing from you. Send your next draft of this if you decide to continue.

—Ira

* * *

Dear Incubator—
9/29

It's about me, Upton. Why does it have to be about all those other things? Can't I write about myself? You sound like you've been teaching too long. And besides, even if you are right (and for all I know maybe you are—you're the expert), what else is there beside dancing?

—U

P.S.   And when will you get the nerve?
P.P.S.   M and W were a couple of mouthy worms.
P.P.P.S. About your book, most of your stories aren't as intriguing as you think, you insecure iguana.

Scientific Cuisine

Abdul simmered the thick soup until the apples softened. Then he added honey, cinnamon, and two drops of blood from his right forefinger. In the den, the two American students, Margo and Margaret, and the Frenchman, Pierre, squeezed together on the brown couch, passing a pipe filled with a half-and-half mix of hashish and tobacco.

"Abdul," called Pierre. "Help us smoke this."

Instead of answering, Abdul stirred the soup several times with a long wooden spoon and then put his nose to the rim of the pot. The spicy, fruity aroma made him confident. The American women had arrived in Tangiers this morning and called from the airport, looking for a place to stay. Abdul had arranged for his protegé, Pierre, to pick them up and show them the city. Now, after a shower and a nap, they sat in the small windowless den, smoking Pierre's hashish, waiting for dinner.

Abdul heard one of the young women laugh and order Pierre to fill the pipe. That was the tall blonde, Margaret, the self-assured one who looked like a model and whose laugh reminded Abdul of a trumpet. The other woman, Margo, was short and redheaded, and was the daughter of Jeffrey Pierce, the neo-impressionist painter from New York. Abdul had met Pierce several times, and all morning Abdul had paced back and forth in his bedroom, his favorite work place, producing a series of quick pencil sketches to better remember him. This afternoon Abdul had filled in the best of the sketches, adding lines and color. Then, after he met the girls, he had drawn more and started cooking. It had been a productive but uneasy day, reminiscent of his past encounters with Pierce.

Their first meeting had been at an early 1960's Greenwich

Village party where Pierce, an art student, had stolen Abdul away from a playwright named Tennessee Williams. Pierce took Abdul to Pierce's Waverly Place apartment, a tiny studio full of cockroaches. Into the morning the two men made wild, sometimes sadistic love. Abdul had never before met an American—man or woman—who made love with the vigor and skill of Pierce. But when Abdul woke in the late afternoon, Pierce was gone, and on the bedstand was an envelope addressed in neat cursive *to the cocksucking African*. Inside were three fifty-dollar bills on which Pierce had carefully drawn penises slit by razor blades.

Abdul had taken the envelope and put it in his pocket. Then he waited for Pierce to return to the apartment and explain the insult. The longer Abdul sat in the apartment that first evening, the angrier he grew. While he knew he would forgive Pierce immediately if he were to come back penitent, he also knew the cruelty had to be repaid. When Pierce didn't return that night, Abdul slept in Pierce's bed and dreamt that both men were enchained inside a kaleidoscope, its mirrors and colors both impossible to escape, yet promising freedom,. Abdul awoke the next morning unsure what to do about Pierce, but knowing he must learn to paint. He remained in Pierce's apartment until noon, poring through Pierce's books. When Pierce didn't return, Abdul went back to stay with Williams, who doted on the Moroccan's swarthy good looks.

That was more than twenty years ago. In his success, Pierce had downplayed the incident, for in their rare subsequent meetings he had been friendly, but guarded. But Abdul, now one of North Africa's premier artists, had not forgotten. When Pierce had planned to visit Tangiers for five days with his wife, he wrote Abdul to ask his opinion of the best hotel in the city. Puzzled by the request, Abdul offered the guest bedroom of his own mountainside villa. Their first afternoon in town, as Pierce jogged around the casbah, Abdul had seduced Pierce's wife, Dorothy. Though it pleased him immensely that she was as good in bed as Pierce, it bothered him that she acted as if nothing extraordinary had occurred, even after they repeated the adultery the next four days as Pierce took his daily run. That was just over six years ago. Abdul lowered the heat, gave the soup one more stir, and laid the spoon on the counter top. Why these people gave their daughter his name as a contact, he had no idea, but he was glad. He still owed Pierce.

As Abdul entered the den, Pierre held the pipe toward him. Abdul pulled a stool to the couch, took the pipe, put it to his lips, and breathed in deeply, like a man about to go underwater. He passed the pipe to Margaret, who put it to her lips, sucked in smoke in imitation of Abdul, and started coughing.

"I had a dog that used to cough like that just before it died," Margo told Margaret.

"Dogs don't smoke hashish. Only people do," Pierre said, smiling.

"Shit," coughed Margaret as she passed the pipe to Pierre, who fingered the pipe, dumped the ashes, filled it with more of the hashish and tobacco blend, smoked, and then passed it to Margo, who had begun telling Abdul about the coughing dog, Zeke. Margo inhaled, held the smoke in, slowly let it out, and continued, with gestures, telling the story how she had wrapped Zeke in a pair of blue jeans before burying him.

"And then what were you wearing?" Pierre asked, and stared at Margo for several seconds. "Underpants?"

"We don't wear underpants," Margaret said, coughing as she laughed.

"No?" said Pierre, staring now at Margaret until Margo nudged him on the arm and gave him the pipe. Pierre lit it, smoked, then dumped the ashes and refilled the bowl. After the four passed the pipe one more time, first Margaret, then Margo, excused themselves to use the bathroom. Pierre sat watching the women leave and come back. Abdul got up to put a CD on the stereo, the music a mix of marimbas, flutes, drums, and vocals. Every so often several voices sang the refrain, "Africa, Africa, Africa, Africa."

"Welcome to Africa," Pierre said when both women had sat back down. "Do you always go to the bathroom together?" He turned to Margaret. "Do you want more hashish? Say yes and you won't be sorry."

"I smell dinner," said Abdul.

"Later," said Margaret. "I'd like to."

"More hashish?" asked Abdul. "Or should we eat?"

"Whatever the ladies say," said Pierre as he led Margo and Margaret to the dining room, a room three times as large as the den, with north and west facing windows overlooking the city and the sea. Pierre opened two bottles of a Spanish Rioja and poured everybody wine as Abdul brought in a big, braided loaf of bread, two kinds of salad, the casserole, and the steaming soup. Then Abdul disappeared briefly, changed the music, and returned once more to the dining room.

"What is all this?" asked Margaret. "I'm like my mom and dad. I won't eat unless I know what it is."

"Moroccan scientific cuisine," said Pierre. "Abdul's a great chef, a master."

Abdul raised his glass. "To Margo, traveling art student, and to Margaret, artist and friend of Margo. May you find in Tangiers what you've come for."

They clinked glasses and drank. Abdul spooned one of the salads on his plate and then passed the salad bowl to Margaret. "Now what is it you want to know?" he asked her.

"She wants to know everything," Margo said. "She's always like that."

"Everything?" asked Pierre.

"Well," said Abdul as he helped himself to the casserole and passed it on to Margaret, "the first salad's a fancy goat cheese with yogurt, raisins, pears, and dressing. The other is a Moroccan peasant salad—marinated tomatoes, onions, sweet green peppers. The casserole you're holding is an original recipe. I call it Homage to Bosch."

"Bosch?" said Margo, and she and Margaret looked at each other. "We just spent two weeks in Madrid and Lisbon staring at his paintings. He's my father's favorite."

"He scares me," said Margaret. "The man must have been sick to paint like that. That head with its eyes open rolling in a frying pan. Those half-human animals. It was one thing to see him in books. But another up close. He knew how to paint, but I'm not ready for it."

"It didn't scare me," said Margo.

"That's because you weren't really looking," Margaret said.

"I revere Bosch," said Abdul, "so I named this dish in his honor. Red and green peppers, celery heart, peas, tomatoes, lots of spices, Dutch cheese on top."

"Without the Dutch cheese, Bosch would be Abdul," said Pierre.

"Pierre's a joker," Abdul said to Margaret. "If he weren't my best student, one with a talent for color, I'd have nothing to do with him." Then he ladled himself some soup. "This soup's a favorite. It's more like a stew, actually. I call it Chicken Tagine with Two Drops of Blood."

"Blood?" Margaret made a face. "Abdul, what kind of joke is that?"

"Abdul's jokes aren't that obvious," said Pierre.

"I put in chicken, naturally enough, some purple onion, parsley, almonds, green apples, saffron, cloves, a few other spices. The blood goes in last, from my right forefinger. I prick myself with a needle."

"What did you do that for?" asked Margo.

"It's a special dish," said Abdul. "For a special occasion. Now hush. I talk too much. Enjoy the food." Then Abdul filled everybody's glasses. He sipped his glass of red wine and looked out the window. Boats sailed in the distance. Margo complimented him on the soup. Abdul nodded and closed his eyes. He ate slowly to best savor the flavors. The Bosch needed more cumin, but the rest was excellent, especially the soup and the cheese salad.

He opened his eyes and cut himself more bread. The young people were talking about New York, Paris, the price and availability of hashish. Pierre looked like he was lusting after Margaret; Margaret looked willing. The Pierce girl looked lost. Abdul reached over, tapped her on the shoulder, smiled, and urged her to take seconds. The night was going well. When the CD ended, he excused himself, went into the den, and picked another. As he sat back down, he noticed Margo looking at him as she sipped her wine. He smiled at her. When she put her wine glass down, he poured more into it.

"So," Abdul said. "You hope to be an artist like your father."

Margo laughed. "Kind of. But Margaret's the talented one. Even my father said so. She's obsessed."

"I'm not obsessed," said Margaret. "I just like to paint." Then she giggled.

"You're high," said Pierre, and reached over and patted her on the shoulder.

"She's obsessed with color," said Margo. "Our first year in school she even went on a color diet."

"Don't say it, Margo. You'll embarrass me."

"She had different colors for every day of the week. Monday she ate only black and white foods. Tuesday, purple and blue. Wednesday, green. Thursday, orange. Friday, red. Saturday, pink. Sunday, yellow and brown. I think that was the order. How could I forget?"

"Really, now," said Abdul. "This is intriguing. A color diet. I've heard of a diet where people eat only round things, or flat things, or raw things. But color, never. Tell me more. How long did it last?"

"She kept it up almost a whole semester," said Margo. "But then she started craving foods that clashed — grilled cheese sandwiches with tomatoes and mayonnaise, things like that. She refused to use food coloring. Since the diet broke down, she's been a glutton."

"A glutton?" said Pierre. "She's too thin to be a glutton." Pierre reached to give Margaret's shoulder a rub. "A glutton doesn't have a shoulder like that," he said. Then he inched his chair closer to her, letting his hand slide to her back. "But tell me, what were Saturdays like with all the pink food? What did you eat? Lots of tongue? I'm curious."

Margaret laughed. "I was eighteen years old, and I wanted to be an artist. I knew I needed color, and I had it in my head, my parents telling me you are what you eat. Poor Margo. My

best friend at college and she had to watch me put color in my mouth. I didn't know any better. That was a trip, going into a restaurant on a Thursdays and sticking to oranges, carrots, and yams."
 "Here," said Pierre, pouring more wine. "When I was eighteen I went to the States to study poetry at Berkeley. My first month I stuck close to campus, but then one Friday I took the subway to San Francisco. When I got there, I stopped some people to find out which bus would take me to Golden Gate Park. Not only did the people give me directions, but they also invited me to dinner at their house.
 "Leaving the park that evening, I decided to go. As soon as I walked in, I could tell this was no regular dinner party. There were maybe fifty people and I felt like the only stranger. Everybody seemed to know everybody, and they all went out of their way to ask me personal questions, especially the women.
 "After dinner everybody kept saying I better hurry because the bus was leaving in fifteen minutes. What bus, I wanted to know. The bus for the retreat, they said. I said I had to go back to Berkeley. But then Genevieve, the prettiest one there, said if I was serious about poetry, I needed to go. Or else I was a coward.
 "What could I say? I thought, what the hell. So I got on the bus and sat next to Genevieve. All I knew was we were heading north. The night was really dark. I wondered what I was doing on this bus. I figured that even though Genevieve was a few years older, we would sleep together. But on the ride up, every time I put my hand on her leg, she removed my hand.
 "Past midnight, when we got to the place, we had to cross a bridge, then pass through a gate with a guard. All the girls left to go somewhere and the bus driver, a big guy, led the men to a gymnasium that had no heat. Lying on the floor, I shivered all night and kept my hand on my wallet. The next morning people started out friendly like the night before, but I could see they wanted something from me.
 "I knew I should have played dumb to learn more, but I wasn't smart enough. First, the big guy, the guy who drove the

bus to the retreat, ordered me to help cook breakfast. When I refused, he summoned Genevieve to talk to me. She said to give it a chance and listen to people, at least until Sunday like I had promised. Didn't I want to be a writer, she said. Because if I did, I couldn't quit now. Then she left me and I saw her huddling with the big guy near the gymnasium, and they were both pointing at me. So that's her boyfriend, I thought.

"Then I saw someone who for some reason didn't look like he belonged up there, and I introduced myself. He was Pierre, from South Africa. When I asked him if he wanted to smoke some marijuana, he smiled and said I was the man he was looking for. As we walked down to a little stream to smoke the joint, Pierre told me he had been up there three weeks and couldn't leave. Every time he asked about it, they talked him out of it some way or other. The place was surrounded with barbed wire and guards with dogs, he said, and there was only the one gate. Don't worry, I said. A bus is coming Sunday to take me back. That's what they told me my first weekend here, he said.

"Me and Pierre smoked another joint. Pierre told me all about the place: how they didn't feed him enough; how he couldn't sleep comfortably; how nobody left him alone because everyday there were hours of lectures and talks. He felt like he was about to go crazy. Just as we came up with a plan, people spotted us talking and separated us.

"That afternoon, whenever Genevieve or any of the other women talked to me, I grabbed for their asses. Whenever the men talked to me, I slapped them on the back and asked them if they wanted to get high. Nobody knew what to do so they let me be. In the middle of dinner, the other Pierre and I acted like we had to go to the bathroom, but instead met near the front gate.

"There, a guard stood in our way, speaking into a walkie-talkie, three pit bulls at his side. For weapons, all Pierre and I had were dull butter knives we had stolen from the kitchen. As we were deciding what to do next, Genevieve, the bus driver, and a few others came running from the dining hall.

The knives would be no good, I knew, and as I looked at Pierre, I thought he was going to cry. Genevieve was saying how she was disappointed in me because I was a quitter. Meanwhile, the bus driver was coming at me. 'Go fuck yourself,' I yelled, and then I rushed at him and started pounding my fists. The big guy fell, and as he did the dogs yelped and started to jump all over the guard. Pierre and I raced across the bridge. We tried to push open the gate, but it was locked, so we climbed the link fence, and vaulted over the little bit of barbed wire. Then we sprinted into the woods.

"After Pierre and I made sure we were all right, we watched to see if anybody was following us. No one was. Then we began walking from the retreat, making sure we couldn't be observed from the road. It was pretty warm, but after a while the sun started going down. We began talking, and I learned the other Pierre also wanted to be a writer. I lit joints, we smoked them, and he told me about all these writers Abdul knows who I hadn't heard of, or at least hadn't read, guys like Jack Kerouac, Bill Burroughs, Paul Bowles, and Tennessee Williams. As it grew darker and cooler, we became hungry, but we didn't have any food except a few oranges and carrots we'd swiped from the retreat. We ate those and then we lay down in a pasture, holding one another to stay warm.

"The next day we walked along the road all morning before catching a couple of rides back to Berkeley. When we told about our adventures to the people who picked us up, they said we had been at the Moonies' programming camp and we were lucky to have escaped. What a great guy that other Pierre was. We saved each other's lives. That Christmas I left Berkeley for New York, and I haven't been back since."

Pierre looked around at everybody, and then at the table. "Abdul, we're getting low on wine. Can I open one more bottle? And Margo, pass me the Bosch."

"So what happened when you got to Berkeley Sunday night?" Margo asked as she passed Pierre the casserole.

"Not much," said Pierre. "After the excitement, I wanted to leave California, that's all. The next week I wrote a story

about my trip for a writing class."
"So the Moonies were right," said Margaret. "You did write about them."
"That story wasn't writing," said Pierre. "It was shit. My teacher liked it, said I learned something. But it was shit. That's why I paint now."
"What did you learn?" asked Margaret.
"That you better watch out who you eat with," said Pierre, laughing.
"What's your painting like?" asked Margaret.
"Tonight he's a better storyteller than painter," said Abdul. "And, of course, an even better eater than storyteller."
Pierre nodded and uncorked the third bottle of wine. After filling everybody's glasses, he helped himself to two more spoonfuls of salad. "My painting's like me," he said as he leaned back. "I have no underpants. Abdul said I should take more risks. What does that mean, I say. He says I should unbuckle, unzipper, take off the pants, and go naked."
"That sounds like something my father would say," said Margo, and Margaret nodded in agreement.
"I'm not surprised," said Abdul.
"Last week Abdul said I must make my paintbrush move like the tip of my penis. It should lead me. I shouldn't lead it."
"And what would Abdul advise a woman painter?" Margaret asked Pierre.
"I say take the last of the Chicken Tagine. It will give you color," said Abdul.
"But my question is do you need a penis to paint. Abdul, do I need a penis?"
"Couldn't you rephrase that?" asked Margo.
"The last of the Chicken Tagine will do it. It will give you color," said Abdul. "It's the same thing."
"I wouldn't say that," said Pierre.
"You would if you could really paint, Pierre," said Abdul. "It has to do with the big picture. For most people, the penis is a little thing." Abdul rose and began stacking dishes. "Pierre, when you see the big picture, you'll paint it, and when that

happens your debt will be paid." Abdul clapped him on the back.

"Am I missing something?" said Pierre.

"Abdul says you are," said Margaret. Then she put her hand on his shoulder as she got up to help Abdul pile the dirty dishes.

"Sit down, Margaret," Abdul said. "Relax. I'll take these back to the kitchen. Sit and drink the rest of the wine."

First Margo, then Margaret, used the bathroom. Pierre sat talking to the one, then the other, as Abdul made three trips from the dining room to the kitchen to clear everything but the wine glasses and the spoons from the table. Then he returned carrying a tray on which he'd set a pot of tea, a jar of honey, four saucers, and a plate with eight small cookies. After pouring the tea, Abdul placed the cookies and the honey in the middle of the table, and sat down.

"Dessert," said Abdul.

"Now it's tea time," said Margo. "I think I like it here in Tangiers. Don't you, Margaret?"

"What's in the tea?" asked Margaret.

"You suspect maybe a penis?" asked Pierre.

"Mint," said Abdul. "From my backyard."

"The cookies?"

"The cookies have kif in them, as well as almonds and vanilla."

"Kif?"

"Kif. It's an herb, like hashish. I call these the White Cookies of Marrakech. I ate them for the first time on a visit there. You girls must go from here to Marrakech. There's a fine camel market there. Palm groves. The mountains rise up in the east like a wall. The activity in the town is beyond description: fire eaters, sword swallowers, snake charmers. The first time I went to Marrakech I was twelve years old. I accompanied my father, who had business there. We spent three days—a Wednesday, Thursday, Friday—and the first two days I went around with my father while he made deals for tribal crafts. That was his business.

"Thursday night my father gave me two of these cookies to eat. They were delicious. We went to sleep later, and that night I dreamt I was making love to my eldest sister, Laila. Her long, smooth body stretched forever beneath me, and she knew how to sway. We made love endlessly through the night. That morning I told my father my dream. He looked down at my pants; they stuck out. My father laughed, clapped me on the back, canceled his business appointments for the day, and took me to his favorite prostitute in the casbah. After I came out, he took me to the La Maison Arabe for the finest meal I had ever eaten.

"'Abdul,' my father said, as we sipped tea at the end of the meal, 'now you are a man.' Then my father put me to work for him and I had to work hard for seven years. Those were hard times. My father was a tricky bastard when it came to money. If I hadn't met Tennessee Williams, who invited me to live with him in New York, and if I hadn't met your father, Margo, who inspired me to become an artist, I wouldn't be entertaining the three of you tonight. I'd be a businessman. A good businessman, perhaps, it is true, but say what you will, a businessman is not an artist."

Abdul picked up a cookie, ate it slowly, then bit into another. He sipped at his tea. The others did the same. No one talked, and for a moment there was silence for the first time all evening. Abdul finished his second cookie and got up to put on another CD and to boil more water. When he returned to the dining room, Pierre, Margo, and Margaret stood by the windows, looking out.

"More tea?" Abdul asked. "Does anybody want more tea? Margo?"

"Sure. More tea," Margo said.

"Anybody else?" Abdul asked.

"I was just pointing out where we were earlier today," said Pierre, "and what it's like at night. The day is one thing: the night is something else. What do you think? Should we go to the Central and drink brandy? That's the real Tangiers—sipping brandy at 2 A.M. in Soco Chico, watching the drunk

Tanjawis and the prostitutes. Or we can go dancing at the hotel. What do you think?"

"Maybe tomorrow night," said Margo. "But you three go. I better stay in."

"Come on, Margo. You've been talking about Tangiers all summer and now you want to go to bed early. Come on. Soco Chico. Cafe Central. We'll smoke more hashish."

"I'll keep Margo company here," said Abdul, "if that's all right. You two go. I'll make sure Margo gets to bed early." He poured himself a cup of tea and blew on it to cool it.

Pierre and Margaret looked at each other and smiled. Pierre went to the bathroom and Margaret began putting on her shoes. "You sure, Margo?" Margaret asked as Pierre returned to the dining room. When Margo nodded, Pierre and Margaret headed toward the driveway, Pierre placing an arm around Margaret's shoulders.

Abdul sipped his tea. Margo sipped hers and kept looking up at Abdul;. After hearing the car pull out of the driveway, Abdul said, "It looks like Pierre likes Margaret."

"And Margaret likes Pierre."

"I thought so. Well, good for them. They'll have fun tonight." Abdul took another sip of tea. "And now we're alone too. Do you want to go to sleep, or would you like to talk."

"Let's talk."

"Then tell me, Margo, what did your parents tell you about me?"

"They were funny. They said if Margaret and I happened to be anywhere near here, we should come to see you."

"And now you're here."

"My father said you and he were kindred spirits. That made me curious. I wanted to see it myself."

"And are you seeing it?"

Margo nodded.

"What else did your father say about me?"

"He said you were an original artist and if I asked the right questions, I could learn something from you. I asked him what kind of questions, and he said if he knew, he would tell me.

When I asked him what I would learn by asking the right questions, he said I'd find out the kinds of things a daughter needs to know. How's that for evasive?"
Abdul nodded.
"I could tell he was hiding something, but I couldn't tell what. I may only be twenty years old, but I feel older than that. My parents don't need to hide things from me. I'm no virgin. I know my dad cheats on my mom and she doesn't cheat back. My boyfriend back home is almost thirty. Margaret and I have been lovers on this trip. Plus we've met guys. What can you tell me that I don't already know?" Margo put her hand out on the table and touched Abdul's teacup.
"Is that your question?"
Margo slid her index finger around the rim of the cup. "Before we got here I fantasized I'd want to sleep with you. Tonight I want to. Would you?" she asked, her finger circling faster.
"Suppose," said Abdul, "I said I'd want to. Would you know what you're getting into? You don't know Tangiers. I might torture you and threaten to cut out your tongue, force you to fuck a billy goat. I could do many things. You think I'm talking, Margo, but maybe I can make myself into things you know nothing about. You are here alone in a strange man's house. However, I am not so alone. After all, I *am* part billy goat, I *am* part barbarian, I *am* a Tanjawi."
"Abdul," she said, and then she got up from her chair and went toward him with her mouth open, waiting to be kissed. Abdul got up, kissed her hard, embraced her even harder, and quickly led her to his bedroom, a big room with a stone floor. Without turning on the light, Abdul threw Margo on the bed and undressed her, tearing off her clothes. They made love immediately, ferociously, and when it was over they slept.
A few hours later Margo stirred. As she shifted her body to press against Abdul, she could tell he was awake. "What are you thinking?" she asked.
"I'm thinking that right now Margaret is in bed with Pierre and they are enjoying one another."

"That's all?"

"I'm looking out the window at the moon. It's round and fat, like a pig's behind. It looks like it's going to take a great big shit."

Margo laid her head on Abdul's chest and put a hand to his thighs, massaging them, first softly, then more vigorously. "So, you want more, Margo? Here. Let me get up. I need to take a piss. When I get back, I'll show you some drawings. Turn on the light over there, will you."

Margo reached over and flicked on the light, a low intensity lamp that made the room shadowy. Abdul got out of bed, put on a robe, went to the bathroom, and came back. Margo was still in bed, lying on her side, turned toward the edge of the bed. When she saw Abdul standing over her, she smiled lazily and raised her arms toward him.

"Little girl, I figured you'd be up studying my room. After all, isn't that what you're here for, to meet your father's friend? There's no better way to meet someone that to stay in someone's room a while, especially after sharing their bed. Didn't you notice the easel over there? There's a drawing. Let me turn on the overhead bulb so you can see." When Abdul pulled the cord, the bright light made Margo squeeze her eyes shut for an instant. Then Abdul dragged the easel to Margo's side of the bed, scraping the stand's bottom on the rough stone floor.

"I apologize, Margo. The light is bright and the noise is frightful. But here. I want to show you yesterday's work. Though they're still in rough form, as a student you'll appreciate the difficulty and ambition.

Displayed on the easel was a three foot by three foot drawing of Pierre standing next to Margaret, holding her hand. Both were dressed in formal attire, and they smiled, as if posed for a photograph. Surrounding them, in a circle, were the figures of the zodiac.

"It's Margaret and Pierre," said Margo.

"Open your eyes and sit up, and I'll show you the others."

Margo sat up in the bed, propping a pillow against her lower back, letting her upper back lean against the headboard.

Abdul removed the top drawing, revealing a second one underneath. In this sketch Margo was lying on her back, naked, legs spread wide amidst intercourse with Abdul, who had propped himself above her. Margo had a look of innocence; Abdul, savagery. As in the previous drawing, smaller figures circled the pair, but instead of a zodiac, the figures spaced randomly on the outer border, were a collection of disconnected human body parts: ears, eyes, noses, tongues, teeth lips, mouths, necks, fingers, hands, armpits, breasts, penises, vulvas, anuses.

"I like it, Abdul, but it scares me. What a look on your face." Margo gripped one of the blankets, and pulled it up to her chest. "You drew more?"

Abdul nodded. "I drew them all yesterday. And you'll see them all. Here's the next one." Abdul removed the sketch of himself with Margo to show a drawing of Margo and Margaret lying naked on a blanket in the grass. Their fingers brushed against each other's breasts, and they were kissing one another. Surrounding the lovers were figures such as teeth biting nipples, feet kicking ears, and fists punching tongues. In addition, Abdul had drawn creatures such as goats, horses, monkeys, bears, lions, tigers, elephants, and wolves in various stages of feeding.

With the blanket draped over her, Margo crossed her arms around her chest. "Why are you showing this to me? What are you doing?" Her voice shook as she drew up her knees and began rocking.

Abdul raised his hand and made a slicing motion. "No more questions," he rasped, "or I'll tie you up in the backyard and have my billy ruin your smelly cunt." Then he revealed the next drawing, which showed Margaret lying in coitus beneath Jeffrey Pierce. Pierce looked disdainful; Margaret, angry. On the border, Abdul had drawn breasts that had grown legs and stilt-walked, noses that had grown arms and performed handstands, eyeballs that had grown penises and fornicated with monkeys.

Abdul unveiled four more drawings, one after another, displaying them quickly, just long enough to make sure Margo saw what he wanted her to see. The next one showed Abdul lying beneath Dorothy Pierce, the two of them in ecstasy. The following one showed a young redheaded girl, the pre-adolescent Margo, naked and blindfolded, about to be penetrated with a dildo. The one after that showed Jeffrey and Dorothy Pierce in the midst of sexual intercourse, eyes wide open, an expression of rage between them. The final drawing showed Pierce and Abdul licking each other's genitals. Surrounding that one, horse hoofs stomped eyeballs, buzzards chewed fingers, fractured bones lay crossed. As Margo viewed each picture, she hugged herself tighter and tighter.

Abdul removed the last sketch, the one of him and Margo's father. "I let my imagination go today," he said. "That's what does it sometimes. That's all it takes. Now here. Take this. It's yours. A little spending money for your trip." He flipped her an envelope: *to the cocksucking African* it read in neat cursive on the outside. Abdul laughed. "You'll remember this night, won't you. Maybe you'll learn something; maybe you won't. Now I need to go to sleep. I'm tired. Do you hear me, Margo" I WANT TO GO TO SLEEP. Now get out of my bed or I'll cut off your tongue."

Margo leapt from the bed and ran out of the room, slamming the door. Feeling a lightness he had thought impossible, Abdul shed his robe and returned to bed. When a door was slammed a few minutes later, Abdul stirred briefly, but hearing nothing more, he fell back asleep, dozing soundly the rest of the night.

When he awoke the next morning, he checked the guest bedroom. Both Margo's and Margaret's backpacks were there, but neither young woman was in. He was glad of it. He fixed himself liver steak with eggs, sautéing the liver in olive oil, then scrambling the eggs in the still greasy pan. Then he made his favorite pep-up drink: a blend of milk, nutritional yeast, and banana. After breakfast, he washed the dishes and then cleaned the house. As he worked, he stayed preoccupied with the problem of how to transfer the eight sketches onto a single big canvas. What would he keep? What would he have to discard?

How would he achieve balance? Perhaps, he thought, a single canvas wasn't the best solution. Maybe he should do a series of small paintings. Or a triptych.

All morning Abdul cleaned his villa. In the early afternoon Pierre called on the phone, and when Abdul answered, Pierre said he would be right over. A few minutes later Pierre knocked once on the front door, then opened it. When Abdul found him, Pierre sat smiling broadly on the brown couch in the den. He was filling his pipe with a hashish and tobacco blend.

"Abdul, today I'm starting to see the big picture. I've come to get Margaret's pack. She's going to stay with me." Pierre laughed as he lit a match. Then he put the flame to the pipe's bowl, inhaled, and passed it to Abdul, who took it and smoked.

"So," said Pierre, "where's Margo? We're going to the beach. I supposed she'd want to come. And maybe you, too."

"Here," said Abdul, passing back the pack. "Smoke the rest. I don't know where Margo is. She's a woman now. Women do what they want."

"Did something happen? Abdul, tell me."

"We got close, and then she got scared. American women. They're so beautiful, but they scare so easily. I love them dearly. But if you frighten them, they break."

"I hope that doesn't happen with Margaret." Pierre fingered the pipe, smoked, and then dumped the ashes in the ashtray. "That woman can smoke and fuck."

"And the American men," said Abdul. "They're even worse."

"What?" said Pierre.

Abdul patted Pierre on the shoulder. "Go in. Take Margaret's things and Margo's too. You'll probably bump into Margo on the beach. She'll be crying, wishing she was somewhere else. That's how young people can be sometimes. Buy her a beer. Make her smoke hashish. Go on now. You have my blessing. Have the women stay at your place.

"Come see me, if you want, after they go."

Hagedorn Brothers

I knocked twice on the door, then opened it. "Mr. Hagedorn," I said. "I'm here with the papers."
"They sent you? Don't make me laugh."
"Mr. Hagedorn."
"Some no name kid fresh out of college? For chrissakes."
"Mr. Hagedorn."
"I'm not a nobody, you know. I'm Earl Hagedorn. The Earl of Hagedorn, they used to call me."
"Mr. Hagedorn."
"Don't you 'Mr. Hagedorn' me."
"Mr. Hagedorn," I said, and stepped forward. "I have your papers."
"Come back later, sonny. I'll talk to you then. Tell your boss I was out, the door was locked, you couldn't find me."
"Mr. Hagedorn," I said, and took one more step. "The papers."
""Don't give me that *bullshit* about the papers. Next you'll be feeding me the mumbo-jumbo about the float or some goddamn liquidity ratio. I'm sick of it. I tell you I don't want any papers. Come back next week. The Earl of Hagedorn is not in."
"Mr. Hagedorn. It's time."
"It's nowhere near time. I got a circus to run."
"Mr. Hagedorn. You have no circus. We took the tiger last week. There's nothing left."
"You gotta be kidding. I'm working on a lease deal. My man in Tangiers got a lead on authentic Siamese triplets — Squish, Squeak, and Squawk, I'm gonna call them. Two gals with a guy in the middle. A terrific sex act. I'll pack 'em in."
"Mr. Hagedorn."

"A day. That's all I ask. One more day. Come back tomorrow. If the Earl of Hagedorn isn't sittin' pretty and smokin' a big fat one, you've got me."

"Mr. Hagedorn. Our numbers say . . ."

"Don't give me numbers."

" . . . today, Mr. Hagedorn."

"Look. Have some lunch. There's a deli on the corner. Tell Manny behind the counter you're on Hagedorn's tab. He'll fix you up. Have the hot pastrami on rye with two dill pickles. Come back when you're in the mood to talk. I can't do business like this."

"Mr. Hagedorn," I said, and lifted my briefcase to the desktop.

"Wait a second there, sonny. Put that thing down. Take a chair. Sit. Show a man some decency. You understand English? Read my lips. I'm not ready."

"Mr. Hagedorn."

"Let me breathe, will you. Let me relax. That's the trouble—you young people never learned how to relax. Your parents never took you to the circus, did they? Let me tell you. You see this photo? That was me, the Earl of Hagedorn. Could I ever clown."

"Mr. Hagedorn."

"No, sonny. You wait a minute. This photo was the old days. I was the best. You can't tell it's me under the paint, but I was handsome. And strong. And could I make 'em laugh. And you see him? That was Buck, my kid brother. What he couldn't do with lions and tigers."

"Mr. Hagedorn."

"Shut up, sonny. Let me finish. Me and Buck ran away with the circus when I was sixteen and he was fourteen. We figured we'd have a few laughs, miss a little school, be back in a couple weeks. Little did I know. A creep named Ford ran it, a short guy with beady eyes. Supposedly a midget who grew. Always liked to wear a huge top hat—thought it made him look taller. Ridiculous was more like it. Ford saw my red hair and made me a clown. Buck had to clean the animal cages.

"For twelve summers and falls we played two-bit towns from Cheboygan to Paducah, winters and springs it was Kissimee across the Florida panhandle to Natchez and Opelousas. Ford was pure jackass shit, but the rest were a good bunch. Bippo the clown taught me to juggle a half dozen swords. Sugarpop Pete, the oldest man in the world, taught me to be a one-man band. On my own I learned to mime — could do Harry Truman, Stan Musial, even Rita Hayworth. She was the topper. I'd put on a wig, stick a couple footballs in my shirt, throw out my ass, and strut the ring like one hot broad. I was so good I had the small-town rubes asking me out. How I loved to give the toughest one my sexy look, then point to Buck and say real syrupy, 'You see the tiger trainer? He's all mine. And if you give me the time of day, Sweetlips, why he'll see you ain't nothin' but a tiger's feed bag.' What I wouldn't say. And since Buck had those animals eating out of his hand, you should have seen the slobs shut up.

"You see this photo? Amazing Amanda the Aerialist. We were going steady my second year and Ford got the idea we should get married during a show. So we practiced an act where both of us would swing, and she'd double-somersault and I'd grab her. When we got that down, we worked it up where she'd take off a little early so I had to stretch as far as I could for the grab. Our last night in Kokomo we tried it. Did that crowd ever hush when it seemed she'd fall, but they cheered like the dickens when I caught her. Then, when we hurried down the ladder, Sugarpop Pete, dressed in a satin robe, stood holding a bible in the middle of the ring with Buck and Mademoiselle Mercedes, the bearded lady, flanking him. Quickly, Amanda and I exchanged vows. Then I took the wedding ring from Buck and put it on Amanda's finger. When we kissed, Mademoiselle Mercedes lit firecrackers as a banner unfurled CLOWN MARRIES ACROBAT, it read. And the crowd, it acted like July 4th had just married New Year's Eve. I got to hand it to Ford. That one worked. We stayed in Kokomo an extra three days and cleaned up. Me and Amanda had to keep getting married every week for a while there.

"After Kokomo, Ford took me under his wing, taught me the business. He thought I liked him, but no way. For one thing, the little fuck was loony over one of his freaks, Myron Pfig, Jr., the Moroccan Monstrosity. You should have seen him, a pygmy with a penis where his mouth should have been, and a tongue coming out of what looked like a vagina. Usually he was curled in a corner of his cage either masturbating or fucking himself. Ford, though, liked to walk with Myron somehow balanced on his shoulder, like a parrot, or else hidden inside that two foot high top hat.

"But Ford's big mistake was trusting me with the money. Every night I'd skim twenty, thirty, never more than forty. Ford never suspected, though I took for years. Along with the salary I did all right, and when I got to twenty-five grand I told Buck what I'd done and said if we pooled our savings we could quit Ford's that spring, start our own circus, and head west. When Buck agreed, I told Amanda, and she was all for it. So the next morning I knocked on Ford's door, walked in his office, and told him that starting in spring we were through. He laughed, opened a safe, and showed me a contract me and Buck had signed years before which claimed we were indentured through '69. If we left earlier, Ford threatened, he'd see to it we'd never get another job.

"I was pissed as shit, and just as I started making counterthreats, Myron Pfig, Jr., who was sleeping on Ford's desk, suddenly opened his mouth and ejaculated. Most of the jism stained my brand new shirt. The goddamned freak. We were in Bogalusa, and as soon as I left Ford's office, I went downtown and bought a truck. After that night's show we threw a party and spiked the drinks. When everyone was asleep—and I mean asleep—Amanda packed our equipment, and Buck led Sylvia, Ford's prize man-eating tiger, to the truck. Meanwhile, I tiptoed into Ford's bedroom, found Myron Pfig, Jr. where I suspected—under the sheets, tongue to Ford's weenie—and took him. Before dawn we were in Mississippi. That afternoon we crossed into Arkansas, parked by a lake, had a picnic. Over tuna fish sandwiches and coca-cola we decided to call ourselves Hagedorn Brothers. Then we drove into town for supplies to paint the truck.

"Business was not good our first weeks in Arkansas—we were hardly a circus what with a tiger, an acrobat, a clown, a freak, and nothing more—but we were happy. All of us, but Myron Pfig, Jr. that is. The penis-tongued dwarf would either sulk close-mouthed in his cage or squirt his juice over anyone who got too close. You wouldn't believe how often we were getting it right in the eye. None of us could do anything with him, not even Buck, who it turned out was no genius with subhumans.

"Our first night in Arkadelphia was another slow one until near the end of the show when Sylvia suddenly snarled, broke loose from Buck, sprung toward Myron Pfig, Jr.'s cage, and clawed the pygmy. Before Buck could grab her, Sylvia tore into Myron again and again. Face, arms, legs—there was nothing any of us could do. Though I had little sympathy for the freak, I have to admit it was bad. After the attack, the small crowd stood clamoring, cheering. Though we ended early, no one grumbled, and as people left the grounds, I overheard several say that seeing that big cat pounce and feed was the biggest thing to ever hit Arkadelphia, and let me tell you Elvis had already been through.

"After everybody cleared out, as Buck and Amanda buried what was left of the pygmy, I paced the ring thinking how this could be the start of something. First thing the next morning I called Chicago and sunk money into monkeys—a dozen males—and had them flown to Little Rock, then bussed them to Arkadelphia. When I told Buck and Amanda what I planned, they didn't take to it at first, but I convinced them.

"Sure enough, my hunch held. Twice the number of people showed up as the previous night. I opened by playing a Sousa march on drum, mandolin, and kazoo, and followed it with one of my new mimes—Frank Sinatra. Then Amanda did a few high wire stunts before I joined her on the trapeze. But when Buck rode Sylvia bareback around the ring, it was obvious what the crowd wanted. And bet your ass Hagedorn Brothers delivered. Earlier, I had Buck drug one of the monkeys, then castrate it, cut out its tongue, and then sew its penis into its mouth and its tongue to its crotch. Then we dressed it like Myron Pfig, Jr. and waited. When Buck and Sylvia were set to climax, I wheeled the monkey's cage into the ring. Buck spanked Sylvia's flanks, first the right, then the left. I barely leapt away as the tiger flew toward the stupefied monkey, tearing into it exactly as she had torn into Myron Pfig, Jr. the night before. Again the crowd cheered. The next day I ordered monkeys to last the month.

"By the time we left Arkadelphia we got the kinks out of the act. There was no need for castration; I convinced Buck it would be more crowd-pleasing if he first trained the monkeys to masturbate on command, and then trained Sylvia to pounce at the first whiff of monkey musk.

"You look at me funny. What do you think? I'm heartless? A jerk? Crueler than cruel? I'm telling you none of us liked the act—hell, every other day Buck talked about quitting, and Amanda pretended not to notice—but we were rolling it in. Rolling it in, I tell you. We could have spent the summer in Arkadelphia—people were coming all the way from Little Rock and Shreveport to see us. But a summer in Arkadelphia wasn't what I had in mind, if you know what I mean. Instead, we crisscrossed the Missouri Valley, making money like popcorn. In late fall, we headed to Arizona and California, Hagedorn Brothers still me, Buck, Amanda, Sylvia, and a cageful of monkeys flown in biweekly from Chicago. That first year we netted a quarter million.

"The next years we went up and down the Pacific Coast. Buck had been after me for more acts so here and there I picked up animals on the cheap: Max the Lynx, a crane named Lucky Jim, and chess-playing chimpanzee named Dotty. When Buck told me he had to have a team of white horses, I bought him one. In Newport I got a tip a small zoo was folding and I bought that too. Meanwhile, Amanda noticed we'd been ignoring concessions so she set up our food, drink, and souvenir business. When I hired more jugglers, acrobats, and clowns, she set up training sessions and ran the practices. As we grew from one ring to two rings to a legitimate three ring circus, the eighteen hours day got to me. I quit clowning to spend more time organizing tours, making deals, keeping the books. Though we were grossing five million annually, we still ended every show with Sylvia, 'Our Ferocious Man-Eater.'

"Then, at our peak, Sylvia died. Who knew what from. Old age? Bad monkey meat? Right after our last show in Bakersfield, we were set to shove off for Fresno, and there was Buck coming to me, crying. My kid brother. I'd never seen him cry in his life. It's Sylvia, he said. She's dead.

"Of course, we couldn't leave like that. The heat that night. The smell would have driven us batty. I gave Buck and his assistant a couple hours to drive out of town, dig a hole, and bury her while I got on the phone and called San Diego. Maybe they owed me a favor, I forget, but wouldn't you know one of their tigers, Dinah, had just that week nipped the hand off an attendant who'd been baiting her. It had been an accident — and documented as such — but understandably they wanted her gone. Of course there was a price, but I had them where I wanted. First I offered Lucky Jim, the crane, one-on-one for the tiger. They laughed, called me a chiseler. Then I threw in Dotty, the chess-playing chimp. I could hear them considering. Then, when I let them have our rhinoceros, Bert, I clinched the deal. Little did San Diego know Bert was this oversexed lummox always trying to make it with the hippo, Larry. But I didn't break that bit of news — for all I knew San Diego was dying for a faggot rhino who liked hippos. Like I said, I had them where I wanted. I even got them to throw Dinah in a truck to meet us in Fresno for the next night's show.

"By the time I got off the phone, Buck had returned, and he stood by himself, sweaty and dirty, sobbing in the middle of the wide-open lot where our tents had been. Then, through the tears, he slowly started singing some spiritual. One by one, the whole circus gathered tight in a circle and joined him. It was a clear night with one of those great big moons, and it gave me the shivers listening, I tell you. Plus with all the damn animals baying and screeching in the background, I swore something had to give. I elbowed my way to Buck, hummed along for a minute, then started waving my arms until everybody stopped. Then I announced we were two hours late and if we didn't want to disappoint the good people of Fresno, we had to get to Fresno first. You should have heard the grumbling. On the ride up, I told Amanda and Buck about the big trade with San Diego. Hagedorn Brothers wasn't going to miss a beat, I bragged. Buck didn't say a word. Amanda rubbed my neck for a second, started to say something about Lucky Jim, and stopped.

"The next year we solidified our position as the top West Coast circus. The money came pouring in. And nobody but nobody had acts that could top us. We had the clowns; we had the acrobats; and, boy, did we ever have the animals. You name it, and we owned it. Personally, once I got used to Dinah, I preferred her. The new cat was bigger, sleeker, and haughtier than Sylvia had ever been. And could she put on a show. Buck would crack the whip—he'd really snap it—and Dinah would fly after the monkey, gut him in no time.

"But Buck had an attitude. He wouldn't have a thing to do with Dinah, except in the ring. With Sylvia, he used to spend an hour or two everyday cuddling and calling her his kitten, his pussycat. With Dinah it was all business. Once he trained her to go after the monkey, that was it. Between shows he'd wander the outskirts of the grounds, talking to the crocodile, Malcolm, or to Quentin, the boa constrictor. Sometimes he'd stop in front of Gabe, the albino gorilla, and make ape noises. More and more often he spent whole mornings babbling to the sea lions, not doing his work while his assistants covered for him. That's when I got worried. The animals were getting more unruly by the day.

"I tried talking to Buck a few times to really understand, but got nowhere. When I offered him more responsibility in the business, he refused me. Then I arranged for Magnificent Millicent, the new trapeze artist, to seduce him. What a mistake. A week later she told me he'd been impossible to corner so she finally just climbed into his bed one night. And then, no matter what she did, he couldn't get it up. After learning that, watching Buck mope *really* depressed me. What was I going to do with him?

"Then one day I spotted him playfully slapping the rump of the grizzly cub, Gus. Gus. Of course. When we were back with Ford, Buck was always telling me when he retired the first thing he'd do was visit Alaska, where the real animals were. That afternoon I got on the phone and in two weeks ironed out a deal. The next summer we'd take the circus north, spend June in Fairbanks, July and August in Anchorage. When I told Buck, he perked up like his old self. And that made such a difference in the circus. You get someone like Buck, who loves those animals, and they respond. I still thought he was a little hard on Dinah. He'd whip her harder than he ever whipped Sylvia. But what did I know? Whenever I'd mention it, Buck would get defensive and ask me about results. And there was never a problem there.

"Next May we drove to Alaska nice and slow, made the trip into a vacation. We had ten trucks, forty animals, fifteen performers, not including Buck, Amanda, and myself. We arrived in Fairbanks a week early and set the tents on a big dirt lot on South Cushman Street. In the evenings, folks would drive by, see the red and white tents, stop, and shoot the shit until 2 A.M. Why shouldn't they have? Hell, the damn place never got dark. One night a newspaperman stopped by and the next day I was front page news. Then Buck and Dinah went on TV and they ran the same footage at six and eleven o'clock three days straight. And when Amanda led a trapeze workshop one morning, more than a hundred people showed up at five dollars a head. The way people talked, it being tourist season and all, we'd fill up every single night. It wouldn't be California, but it would do. And best, Buck was at peace. In fact, everybody was, except Dinah, who appeared edgy, and the monkeys, who *always* seemed nervous, if you know what I mean.

"Even though I felt good about being there, the first night of business exceeded expectations by 100%. Eight o'clock, and you'd have thought it looked like three in the afternoon. That's how high the sun was. Sure, it was cool, about sixty, but you'd have thought it was ninety out the way those Alaskans dressed. And whatever we did, they'd stand and applaud. It almost got embarrassing because we weren't doing anything special. But those people were starved up there. Starved, I tell you. You know how starved? First night, we broke our record for hot dogs and hamburgers. Ha. And during the finale, when Dinah lunged, clawed the monkey with one of her big forepaws, bit its head off, and started to chew, the crowd started stamping their feet, yelling: 'Raw Monkey, Raw Monkey, Raw Monkey.' All my years with the act and that was a new one on me.

"Every night we increased business. First, we had to add several rows of bleacher seats. Then we started selling standing room tickets. 'Raw Monkey' was the Fairbanks rallying cry. I can hear it now. The end of every show the crowd would chant from the time Dinah stepped into the ring until she gobbled every last bit of monkey meat. Amanda was radiant. To please her—and the good people of Fairbanks, I should add—I applied the greasepaint for the first time in three years, juggled a few knives, bowed some fiddle tunes, did the old Rita Hayworth routine. The Earl of Hagedorn was back.

"But I was happiest for Buck. At the end of the first week he came up as I was counting the night's till and asked if I remembered offering him more responsibility in the business. I nodded. Then he mentioned if the offer was still good, he'd be interested. I told him I'd think about it, but as soon as he asked I knew what I'd do. I'd been hearing stories about the freaks in Eskimo villages. Supposedly there were half-man, half-reindeer creatures; eight foot tall giantesses who gave birth to nine babies at a time; three-hundred-year-old men who flew like eagles. The next morning I told Buck if he was serious about wanting responsibility, he could run the circus the last two weeks in Fairbanks and the first week in Anchorage while I was gone visiting villages. The next week I bought a plane, took flying lessons each morning, then spent the afternoons briefing him and Amanda on what had to be done in my absence.

"Say what you want. No one told me exactly what would happen when I flew into those little villages. The first place I went, I jumped out, did a little clowning, played a little music. The whole town must have shown up laughing and pointing. A little while later, the mayor, I think it was, invited me to dinner and offered to put me up for the night. I accepted the hospitality and in return gave the whole village lifelong passes to Hagedorn Brothers. Did they love me. The people were great, I tell you, normal as you and me, except they were hiding something. I could tell. But though I took it slow for a couple days and looked real close, I couldn't find a freak, not one. Then I asked a few of them about it. That's when they got quiet, real serious, and I knew I was on to it. Next village downriver, they all said. I refueled and flew off. Downriver was always the same: spend a day or two getting to know them, ask the same questions, get the same answers. I must have hit a half dozen villages. The strangest sight I saw was my own face in glass—the only white face in more than two weeks. It got to me, I tell you. I left a few days early, eager to meet the circus in Anchorage, even without a village freak to show off.

"I got into Anchorage past midnight, and the first thing I did was buy a local paper. There we were, Hagedorn Brothers, front page news. Buck had done good. I could tell. I skimmed the article: sell-out crowds, dangerous tiger, a reference to an accident. I caught a cab, asked the cabbie if he knew about the circus that was supposedly in town.

"Circus? he said. You mean Hagedorn Brothers? You oughta go. What a tiger. The monkey-chomper, the radio's calling it. 'Raw Monkey,' everybody yells. One night in Fairbanks it took a swipe at one of the Hagedorns, Tore off a thumb, I hear.

"Take me to the circus grounds, I told him. Fast.

"We ran a couple lights and I tipped him big when he let me off at the front gate. The Hagedorn Brothers banner stretched high over the entry. Almost 1 A.M., it was darker than it had been in Fairbanks or the villages. I could still see though, and could tell that everything had been properly shut down for the night. I kicked at a beer can, picked it up, threw it in the trash. I wondered whether I should knock on Buck's trailer now or wait until morning. My kid brother. As soon as he took charge of the circus—bam, his first accident. What dumb luck. I paced the grounds. Yes, everything was in order. Whatever had happened, he hadn't neglected the business. Maybe the cabbie was exaggerating. I decided to go to bed. I'd get the report from Buck in the morning.

"So I went to my trailer. Getting close, hearing a soft moan, then a loud deep one, I couldn't help but smile. So, she was lonely for me, couldn't get to sleep. I thought of calling to her, but, no, I'd surprise her. Then, about to enter, I heard grunting, Buck, and I felt my ribcage split. Sonny, I hope you never know what it's like to find your wife in bed with another man.

"I stood by the door listening for a minute, then put my hand on the knob, turned it, and cracked the door. They were licking each other, and I was watching. I felt this blood vessel in my forehead pop. My skull was exploding, I thought. I was glued to that doorway, watching, thinking that this was my brother, this was my wife, and they were enjoying it. Goddamnit, they were enjoying it. I held my breath, listened to their breathing, listened to more sucking and licking sounds.

"Love me, Buck, I heard her say then, and she was pulling him toward her, opening her legs wider. Love me, Buck. Just the sound of it. The sound of those words. Then he got on top of her, and when he did, I just closed my eyes, took a deep breath, put this grin on my face, and sort of tap danced into the little room, started doing a strip-tease as I sang this old show tune that just came to me:

> Pack up your troubles in your old kit-bag,
> And smile, smile, smile,
> While you've a lucifer to light your fag,
> Smile, boys, that's the style.

What's the use of worrying?
It never was worthwhile, so
Pack up your troubles in your old kit-bag,
And smile, smile, smile.

"Did that ever stop them. After I finished the second time through, I slipped off my underpants, and dived into bed, landing so I was on one side, Buck on the other, Amanda in between. A Hagedorn sandwich—you're getting twice the meat, I teased Amanda. When I started pawing, she turned away. Buck began explaining, showed me the bandaged left hand, said something about having a thumb sewn, kept talking, but I wasn't listening, wasn't going to listen. A Hagedorn sandwich—what an idea. I couldn't let it go. I kept it up until I fell asleep. When I woke, Buck and Amanda were gone.

"Lying in bed the next morning, thinking, I felt terrible, awful, but I knew I had Buck where I wanted him. Noontime, I followed him to the horse stalls. Buck, I said. You like it here in Alaska?

"He nodded warily.

"Okay, here's what I'll do. A quarter of a million right off the top, plus 5% the next five year's profits. Enough for you to retire on.

"He kept nodding, looking at me funny.

"I'm taking the circus, I said. You're going to stay here. Then I glanced at his bandaged thumb. And of course I'll pay your medical. Dental too. I'll even throw in ten years Blue Cross, Blue Shield. Here. Make it official, I said, and handed him a pen, thrust a paper at him to sign.

"That afternoon Amanda burst in the trailer, calling me a creep.

"So I'm a creep, I said.

"Creep, she said. Jerk. Buying out your brother.

"Aren't you quick to take his side.

"Look at you. He's feeling terrible and you make it into a

business deal.
"Shut up, Amanda.
"Listen to you.
"Listen to what?
"Nothing.
"Come here, I said. I want to fuck that nasty look right off you. Bitch.
"Don't you ever call me that.
"Come here, I said, lunging at her.
"What are you doing? You're sick, sick, sick.
"Come here, I said, catching her. I'm going to fuck your eyes out. Just like Buck was about to do last night. Like he probably did this morning.
"No, she screamed, hitting me. No.
"I forced her to the bed, started working off my belt and pants, then ripped off her skirt and panties. She was dry, but I muscled in. Now move, I commanded. I saw you with Buck. He made you so hot. Well, I saw. Things are going to be different with you and me, baby. Now move. I want you to move.
"Even though I hit her, she stayed limp underneath. Did I ever come. I came and came. It was like milk. And still I came. So this is what being a woman's like, I thought. But she didn't move, not until it was over. After I rolled off, she looked at me, got up, and slowly, deliberately, put on her panties and skirt, making it into a show. When I clapped my hands, she looked at me, and her blue eyes shone like sapphires. Earl Hagedorn, she said. You two-bit sicko. I hope you die.
"I laughed. She'd be back that night, I knew. I may not have been the greatest husband the past years, what with building the business, but now I understood what needed doing. If she wanted to be treated like an animal, I was the man.
"But she didn't come back. According to Sir Waffle, one of the clowns, Amanda went straight to Buck's and that was that. They cleared out during the night's performance and never came back. The tough part was we still had seven more weeks in Anchorage so were in a lurch. But the rest of the circus pulled through superbly. With Buck gone, his assistant, a skinny guy

named Butcher, took over most duties. And I found myself hanging by Dinah's cage more and more. Within a week I felt comfortable going in the ring with her. We weren't the same circus without Buck and Amanda, far from it, but Anchorage didn't know a thing. Raw Monkey. That was what they cared about. And we delivered. We packed them in through Labor Day.

"That was fifteen years ago. For a few more seasons I held my own. But the damn animals kept giving me trouble. No, it was the trainers. Butcher was a thief—stole a few hundred thousand before I canned him in Idaho. Then it was his assistant, an Italian gal named Romero. She got stomped on by the horses in The Dalles, and died a week later of internal injuries. Because of a lapse in the insurance, I had to pay a bundle, which meant selling the plane, and letting go a few acrobats and clowns. Then, I forget, we were going through one or two trainers a year for a while. I was doing fine with Dinah. All I had to do was whisper in an ear, squeeze a haunch, and there went another monkey, gone. But the rest? Shit. You don't want to hear it. One year I lost two trucks and all my horses in a bad wreck near Tonopah. The next, I had that fire in Yuma where I lost the monkeys, the reptiles, the birds, and the midget elephant, Bonsai. The goddamn Yuma paper. 'Circus Fries' was the front page headline and underneath they ran a photo of the burnt monkeys. 'Grilled and ready to eat' was the caption. The bastards, making a joke out of it. Of course I got more monkeys. The others I didn't replace.

"And the malls were hurting me. And television. I couldn't pick up a decent new act, and to get even one truck painted, much less ten, it was costing me a grand. Everything needed replacing. My equipment was getting old. Shit, *I* was getting old. A few years ago, when my top clown, Munster Bader, quit with no notice whatsoever, I went back into the ring myself. You know, I did great until I pulled the hamstring. I could hardly walk for two months, I tell you. The right leg stiffens if I'm not careful.

"Wait a second now, sonny. About five years ago I pulled

in for gas, the outskirts of North Las Vegas. We had a show that night in Needles. Filling up, I got tapped on my shoulder so I turned. It was Ford. He was old and wrinkly, but it was him, the jackass, still wearing the top hat. Bowing, he doffed it and gave me this big smile. On his head was a midget, couldn't have been more than eighteen inches high, no arms or legs, and it was completely covered with hair. I could barely make out the eyes, nose, and mouth, for chrissakes. Then the thing talked. It said: The Earl of Hagedorn. That's all. But the midget kept repeating it in this low, low voice. And Ford just laughed and laughed, told me he'd followed my career with interest. Then he asked me where I was going next. Needles, I told him. And then Ford just laughed one more time, said if I was on my way to Needles, I was out of luck, because he'd just spent a week and had taken every cent the town had for circus. Then the little turkey buzzard stuck his top hat back on and walked off, laughing.

"And since then we've lost acts right and left until it was just me, Dinah, and the monkeys. And Dinah's missing some teeth, her coat's mottled. Last week I had to call in a specialist, who's been treating her. I'm no vet. I'm a clown. And what did you say earlier? You say you have her now?"

"Mr. Hagedorn."

"Shit. You interrupt me one more time . . ."

"Mr. Hagedorn, I need the photos. And the keys. We're closing you up, Mr. Hagedorn. Closing you up."

"You wait, sonny. I'm not through."

"Mr. Hagedorn."

"No."

"Yes, Mr. Hagedorn. Now." I set my case on the desk, put thumbs to the clasps, unsnapped.

"No."

"Mr. Hagedorn," I said. "Your papers."

My Grandfather's Story

For my grandfather Val's eighty-first birthday, I took the bus downtown and let him buy me lunch. Arriving at our agreed meeting place, just outside the entrance to the Athenian, a cafeteria close to where he lived, I busied myself watching women. Seattle was so perfectly full of them these days. A few minutes past one, when my grandfather tapped me on the shoulder, I was looking the other way, following a blonde.

"Romeo, oh Romeo," he said, chuckling. "You ready to have some lunch with your old grandpa?"

I turned. My grandfather was wearing a white Stetson, a cowboy shirt, stiff new jeans, and pointed boots. A red carnation, pinned to his shirt pocket, made me think of a heart. On almost any old man the outfit would have looked ridiculous, but on Val, who as far as I knew had never ridden a horse, the clothes seemed not only appropriate, but stylish. The man looked sixty-five or seventy, in peak health except for an absurdly big, veiny, reddish-purple nose. But even with the nose, Val had bearing.

"You're looking pretty sharp, you old cowpunch," I told him.

He smiled, pleased. "New duds," he said. Taking off his hat, he motioned me to follow him into the cafeteria.

The lunch rush had passed so there was no line. My grandfather picked up a tray, quickly chose the liver and onions special, and ordered a beer. Just as quickly I settled on the shrimp newburg and a glass of apple juice. For dessert we decided to share a piece of coconut layer cake. After grandfather paid, we found a window table, the view overlooking the sailboats, ferries, and freighters crisscrossing the sound. In the distance, the Olympic Mountains jaggedly rose. After we set our food on the table, I carried our trays to the counter. Both of us had forgotten silverware and napkins so I grabbed some.

"So how's the young writer?" my grandfather asked once I returned. He pointed to my drink. "Can't you even join your grandfather for a beer on his birthday. For crying out loud, what are you, some kind of saint?" He coughed as he lifted his glass, then signaled me to lift mine. We clinked. "To me and you, sonny. May we both live to be a hundred."

I nodded and we drank. "I'm writing," I said, and realizing that wasn't explaining it, added, "No alcohol when I'm working on a story."

Confused, my grandfather looked at me.

"But it's a story about *you*. Understand? I'm working on a story about *you*. For your birthday. That's why I'm not drinking."

"Oh," he said, eyebrows raised, and his cheeks reddened. "Well, I'll be. About time." Then a tic swept the right side of his face, beneath the eye. He dropped his fork, put his right palm to the spot, and pressed.

"Grandpa Val."

"Don't get old, sonny. Don't get old," he said, voice quivery, once the attack passed. He put a forkful of liver in his mouth and chewed. "Now tell me about this story. Is it done? You know damn well this old bird's impossible to catch. It better be a good one."

I nodded. I *had* been writing, but not about Val. I'd only been teasing, saying the story was about him. In my current one, titled "Snakebit," a wilderness guide, bitten by a rattlesnake, gets nursed to health by a young Navajo woman, a physician's assistant. She's engaged to marry a doctor, who she thinks will support her through medical school. In my outline, the guide gets involved with the Indian. But on paper the story was bogged on page ten and going nowhere. I couldn't get the physician's assistant romantically interested in the guide without ruining things. I looked out the window. A ferry had docked, and cars were spilling out Alaska Way. That gave me an idea. For the next development I could have the guide, snubbed by the Native woman, but now at full strength, return home to Seattle. There he'll begin leading climbing expeditions to Alaska. On one of the trips, there's a woman . . .

"Sonny, didn't you hear? Tell me about the story."

"Oh, you know. It's about your life, about all your comebacks," I shoveled in a couple of mouthfuls of shrimp newburg.

"Speaking of comebacks, you planning another one?"

For years my grandfather had played folk music throughout the West, and the past decade he'd made a career out of his "comeback" tours. For his eightieth birthday he came out of retirement yet again to play in Los Angeles, San Francisco, Portland, and Seattle. My grandfather was still relatively famous—as a young man, he'd performed all over the country, and even in Europe. Fans still wrote.

"You see this?" He laid his left hand on the table. "It's getting to be like a claw. Takes me forever to make the changes. I can't do it any more."

"You can still sing."

He laughed. Then he put another forkful of liver and onions in his mouth, chewed, and swallowed. "Yeah, I can sing. I'll sing even after I'm dead. But what does it matter? I got nothing more to prove." He drank more of his beer. "Your grandpa's tired today," he said when he put down the glass.

"You sound depressed," I said.

"Sonny, believe me. I am not depressed."

"So what are you doing with yourself then? You have a new girlfriend? Or are you just reading a ton of books?" I ate the last shrimp of my newburg. Besides performing on stage, women and literature were my grandfather's passions. And periodic depressions were his great demon. And lately, ever since I'd moved to Seattle, he had taken an interest in me. Two or three times a year we'd get together for lunches in which he'd tell me stories, offer advice, and end by writing a big check "to help with expenses." As he saw it—and so often told me— I was the only one in the family "who understood," the only one in the family "with a chance."

"I haven't read a book in a month," my grandfather said.

"So, do you have a new love?"

He blushed. An eighty-one-year-old man—it was so sweet. "Tell me about her, " I said as I pushed aside my plate, and with a clean fork picked at the cake in the middle of the table.

"You'd approve, sonny. Her name's Theresa. She's a widow, born in Kentucky, a redhead, and only sixty. Only sixty," he mused, grinning, as he looked out the window. He put a finger to the glass. "Pretty face," he said. "A little pudgy. We met at a party in Portland after my show last April. In July she wrote to say she'd be in town visiting her daughter." My grandfather then pushed aside his plate.

"Tell me more about Theresa," I said. "And how come you didn't mention her before?"

My grandfather shrugged. "She sings and plays the piano. In October I took the train down for a visit. She just spent January at her daughter's—a very pretty girl by the way. And you know what?" My grandfather grinned broadly.

"What?"

"We're getting married on Easter. That's exactly two months and one day away," he said, beaming.

"You and Theresa are getting married?" I shook my head. "Isn't this a little sudden, grandpa?"

"Not at my age, sonny. I'm eighty-one, goddamnit." Holding his fork upside-down, he triumphantly stuck it in the coconut layer cake. "You see that?" he crowed.

"What? I see a fork sticking out of piece of cake."

"You don't see a thing yet, sonny. You don't see a thing. Now how about going up to the counter and getting your old grandpa a shot of coffee with just the littlest squirt of cream."

For the rest of the lunch, as I grilled grandpa about Theresa, he grilled me about my writing goals. Finally I grabbed a fresh napkin and mapped out a plan for the years ahead. He approved. Rising from the table, he handed me a check. "Keep writing," he said.

Just outside the entrance to the cafeteria, Val fit the Stetson on his head. Then we hugged. As always, I offered to walk him to his place. And as always, he politely declined. But be-

fore he left, he said, "Sonny, four weeks from today, same place, 1 P.M. sharp. I'll take you to lunch."
"Sure thing," I said.
Turning to go, he said, "And finish the story you're working on." He winked. You know the one I'm talking about." Chuckling, my grandfather slowly walked away, an exaggerated bowlegged gait that I guess he picked up from the movies.
The next week I wrote the last two thirds of "Snakebit." I had the guide lead a successful winter ascent of Mount Baker before going to Alaska and attempting Denali. On this expedition one of the climbers is a doctor, a woman surgeon who's recently divorced. After a few setbacks—she loses her balance and nearly shoves him into a crevasse; the next day, making sure she overhears, he refers to her as the East Coast bitch— the guide and the doctor hit it off. After spending several nights in his tent, they make plans for when they're off the mountain. On a clear, relatively windless June morning, they reach the summit, and on the mountaintop they kiss. Two days later, the woman doctor slips, falls, and plummets to her death. The grief-stricken guide is disconsolate for months. One night, drunk, he writes a maudlin letter to the physician's assistant, the woman from before. Her doctor, too, is now out of the picture, and she invites him for a visit. The story ends with the guide driving through a lightning storm en route to her. As he reflects on how strange life is, every so often a bolt illuminates the night.
After the initial joy of finishing, I was depressed as I usually was once I completed one. Life was strange, and though I was acquiring enough technique to make even the strangest plots seem feasible, I no longer cared. Why do this, I wondered. Once I had liked writing, so had wandered into it. And thanks to my grandfather, I kept at it. But now it was a job, in many ways like any other. Stuck, I needed a break.
The end of February I drove to Eugene to visit a girlfriend, Janet. For one weekend we were quite the pair. She, too, was drifting, in her case attending law school, not because of passion, but because the degree would make her employable. A talented actress, she was tired of being poor.

For three days we drifted together, she ignoring her schoolwork, me ignoring the big questions suddenly dogging me. Our last morning together, she told me a man she'd never met, a friend of her father's, had started writing in December and the past week had asked her to marry him. He was lonely, rich, and from his picture wasn't bad-looking. She was thinking of accepting. Then she cried for a while and I held her, saying nothing, hoping that was enough because that was all I could do. That afternoon I left, relieved to be on my way home, but at the same time not looking forward to arriving. I was tired of writing, tired of being supported by my grandfather. It was time for a change. Driving back, I bought a motel room in Longview, and the spent the evening watching television.

When I reached home Monday, not knowing what else to do, I began writing about my grandfather. But no sooner had I started that I saw Val was right: he was a tough old bird to capture. There was the boisterous, happy-go-lucky public side of him, the folksinger who liked to tour true to his carefully cultivated image of a hard-drinking, hard-loving rover. And there was the quiet, private side, the man who loved nothing more than to stay in for weeks at a time playing guitar and reading books. The same man who had been my generous, good-humored benefactor the past three and half years was not only estranged from all seven of his children, including my father, but also had been married six times, and had, in two of the divorces, including his first one, to my grandmother, been cited for "extreme mental cruelty."

I began to write, deciding on a first-person narrator, a character similar to me, the grandson. I'd begin with the lunch I had at the Athenian and tell of his latest comeback.

By the weekend I was well into it. The main plot was my grandfather's career, which I quickly traced from his first guitar, which he salvaged from a trash can, through the years of practice, the songwriting, the touring, and the latest comeback-to-be. The tougher part was weaving in the two main subplots. First, there were all the women. Val had once told me except for his first wife, he'd never pursued a woman in his life and that his subsequent marriages, as well as his many affairs, had been "accidents." Accidents. That was my grandfather's euphemism for shirking responsibility. So I exaggerated his love life, made it comic. But I couldn't write the story strictly as comedy. And that was where I stuck in his eldest son, my father. I made my dad a bitter low-achiever, a man who had reached out for his father time and again, and had never found him.

By Sunday night, I had managed a cohesive draft except for two problems: the proper tone for the grandson-narrator; and the ending, which for this story had to veer toward, but avoid, sentimentality.

That evening, going to bed, I remembered back to when I was twenty-two, and finishing my English degree at Boulder. That spring I saw an old folksinger performing at a club on Pearl Street. For an encore, the performer announced he'd sing a song he'd recently written for his grandson, Lance, who he'd never met. Lance, that was my name. Listening to him sing, I trembled as I recalled the last time I saw my grandmother, Eva. I was eight years old. She was in the hospital, dying. My mother and father were out in the hall with my sister. It was Saturday morning and the cartoons were on. I was watching with my grandmother, and trying not to breathe the air. Then I felt her fingers on my scalp. You need to know the truth, she said. Your grandfather isn't really dead; he's a singer. He's in your blood, and if he ever comes calling, you'll know it. My grandmother died the next day.

Until that encore, I'd forgotten the memory.

Afterward, I wandered backstage to meet the folksinger. A woman my age was on his arm. "I'm Lance," I said.

"Lance who," he said.

"Your grandson, Lance," I said.

The folksinger studied me for a second, then whispered something to the woman. When she left, he asked, "Who're your parents?"

"My father's Bill," I said. "My mother's Rosie. Both of them hate your guts."

"Is that so?" Then the folksinger smiled and said, yes, he was now quite sure I was the one he'd written the song about. This was a special occasion, he said, and he'd like to take me out drinking for a night I'd never forget.

The next morning I woke in a hotel room with the worst hangover I'd ever had. I smelled vomit, and after stumbling to the bathroom I saw why. My chest was smeared with it. Nauseated, I puked again, this time into the toilet. After showering, I put on clothes that smelled of cigarettes. Leaving, I found a note tacked to the door: *Meet me six months from today, Seattle, 1 P.M., the Athenian, lunch.* It was signed, *Your grandfather, Val.*

I met him then, soon after moved to Seattle, and had been meeting him since. And now I was writing about him. Falling asleep, I was undecided whether to throw in the Boulder episode, but the next day I wrote it, and then added a few of our lunch meetings. That would help explain the narrator. Ambitious, troubled, unreliable—no wonder he was taking over the story. Tuesday afternoon, I tackled the ending. That was easy. I finished in time for our Wednesday lunch date.

Late morning I took the bus downtown, proofreading my story on the ride. So far my grandfather had liked everything I'd shown him, or at least said he had. But this one was different, and I was wary. Getting off the bus, I stuck the story in my pack. Like the month before, I arrived early at the Athenian and waited by watching women pass. This time I saw my grandfather approaching from across the street. Seeing me notice him, he waved. I waved back. He was flanked by two attractive women, one much older. The redhead, I guessed, was Theresa. I wondered if the younger one, a dirty blonde, was her daughter. From a distance she looked like Janet, only taller. Both women were wearing classy dresses. My grandfather, who usually favored jeans, wore a black suit, a starched white shirt, and a red and green striped tie. All three had on dark, shiny shoes. In tennis sneakers and old blue jeans, I felt out of place once the three closed in.

"Theresa, Sara, my grandson, Lance," Val said proudly.

I shook hands all around. "What's the occasion?" I asked.

"New policy at the Athenian?"

"He didn't tell you?" Sara said.

My grandfather shook his head. "I couldn't wait until Easter, sonny. Me and Theresa are getting married today right after lunch."

"Today? You're getting married this afternoon?"

He nodded. "Let's eat," he said. "I'll tell you more at the table."

In line, grandfather insisted on ordering for all of us: grilled sole with sides of french fries and cole slaw, Red Hook Ale to drink, a piece of chocolate cake to share four ways. We found a table by the window. Val and Theresa sat on one side, I was next to Sara on the other. I kept waiting for an explanation, but my grandfather kept whispering into Theresa's ear, or giggling as she whispered into his. As they began playfully tickling each other, I suddenly realized except for the first time I met him, when he dismissed the young woman he was with, I'd never been with him when others were around. Was that part of what was making me feel so strange here, I wondered.

Then Sara's hand was on my knee as she whispered in my ear, giggling. "You know, I just thought how in a few hours I'm going to be your aunt once removed."

"Is that what it's called?" I said, and that instant felt like I was talking to somebody I had known all my life. Her hand was still on my knee. I could feel her warm breath in my ear. I looked at her. Her gray-green eyes seemed familiar and were opening me up. My leg muscles tightened. Sara let her hand linger a second more, pressing with her fingers before letting go. Then she chuckled. And then we were staring at each other. When I looked away, I noticed Val and Theresa were grinning at us.

"Mom," Sara said squirming. "Don't say a thing. You two just go on being lovey-dovey. Me and Lance don't even know each other yet." Then she looked at me again, and again I felt like I was with someone familiar, who was somehow inside me.

I looked down at my food, tried concentrating on eating

and drinking. In a minute my grandfather was snuggling with Theresa. I stole a look at Sara. She was looking at me, waiting.

"I hear you're a writer," she said.

I nodded. "And you? You write too?"

She shook her head. "Maybe someday. I sing and play guitar. I substitute teach high school French. I like to read." She shrugged. "Actually, I'm kind of drifting."

"To what?" I felt her eyes pulling me. Under the table, my left hand accidentally touched her knee.

After lunch, the four of us crammed into a cab and rode the several blocks to the courthouse. A skinny man with glasses met us in the lobby, led us into a chamber, and with Sara and I witnessing, quickly married Val to Theresa. Kissing her for the first time as a husband, my grandfather slipped his hand down his new wife's backside. Not breaking the kiss, Theresa took that hand and moved it to a fleshier spot.

"A lusty old lady I got for a mom," Sara said.

"Number seven and maybe he's finally gotten it right," I said.

"Maybe," Sara agreed, bumping me slightly.

After the ceremony, we squeezed into another cab, this time my grandfather on Theresa's lap, Sara on mine, as we rode to Sara's apartment on Capitol Hill. There we drank champagne and listened to Sara play and sing songs I recognized as my grandfather's. She was good, I thought, as I uncorked a second bottle and filled everybody's glasses. Then I used the bathroom, which adjoined Sara's bedroom. On the way back I snooped through her bookshelves: women novelists, nature writers, a number of field guides and songbooks. Scattered around the room were a few framed pictures. Only one had a man in it, and he was much older. As I returned to the living room, Sara was pushing her guitar on my grandfather.

"Why don't you play something pretty for Lance over there," he said, refusing the guitar, and pointing to me.

"Val," Theresa said, smiling. "Play something for me. Send me to heaven."

"Oh, all right, my love," Val said. "I think I got one." He

took the guitar, strummed a D chord, another D chord, tried to make his fingers move to G. "Ah shit," he muttered as he closed his left hand around the neck and thrust the instrument back to Sara. "Fingers don't want to move. I'm through playing."
Theresa put an arm around him and kissed his cheek. "Honey, sing me the one where the girl disappears and you go from place to place, looking for a trace of her. Sing it like the night you proposed. Sara can back you up."
I saw my grandfather frown then, a frown that seemed to expand and expand under that big, veiny nose. What was he thinking? Of Theresa, who was regarding him so warmly? Of Sara, who could play guitar like he once could? Of me, Lance, still observing from the doorway?
Suddenly I felt inadequate—the grandfather story was still in the backpack. I shivered. And the next instant I shut my eyes, could feel myself sail into his frown.
Evangeline was her name. Evangeline Stoddard. She was pretty like a wisp of candlelight, always flickering somewhere or other. All of us were after her. I found a guitar in the garbage and fixed it up and learned to play so I could court her. All I did was play. It didn't mean nothing, not at first. So I was the guitar player, the singer. She had her choice: the ballplayer, the brain, the artist. But I had that guitar and I had my songs. I kept practicing. She was the one for me, that wisp of a girl, pretty, and every time I looked at her, she was always different. No way she could avoid me forever.
We started going out. Still, it took a while. I had to say things just right to her mother, just right to her father. But Eva, Eva, I started to understand Eva. I knew I had her when as soon as I started playing her eyes went a little crazy. Nobody ever did that before. I love you, Val, she'd say. I love you, Eva, I'd say. Forever and ever. I'd hold her and sing for hours. It got so I didn't pick the guitar any more. I'd just sing and sing. That's all I wanted. She was so pretty. How we burned together. No one else mattered, none of them more than wisps. Eva and me. I couldn't stay away,. The next thing I knew she

was pregnant.

When she broke the news, she said she understood how young men like to run around and that I wasn't fit yet to be a father. She had this to say: I want your baby, Valentine, more than I want you. If you ever plan to run around on me, get out now.

The way she said it. That look in her eyes. I asked her to marry me. She refused. I kept after her, asking and asking, promising I'd be the best husband and father the world had ever seen. We married in her sixth month. That wedding day. That was the happiest day of my life. Eva. Everything was on fire.

To support us I had the music. It was the only work I could get. First, I'd be gone overnight, sometimes a weekend, and then a couple of weeks. I'd get lonely. At home, if the boy cried, I got mad. Eva got pregnant again. The boy was always crying. I blamed everything on that boy. Everything. Eva really loved me. I loved her. But I was gone. And I was young and dumb. Young and dumb. All I've ever had is a guitar. And a guitar's nothing but a box.

That frown of Val's. I understood. And I understood why, an instant later, when he opened his mouth to sing, only a confused squeal come out, and then a great grunt of frustration as he put his hands to his face, and pressed.

"Val," Theresa said.

""I'll be okay, he growled, rising. Then he staggered toward me. "Marry her, boy," he whispered to me fiercely. "Marry her, boy, and stay married. She's pretty and she'll love you forever. Don't make my mistake. Sing to the same one over and over. That's what love is, boy. That's what love is."

Then he fell at my feet.

As Theresa and Sara helped him to the sofa, I phoned for an ambulance. When my grandfather opened his eyes, there was first a dazed, baffled stare, then the slow realization. And then I saw the terror.

Looking from mother to daughter, I nodded. Then I tenderly approached.

Whitemarsh

At 4 A.M., you're downstairs reading year-old magazines and watching a movie, something about a murder. You wonder if this is one more part of the grief process: sipping a beer somewhat pleasantly, letting your mind go. It's Sunday night. The guests are gone. Your mother, aunt, sister, and baby niece sleep upstairs. The funeral's over. You are the only one awake, the man of the house.

You put down *Sports Illustrated*, pick up a *New Yorker*, and flip pages, stopping at a cartoon of an embalmers' convention. One embalmer, a zombie-like woman on his arm, says to a second embalmer, who is stirring a drink, "Grimsley, the business is coming alive. The word is growth." You put down that *New Yorker* and pick up another, by chance turning to a poem titled "The Death of Not Just Any Zebra." You read the poem, a sonnet which ends with the line, "the black to be matched with intelligence."

Black seems to be your color today. As you ponder this, you hear swing music and look to the television. There's a dance scene, and the character you recognize as the suspect is jitterbugging with the love interest, a beautiful, dark-haired reporter, while a tuxedo-clad big-band plays in the background. The musicians are all black. Amused, you stare at the screen and tilt a half-full beer bottle to your lips.

After receiving the early morning phone call informing you of your father's death, you spent all day Friday putting your affairs in order so you could take the following week off and go back east. Then you flew a red-eye, changing planes in Detroit, arriving just before noon on Saturday, carrying with you a large suitcase and your fiddle. Your sister, Tina, picked you up at the airport, her nine-month-old baby, Roxanne, strapped in a safety seat in the back. Carl, her husband, was in Phoenix on business, Tina explained as she started your father's car, a dark brown Mercedes, its odometer registering less than 10,000 miles. Your father had been proud of that car. Two weeks earlier, the last time you talked to him on the phone, he mentioned how the Mercedes was handling like a dream.

Riding back to the house, the air conditioner blowing, you kept looking out the windows, amazed that though your rarely returned here, the route was familiar, this zig-zag through Manayunk, Roxborough, Ivy Ridge, back to Whitemarsh. As you and your sister took turns asking one another how things had been the past eighteen months, you tried to draw memories from each passing intersection, each passing shopping center. So often your father drove these roads, you with him. When you weren't looking out the window, you looked behind at Roxanne.

As you reached the house, your mother and your father's sister, your Aunt Sally, were outside, waiting. Even before you could get out of the car, they were telling you what had happened and what would happen next. Your father died just before sunrise Friday. He had gone to the bathroom, and when he hadn't come out your mother grew worried. Arthur, she called. She got up, called once more, and when he still didn't answer, she knocked on the bathroom door, cracked it open, then pushed. There he was, your father, sitting on the toilet, dead. After dragging him back to bed, she tucked him under the sheets, laid his head on the pillow, and began the phone-calling, first the doctor, then the family. You were the last to be called because of the time difference. And now you were the last to arrive, because you had to travel the farthest.

You gave your mother a hug and kiss, and told her she looked remarkably well. Then you hugged and kissed Aunt Sally. The three of you stood awkwardly for a minute. Then your mother said the autopsy had listed heart failure. She wasn't looking so good, your mother; you didn't know what to do, what to say. But you had to say something. What was next, you asked.

A few close friends would be coming by this afternoon, she told you. There were already dinner reservations for tonight. The funeral would be tomorrow, Sunday. Then, the cremation. Your father requested that his ashes be placed in two urns: one to be kept on the fireplace mantel; one to be buried in the backyard. Afterward, there would be a gathering here. Your mother sniffled when she said that your father asked you give a eulogy at the funeral and that you bury the one urn. He loved you so much and was so proud of your story writing, your father. Then your mother began crying, and you moved closer to touch her.

After lunch, while your mother and Aunt Sally remained at the house to receive condolence visits and babysit Roxanne, Tina drove you to the funeral home, a downtown building made of granite, that from the outside reminded you of an art museum. An assistant funeral director, a big and hearty man, told you what preparations had been made as he led you to the casket. Then he left the two of you alone to breathe in the flowers and view your embalmed father, his eyes closed, face clean-shaven, a jowly sixty-five-year-old man wearing a starched white shirt, solid red tie, a perfectly tailored black suit.

You didn't stay long. From there you rode to the crematory, and after being assured the arrangements there were in order, you asked your sister if you could drive back. She let you, and you decided to go roundabout, past every meaningful landmark you could think of. Turning off Henry Avenue, you drove along the Wissahickon through Germantown and Flourtown before returning through Blue Bell, Broad Axe, Plymouth Meeting. It was warm and sunny, not too humid, a wonderful Saturday afternoon, and you shut off the air conditioner and rolled down all the windows to take in the breeze. Neither of you said much much, not even when you passed your old schools, your camps, your sports fields. When you drove by Miles Park, where you once pitched a shutout in American Legion ball to clinch a district title, your sister asked

what you were thinking. Nothing, you answered.
You spent the rest of the afternoon puttering around the house, avoiding your family. You tried to nap, but all you could do was lie there thinking how you never liked it here, how you never learned to act properly, how your father was dead. You thought about what would happen when your mother died. Only your sister would be left, someone you liked, but could never talk to. You wished that this had happened years ago so now you would be over it. You wished your father was still alive, or at least had warned you somehow. You wished you were home in Seattle, doing something fun. Life was fun, you repeated. You got up, and for an hour you sat in a chair on the back patio, your shirt off, reading a *Sports Illustrated* article about last fall's World Series. Then you threw down the magazine, went inside, drew a hot bath, and soaked in the tub.

For dinner the five of you drove to a fashionable Blue Bell restaurant that your mother said had been your father's favorite the past few years. As soon as you walked in, you could tell the choice was wrong: the restaurant was loud, crowded, pretentious. When you asked politely if perhaps it might be more appropriate to eat elsewhere, your mother flashed you a murderous look. At that moment you vowed to drink your way through the meal, and you wished you had looked into the details of this outing earlier in the day.

As you expected, the meal went badly. Your mother saw Aunt Sally smother a roll with butter and immediately accused her of not watching her cholesterol—she was as bad as Arthur. Aunt Sally accused your mother of nagging Arthur into an early grave. Your mother looked at you as if appealing for a defense. You made meaningless small talk with Tina, anything to deflect the squabbling. Meanwhile, the service was indifferent, the waiter taking far too long to deliver the drinks. Later, he forgot your salads, and insulted you when you mentioned the oversight. When the main course arrived, the portions were small, your fish overcooked. Only the baby, Roxanne, sleeping in the high chair, appeared content. When the check came, you reached for it, and since your father wasn't around, it was yours. You paid with your charge card, the same one that paid for the flight, and you cringed as you signed the bill: over two hundred dollars. Just paying the minimum next month was going to be a challenge. For the first time, you wondered how much you might inherit, and felt guilty. Looking around to see if anybody noticed your sudden discomfort, you judged no one had. Relieved, you stared down at the cloth napkin covering your lap.

You drove home. Though it was already late, as you pulled in the driveway you invited your family to stay up and hear you play fiddle. Despite pleading tiredness, the women sat in the living room as you got the instrument, tightened the bow, put the chin rest to your your chin, and played a medley of square dance tunes. Though they clapped when you were done, you could tell they were only humoring you. You put your fiddle away as they went upstairs to bed. Then you composed the eulogy as you stayed up watching movies and leafing through newspapers. When you spotted your father's obituary, you began crying softly, aware that if you really let yourself go, you'd wake the others.

That cry got you started. With tears in your eyes, you finished the eulogy and quickly wrote two poems, first a sestina, then a villanelle, scribbling the lines so quickly that you felt that you were not the poet, but the stenographer for some other poet. When you finished that second poem, you set down the pen, turned off the television, and went upstairs to bed.

You look at the clock: almost 4:30. 1:30 Seattle time. You rise, put the empty bottle in the trash, open the refrigerator, grab another beer, twist off the top, and drink. The suspect's in court, and the preliminary evidence is against him. The victim, a wealthy civic leader and tennis enthusiast, owed the suspect, a tennis pro, more than a quarter of a million dollars, money the pro won in an elaborate swindle. The civic leader didn't want to pay. However, the tennis pro, with gambling debts totaling over one hundred thousand dollars, and pressured by loan sharks, apparently threatened, then shot the civic leader, who was found in his car, a bullet in the head. The caliber of the weapon was identical to the tennis pro's handgun, which was lying on the back seat, the tennis pro's fingerprints on the trigger. That's the prosecution's case, establishing both motive and method. The tennis pro's lawyer, though an honest man, is an alcoholic who's thoroughly overmatched here. All the tennis pro's got going for him is the love of the beautiful reporter who's risking her job, and her life, to investigate this case she's already been warned off of.

You pick up the TV page and read the blurb for this late-night movie. Handsome gambler and tennis pro must depend on attractive journalist to set him free. Three and a half stars. You think: If this is three and a half stars you're wasting your time in Seattle trying to write literature. You should go to Hollywood, live in a bungalow, and write screenplays. You can do better than this. As is, poetry editors tell you your poetry's glib, fiction editors say your fiction's false, nobody's publishing you, and everybody agrees your fiddling lacks something essential. Except your father, no one thinks you will ever amount to much. And your father is dead, cremated.

After getting up this morning, you put on a stiff white shirt, and then the charcoal-colored three-piece suit your father bought for you ten years ago, your college graduation present. You fingered the wool, wishing it was cotton. But this was the only suit you owned so you got on with it. You knotted your black tie, laced your black shoes, went downstairs, and as you sat in the living room waiting for the women, you impatiently glanced at the Sunday paper, then at your notes for the eulogy, then outside. It was another beautiful day. Seeing a shaft of light brighten a row of houseplants, you wanted to cry as you remembered how your father loved sitting in this room, especially on Sundays as he read the paper. You sat for a few more seconds, then went to the kitchen and poured yourself orange juice.

The women found you there, drinking juice at the kitchen table. They were all dressed in black, even the baby. Your mother, black hair streaked with gray, her lips and fingernails painted a gaudy purple, gave you the car keys. In silence, you drove to the funeral home, arriving more than ninety minutes ahead of the scheduled start for the service. As soon as you arrived, the assistant funeral director greeted you, briefing you again on the arrangements. You wished you could follow him to his office and spend the day sitting at a desk, enclosed by four walls, only a telephone for company.

Instead, you stood dutifully by the casket, your mother on your right, your sister on your left, your niece asleep in your sister's arms. For what seemed like a long time you accepted condolences. Your father's business associates, their faces hard and somber, clasped your hands tightly. Women you didn't know, their make-up thick, hugged you, murmuring they were sorry. You breathed in the sweetness of the flowers, looked at them, and wondered how you missed noticing the colors yesterday. The blues, yellows, red, and purples, though overdone to your taste, were beautiful. You saw your mother talking to Rabbi Elias, an old family friend who would officiate the service. Then, looking at your niece, you knew that baby girl was going to wake up and cry, and she did. And as she started crying, you cried too, but softly.

When the service began, you sat in the front row, felt hot in your suit, and couldn't listen. Then Rabbi Elias nodded, and you walked to the pulpit, put your notes on the podium, and looked toward the people seated on the brown folding chairs in front of you.

As you stood there, prepared to speak, you felt as if your wool suit was swallowing you up, and instead of eulogizing your father, you wanted to tell a different story: how you and your girlfriend, Jessica, had planned to go to Florida for Easter vacation your senior year of college, and how your father had forbidden the trip. In fact, he had ordered you to come home, threatening that if you refused his request, he wouldn't attend your graduation. Though it made no difference to you whether you attended your own ceremony, you knew the ultimatum meant your father had something to tell you.

Your father had quit college his sophomore year to fly planes in the second world war. When he returned from the war, the first thing he did was marry his childhood sweetheart, your mother. The second thing he did was go to work for his father, your grandfather, a printer. Though he always meant to go back to college and finish his degree, he never found the time. The business prospered. He had two children, yourself and your sister. He was proudest not that he had made a lot of money and established himself in the community, but that both his children would graduate from college and surpass him. He insisted on paying every cent of tuition, and he always told you how he would cry when he saw you, his only son, graduate from college.

So, in deference to your father, you went home that vacation, perplexed. For five days your father hardly spoke a word to you, and you spent your time reading magazines and fantasizing what it would have been like to have been in Florida with Jessica. Then, on Thursday morning, your father called you at the house and told you to take the train downtown to meet him at the office. You did as you were told and met him in time for lunch.

He took you to a seafood restaurant called Bookbinders. There he told you about the war: how in Hawaii he had fallen in love with a Japanese-American girl name Lois, who later disappeared; how it felt to be a bombardier; how he had contracted an insomnia that plagued him still. About the insomnia, he had said something you would always remember, "I got it from smelling people die."

You both had chowder, the flounder, and coffee. Afterward you smoked your first cigar. Throughout the meal, your father never stopped talking. And you, you listened, never once interrupting or questioning. Finally your father walked you out of the restaurant, around the corner, and down some steps into a tailor's shop, a single room not much larger than a cubicle. The place smelled of must and sweat, and as your father watched, the tailor, a man with a cadaverous complexion and bony wrists, introduced himself as a friend of your grandfather's. Then, as he talked about his childhood in Poland, he took your measurements and made you select cloth for a suit. Though you looked at your father pleadingly, he disregarded you. Feeling trapped, you chose the charcoal-colored wool. After the tailor chalked the cloth, he put a hand on your shoulder, looked at you kindly, and said, "Siegfried's grandson, once you put on my clothes, you can never go back." You shrunk under the tailor's hand and stared at the concrete floor. Then your father took care of the payment and you left. Two months later your father and mother attended your college graduation, and after the ceremony your father beamed as he walked between you and your mother to your dormitory. There, he told you to wait with your mother, and he returned a few minutes later with the tailored suit. He asked you to try it on. You refused. He asked you again. You refused once more, and thought that would be the end of it.

But that night over dinner, though the suit was never mentioned, the two of you argued bitterly, mostly about your future. Your father insisted you join the family business, if only for six months; it was important to him. You refused; you wanted to travel. He kept insisting, you kept refusing, and for the next several years, as you changed jobs and addresses once, twice, sometimes three times a year, your relationship with your father was badly strained. Still, through it all, you made sure to take the suit with you. Then you moved to Seattle, began writing more seriously, and when you wrote a story you were proud of, you tentatively sent it to your father. He responded positively, and then you grew closer. The other day, you'd packed the suit in your suitcase. Today you were wearing the charcoal-colored suit for the first time.

You wanted to tell that story, but did nothing of the sort. Instead you talked of how your grandfather, Siegfried, had come to the United States from Poland and started a printing company, Goldman Printing, and how your father, Siegfried's son, had gone to war, come back, married your mother, and begun working for his father. As your father, Arthur, took on more and more responsibility, the business prospered, merging with other small firms as it became a much bigger firm. Your father worked hard, was a fair man, had provided a comfortable life for his wife and children. For that you were grateful.

But it was not always easy being his son. Though your father wanted you to continue in the business, you could not. You simply could not—it was not your nature—and though your father let you know time and again that nothing would have pleased him more, he knew when it was time to let you be. Your father loved you for being yourself, and for that you were thankful, and you were able to love him more.

In your own way, you could say you were following both your grandfather and your father. Just as your grandfather had emigrated seventy years earlier to find a new home and start a new business, so, too, had you left one coast for another. Just as your father succeeded at a life that was a continuation of his father's, so, too, were you now writing, practicing the craft that made it possible for Siegfried Goldman to go into the printing business in the first place, and allowed Arthur Goldman to follow. Your family was a circle.

Then you reached into your pocket, pulled out the sestina you had written the previous night, and read it:

> Father, today we send you home.
> How it would please you to see your son
> speaking, your friends listening, the sun
> shining. A ceremony is a kind of art
> and this afternoon the god
> of funerals blesses you, father—
>
> all is perfect. I remember when your father,
> Siegfried, died. It was at home,
> a slow, painful, cancerous dying that god
> prolonged. As death neared, you, Arthur, his son,
> sat at the bedside and waited. "Art,"
> he said, reaching for you. "The sun

comes for me. I am flying. The sun."
And then he died, Siegfried, your father.
At his funeral you told of his art:
how he left Poland, his father's home,
to come to America; how he fathered a son,
a daughter, a business; how he loved god,

baseball, cigars, his garden. Oh my god,
you cried. How he'd love today, the sun
out, tomatoes ripening, a game on TV, his son
speaking. Now, twenty-two summers later, father,
amidst ripening tomatoes, you, too, are flying home,
and I've been called to practice my art:

the storytelling. Father, my art
saddens me. I cannot play god.
I cannot bring you back. Your home
is now upward, where the sun
rises, where your father,
Siegfried, awaits you, Arthur, his son.

Father, I hope I've been a good son
because being one is a great, great art.
I will always love you, father.
You were a good man. I only hope god
saw you in our yard, crouching in the sun,
thrusting a catcher's mitt behind an improvised home

plate. "Right here, son. A fastball so fast god
won't see. Don't worry. Art'll catch it." The sun
was shining, father. That was our home.

   As you finished reading the sestina, you were crying, and though you had more to say, Rabbi Elias stepped next to you and announced the gathering at your house that would take place this coming evening. Then people surrounded you, consoling you. You let them. You remembered you were supposed to help load the casket in the hearse and you did. The box felt weightless. You let your sister lead you to your father's brown Mercedes, and you held her hand as she started the car and followed the hearse to the crematory. As you waited there, you spent the time sitting nervously in a straight back chair, feeling like something was growing inside you, and something else was leaving you. After the cremation was complete, the cremator gave one urn to you and one to your mother. They were big and silvery, heavier and more ornate than you would have thought.

The five of you returned to the house in your father's car, your sister driving. The caterers were already there, two young women busy in the kitchen. Upon walking in the front door, your mother put the one urn on the fireplace mantel and then went to check the food preparations. You brought the other urn upstairs and gazed at it as you took off your suit, bathed, shaved, and changed into blue jeans and a tee shirt. When your mother saw your outfit as you approached her downstairs, she started to say something. You interrupted, told her you had a hole to dig, these were the clothes for it, and you weren't going to argue.

Carrying the urn, you went to the shed, grabbed a spade and shovel with your free hand, and walked out and around to the backyard. There you stood, surveying the property, the late afternoon sun sinking, trying to imagine where you should dig this hole. Then you set down the tools and the urn, and began pacing, first back and forth, from the peach tree toward the vegetable garden, then down near where your father had erected a swing set when you were a child. You felt like a hunter, sniffing the air, gauging the breeze, watching the shade slowly envelope the yard. Then you knew. At this time of year the last rays of evening light would fall in the southeast corner. You would bury the urn there, and as you decided this you felt a pang: that was where your father used to squat, punching his old catcher's mitt, squinting into the sun, encouraging you to give it your best heave.

The mourners began arriving at your house. A few of them

stood on the patio, drinks in their hands, cigarettes in their mouths, watching you dig from that distance, not wanting to disturb you. There was not much to your task. The grass at this spot was lush. The ground beneath was fairly moist. The hole didn't have to be deep. You gripped the spade hard and kept thrusting it in the ground until the earth gave way. Then you thrust deeper and deeper, pressing the blade with your foot, leaning on the handle until you turned over the dirt, throwing it over your shoulder. As you worked on, four men ambled over, your father's business partners. When they offered to help, two of them with cigars in their mouths, you let them. Each man took a single turn, handling the spade like a golf club before giving it back to you.

Toward sunset you had a hole that could have buried a half dozen urns. You laid down the tools, drifted into the house, and told your mother that were ready to bury the urn. Your mother made the announcement and soon the party gathered in the shadows of the yard's southeast corner. As you stood in front of the people, you said only that you had written a second poem for your father and wished to share it:

"It's all part of the journey,"
my father used to say. "So don't mourn
the comings, the goings, the twists and turns

of age." From him I learned
what it meant to be reborn:
it's all part of the journey

home. Earlier today we burned
his corpse as specified, my feelings torn—
the comings, the goings, the twists and turns

of our lives cut. We had earned
our love late, he and I, like October corn.
"It's all part of the journey" —

those words echo from this urn.
I remember too little time, too many thorns,
the comings, the goings, the twists and turns

of unmet desires. The echo back I yearn
to change. "Yes, father, I will mourn."
It's all part of the journey —
the comings, the goings, the twists and turns.

When you finished reading, your eyes teared, and you bent over, placed the urn in the hole, took hold of the shovel, scooped a small heap of dirt, and dumped it on top of the urn. The earth hit the metal and barely made a sound. You paused, then repeated the procedure: scoop, then dump; scoop, then dump. The evening seemed to darken quickly then. A few fireflies blinked. The mourners left you alone, almost all choosing to return inside. You continued working, every so often stopping to pack the dirt with the shovel's bottom. Almost finished, the darkness almost total, you scraped together a last pile of dirt, and just as you were about to toss it on top of the rest, you thought better of it, and began walking northwest, counting approximately sixty and a half feet from the hole. On that spot, somewhere near the middle of the backyard, you dropped the dirt, knelt, then smoothed the soil with your hands, making a miniature mound.

Feeling empty, you wandered back to the shed, leaned the tools against the wall, walked across the yard, and entered the house through the kitchen. After washing your hands and face in the kitchen sink, you looked around. You smelled food and were surprised to realize you were hungry. On the other side of the room, someone wearing a striped dress was beginning to carve a turkey. She had black hair, a pretty face. You reached into the refrigerator, twisted open a beer, and stood next to her, wishing you had something to say.

"Who are you?" you asked a moment later. "Someone from the office getting put to work?"

"Donna, one of the caterers." She looked at him briefly.
"Who are you? The gardener?"
"The son," you said.
"That's funny," she said. "I wouldn't have guessed." You stood beside her, holding your beer, watching her work her long knife, her long fork, watching her slice the thigh from the bone. You put down your beer, stuffed a hunk of dark meat in your mouth, watched the other caterer, a blonde, bustle in, then out of the kitchen, and when you finished chewing, you picked up your beer and drank. You wondered what other kind of work this woman did. She didn't look like a caterer. And then you asked, and as soon as you did, you realized you had spent your whole life getting to know strangers, not family. And now you were doing it here, tonight, your father dead. Some things would never change.

"I sing blues," she said. "Do it pretty regular in some of the clubs. Most Tuesdays with one group, Wednesdays and Fridays with another."

"I'll be in town all week," you said. "Maybe longer. I'll want to see you somewhere."

"I do more than sing," she said, laughing.

"I can see that," you said. "The turkey's proof." Then you put your index finger to her neck and she let you keep it there. After you exchanged phone numbers, you moved into the living room, a beer in your hand.

For a while you walked around, listening. In one corner, several men rattled off baseball statistics. In another, some women compared the managerial staffs of the different country clubs. One by one, as they spotted you circulating, your father's business partners, his long-time childhood friends, the relatives you barely knew, came up to you, shook your hand, complimented you on being your father's son, and told their favorite story about him.

When you finished your beer, you went into the kitchen and found another. For a couple of minutes you picked at the turkey. Donna was elsewhere, so you talked with Freda, who owned the business, and was also a singer. When you returned to the living room, you saw your sister sitting on the sofa, holding Roxanne. You offered to take the baby, and for several minutes you held her, feeling pleased until she started squealing and you couldn't quiet her. Fortunately your mother took the baby from you. As she did, you wanted to thank her, but you didn't know just how, and the moment slipped past. You went back to your beer.

The guests began leaving, first in couples, then in groups. Only a few close friends lingered, seated in the den watching the eleven o'clock news. As Donna and Freda put away the food, you went to the refrigerator, grabbed another beer, and asked if they needed any help. Donna shook her head, looked at you funny, then smiled, and you thought: You're going to call her tomorrow. You had a feeling, and already you were imagining seeing her two or three times this week, then the possibility of long-distance phone calls, cross-country visits. It made no sense. But so little did. As you left the kitchen, your left eye twitched.

You went into the den and watched the television for a few minutes. Then you walked around. Your sister had already gone to bed. So had Aunt Sally. Your mother was still up, straightening the living room. You went over to her and stood beside her. What did you want, she wanted to know. She sounded angry. Nothing mother, you mumbled, not knowing whether you wanted to touch her, or not. Then you sat on the sofa and watched her. Before she went upstairs, you got up and gave her a kiss on the cheek.

In the next minutes, the remaining guests left and so did the caterers. You sat on the sofa for a long time, thinking of nothing, looking at the house plants, sipping your beer. Then you went to the den, turned on the television, grabbed a stack of old magazines, and riffled through them as you watched the last half of a bizarre screwball comedy, then a movie about a lynching, then this murder-mystery.

The movie is ending in another twenty minutes, at least according to the TV page. You can put this much together: the tennis pro, who is now awaiting the verdict, has been framed. He loves the reporter and the reporter loves him. She's got the goods to crack this case, but some higher-up has decided the information can't go public. The corruption goes deep. The managing editor is in on it; so is the congressman; so is the foreigner, the chief executive officer of a multi-national company. Meanwhile, the reporter has gotten in even deeper—her life's been threatened for a second time—and she's continuing despite little help from the lawyer, who is on his worst drinking binge yet. The tennis pro can only brood and wait as he continues to plead innocence. The prosecuting attorney seeks a life sentence.

Now, as you view the screen, you see a flashback: the reporter's a young girl and she's riding a horse across a meadow. The flashback is a bad move this late in the story. You only wonder who wrote the screenplay and how much they got paid. And then you realize you don't want to know. It will only anger you. You think: thank god for literature; thank god for intelligence. You get up and turn off the television. It is a quarter past five.

You move a few steps and stand by the window. The night is full of stars. Quickly you go into the kitchen, open the back door, and stride to the edge of the patio. You look up to see stars swarming like fireflies, a lone cloud far to the west. The night sky is beautiful, and as you stand there gazing and admiring, you wish you had your father here with you to see this.

Then you think: you didn't play music all day and now you feel like it. You go inside, find your fiddle, and return to the middle of the backyard, the spot where you made your little pitcher's mound. Then you face southeast, to the corner where you buried the urn. Thinking of your family, you bring your fiddle up and begin playing soft and slow: soft so you don't wake anybody in the house; slow because it's one of those bluesy modal ones from the West Virginia mountains. It's a haunting melody that legend says will raise the dead. Catch that, father, you think. Catch that. The day is breaking. You are flying.

And then you begin to play the music even slower, your fingers sliding up the strings, making each note spook.

Tongue Talk

I went to bed feverish and woke shivering a short while later, my sheets and pillow wet. I got up, made it to the kitchen, drank a glass of water, and, as I swallowed, felt a disorienting heaviness in my mouth. I went to the bathroom, flipped on both lights, and stood in front of the mirror, and opened my mouth. Immediately I located the problem—my tongue. I stuck it out to examine it more closely.

I wasn't sure if it was swollen—I had never examined my tongue for swelling before—but it was pocked by pasty-colored splotches and it hurt to wiggle it even the littlest bit. I stood there for several minutes wiggling my tongue, thinking of things I had never thought about, things like tongue paralysis and no more tongue kissing. Then I took out my thermometer. The glass felt cool and silvery under my tongue, and I left it there longer than necessary. My temperature: 102.1. I shuffled back to bed, my forehead hot, my tongue achy.

Most of Sunday I slept, too ill to get out of bed except to urinate. Monday morning my fever still hovered near 102, so I called in sick to work. When I talked to the secretary, I had trouble identifying myself because my tongue hurt so much it felt like it was blackening with every word, every syllable even. I decided to call my doctor. He listened to my slurred explanation and advised me to call my dentist, or else "a mouth man." I called my dentist.

She told me she couldn't help, but gave me the number of a friend who specialized in tongue disease. Great, I thought. Tongue disease. I called the number and got an answering machine: the tongue specialist was at a convention in Hawaii. Then I thumbed through the yellow pages, looking first under "mouth men," then "tongue men," then physicians. There were no "mouth" or "tongue" men anywhere, but I wondered if what I needed was "an ear, nose, and throat man," an otolaryngologist. I hoped not. All I wanted was a doctor. I decided I'd wait one more day before trying a walk-in clinic.

I spent the morning propped in bed, drinking water almost non-stop, and either watching television or reading. Often I had to get out of bed to urinate, and by mid afternoon I'd gotten in the habit of lingering in the bathroom. First, I'd stick out my tongue and exercise it in front of the mirror, doing a kind of lingual calisthenics. Then I'd massage my tongue with my fingertips, probing gently, hoping to discover the one sorest spot. I had no luck. The whole tongue was the sorest spot, and the splotches I noticed earlier had grown into chalky scales, so it looked as if thick layers of partially dissolved aspirin coated my tongue. It was a depressing sight. When I grew tired of it, I returned to bed to drink more fluids.

Early in the evening, the telephone rang. "Heh-oh," I answered.

"That you, David? Fred here. We were thinking of surprising you, and Gina said we better call first. "So," he said, "you want company tonight?" Or do you already have company?" He laughed.

"Freh," I said. "Freh, I . . . Fred, my uhn hurh."

"David, if that's you, I think you better repeat that."

"Freh, I szick. My tongue hurz." The d and t sounds were a couple of killers and it had gotten worse since I last tried to talk. I readied myself to grunt more of an explanation, but I could hear Fred cracking up over the phone. Then I heard him yell something to his wife, probably some mistranslation of what I was up against here.

"David," he chuckled, "it's all set. We'll be by in an hour. Gina says ice cream 'll be good. What'll it be—vanilla or chocolate?"

"Ha-eh Oz," I said. I figured if they were going to visit somebody who couldn't talk, they might as well humor him with the gourmet stuff.

Sometime later I heard the knocking. I got out of bed, put

on my robe, and opened the front door. Fred walked in, holding a book. Gina smiled at me as she carried in a sack of groceries.

"Heh-oh," I said.

"Heh-oh yourself," Fred said. He put the book on the couch and threw his hunting cap and army jacket over them. So, got yourself some tongue problems, huh? The kind of mischief you've been getting yourself into you're lucky if it's only tongue problems. "Say," he said, giving me a good, close look. "Nice robe. Where'd you get it?"

"Ammy ave ih oo me."

"Who?" said Fred. "Amy or Tammy? Which one? Or did your mammy give it to you last time you were sick?"

"Tammy," I winced, spitting out the *t* sound. "For my birray las year."

"It looks really nice," said Gina. "All cotton?"

"Tammy, I remember her. You and Tammy never had a chance. I knew it the first time I saw you two, that time at Hank's." He gave me a funny look, which meant he would have said something particularly outrageous if Gina hadn't been standing there. "Ol' Tammy," Fred said. "She was a cutie, though. What's she up to now?"

I shrugged.

"Bet whatever she's up to, she doesn't have tongue problems," Fred said. "I declare. You sure this isn't gonorrhea, syphilis, or you know what?" Fred grinned over at Gina, who gave him a nasty look. "Don't you worry, ol' buckaroo. Me and Gina here 'll fix these tongue problems of yours. We're experts in matters of the tongue. Isn't that right, Gina?"

Gina was still holding the groceries, but had stopped smiling and was shaking her head with a kind of wariness I had seen before in women who saw my living room when I hadn't cleaned. "This place is a *mess*," she said. Then she turned to me. "Doesn't this *bother* you?"

Fred was an ex-housemate of mine. He understood my ways. But Gina was different. I looked around the room, trying to see it as Gina did. I saw unshelved books and maga-

zines, papers scattered about, vacuumable material all over the floor, dust on every wooden surface.
"Eh-ee-way, my uhn ihz worz tha thihz room," I said, shaking my head. "Tal-king reel-ee hurz," I added, wishing it wasn't so much trouble to tell Gina to put the groceries down and stay a while. The living room had looked worse.
"Let's see it then," said Fred, and he snapped his fingers like he always did when he got an idea. "How about it, Gina? Judge tongues. Peterson 'll stick out his, and I'll stick out mine. Gina, tell us what you see. Maybe we'll make scientific history here tonight."
"Fred, I don't want to see yours or his."
"Gina," said Fred. Then he stuck out his tongue, letting it droop over his lower lip. I looked enviously at its salmon-colored flexibility. Then I stood shoulder-to-shoulder to Fred and stuck out my tongue. When Fred saw mine, he immediately rolled his back in. "I do declare," he said.
"You must not be feeling too good," Gina said, glancing at my tongue. Still holding the groceries, she went into the kitchen and turned on the light. Fred and I followed. We watched Gina set the bag on the kitchen table, open the refrigerator, and find nothing but beer, champagne, and mustard. Frowning, she cleared dirty plates off the counter into the sink and transferred the grocery bag onto the counter. Fred and I sat as Gina started boiling water for tea as she unpacked the bag. First she took out a small chicken, then some onions, celery, two bags of flour, butter, honey, yeast, spices, some teabags. Then she took out a white plastic bag which contained two pints of Häagen-Dasz ice cream: one of vanilla and one of chocolate.
"Whah'z uh pla?" I asked Gina after she found the bowls and began scooping the ice cream.
"What?" said Gina.
"What's the plan? That's what he wants to know," said Fred.
"Plan? No plan. First we'll have ice cream and peppermint tea. Plus I've got a kosher chicken here for chicken soup. That's for tomorrow. Also I'm going to bake rye bread." Gina searched

the cabinets until she found two large soup pots. "One of these will have to be a bread bowl because you don't have one."

"You're oowizsh?" I asked, pointing to the chicken.

"She's ooh-ish, all right. And ticklish. And that's not all."

"Joowizsh," I said, struggling for the *j* sound. I nodded to her as she set bowls of ice cream and cups of tea on the table.

"My mother was Jewish," she said. "But except for chicken soup and rye bread when we were sick, we never practiced."

I tasted the ice cream while Gina skinned and washed the chicken, stuck it in one of the pots, and filled the pot halfway with water. The vanilla was delicious, and I let the coldness dissolve on my tongue. Then I sipped the tea. It was almost too hot, but bearable, and I savored the extreme from cold to hot. Then I spooned chocolate ice cream onto my tongue and watched Gina drink her tea as she stood at the counter. The next moment she was pouring flour into the other soup pot. Fred, who had already finished his bowl of ice cream, stood beside her and chopped celery and onion for the soup.

When Fred finished, he laid down his knife, pushed the vegetables into the soup bowl, and helped himself to seconds of the ice cream. "Whatever happened to that girlfriend of yours who liked tomato sauce on ice cream?" he asked, his back to me. What was her name? Sonia?"

I waited for him to sit down. "Ah-ya was uh one who ike Shineeh foo." I said.

"What?" said Gina.

"I'm not getting this one either," said Fred. "Maybe the ice cream isn't shiny enough?"

"Sonia liked *Shineehz* food," I said, discovering the combination of hot and cold made my tongue move a bit easier. "Jan puh salsa on ice cream one ime only."

"That's right," said Fred. "Ol' Jan. I forgot all about her. What's she up to?"

"Why'd she put salsa on ice cream?" asked Gina. "What was she? High?" Quickly she ladled off the scum that had formed in the chicken soup, lowered the heat, and put a top on the kettle. Then she brought the rest of the ice cream and tea to the table, and sat down with us. As Fred leaned over to kiss her, she leaned toward him, her lips open, her eyes closed. "She was high," I said when they finished the kiss. "and wan-ned combine her favorih foosz. I ha a bih, an ih was awful." I made a face. "Ih ru-ih both, speshly the ice cream. Now she's ma-ree and lives in Porland. We wri leh-ers."

"Did you say 'Poor-land?'" asked Fred.

"Speaking of writing letters," said Gina, "how's your writing going?"

"Actually," said Fred, "what I'd like to know is what you've been reading in the throes of this tongue problem."

"Reree-ing Henry mih-er," I said. Then I turned to Gina. "I'm not wri-ing. I can harly even alk thihz week." I dug my spoon into the vanilla and came up with a big white chunk before scraping the bottom of the container.

"Then how's it been going lately?" Gina asked.

"What he's trying to say is he's had nothing much to say and he's sick of it. So now he's reading sexy books to get better. Isn't that right, bucko?"

I nodded and ate more vanilla ice cream.

"How are you feeling right now then?" asked Gina. "Better?"

"A li-uhl, I hink."

"You ever bake bread?"

I shook my head.

"Well, if you feel up to it, you can help me knead the bread, and then, after it rises, we'll stick it in the oven. On the ride over Fred was telling me he'd like to tell you a bedtime story. How does that sound?"

I looked at Gina. She was tall and pretty, and when she smiled a certain way, as she was doing now, she reminded me of a big happy cat leaping out a window onto a tree branch. "You're bui-ful," I said, and kissed her cheek.

"I think he's up for it," said Fred, grinning from the kitchen table, digging up the rest of the chocolate ice cream.

I stood next to Gina at the kitchen counter as she pointed at the makeshift bread bowl. "You see that?" she said. "That's called the sponge. I put in warm water, yeast, honey, and wheat flour, then stirred and waited. The yeast is alive so you need to be careful. Now that all the ingredients have gotten used to each other we can add the rest and have some fun."

I watched Gina slice a half stick of butter in squares and stir them into the mix. Then she added caraway seeds, then equal parts of whole wheat flour and rye flour, and then she began stirring."

"You see what I'm doing, don't you?" she asked.

I shook my head. I had no idea.

"I'm thickening it. Here, you stir and I'll add a bit more flour. Try to keep the spoon moving, and mix everything so there aren't any wet spots." Gina poured rye flour, then wheat flour into the pot, little by little. I kept stirring.

"Okay," she said. "Watch this." Gina sprinkled flour on the countertop, took the pot, and turned it upside-down to the lump of dough landed on the flour. After sprinkling flour on her hands, she began playing with the dough, pushing it down and forward with the heels of her hand, then turning it, folding it, then pushing it down and forward again.

"You know what this is?" Gina said.

I stood there watching her hands move.

"You know too what it is," said Fred.

"This is kneading. It's like massaging one of your girlfriend's rears."

"See?" said Fred. "She's saying now it's your turn."

Gina stepped aside and I stood in front of the dough. I took a breath, and then put my hands on it and began to knead. After a few turns, my palms were covered with flaky wetness. "Wha ow?" I asked.

"Get that stuff off, add it to the dough, and then put some flour on your hands. That'll keep them dry."

I scraped my palms clean with a knife. Then I dumped some rye flour on the counter, spread my hands in it, and started to knead again. Gina was right. The flour kept my hands dry and that made it easier. Then I had to concentrate on the rhythm. For a while I alternated between pushing and folding

too hard, and then not hard enough, but then I understood. Kneading was easy.
"Okay," said Gina. "Enough. You can keep kneading, but it'll tire out the yeast, something you don't want. What we need now is to smear butter all through the bread bowl and then stick the dough in it. It'll rise for an hour and then we might as well bake it. At home I'll let it rise twice, but this'll work mainly because of your great kneading." She gave me a look. "So, okay?"
I nodded, not sure what she was talking about.
"You okay, honey?" She looked at Fred and then at her watch. "It's almost nine," she said. "Why don't you tuck David in. I'll just be a couple minutes in here." She lifted the lid to the chicken soup, ladled a spoonful, tasted it, added a few spices, then put the lid back on and turned the heat down. Fred led me out of the kitchen as Gina began greasing the pot for the bread.
"Well, bucko, you ready for bed?" Fred stood in the living room, snapping his fingers.
I shrugged. "Lez sih ow here."
"Let's see your tongue."
It felt rawer than ever as I stuck it out.
"I declare. Now I know it reminds me of—a doormat covered by a half foot of dust. To the bedroom," he ordered, taking my hand and walking me to the bathroom door. "If you need to use the bathroom, use it. I'll go find the book. Gina said I should tuck you in, and I will if she doesn't change her mind and decide to do it herself."
Fred left me there, and after I used the toilet, I washed my hands and brushed my teeth. Although I had felt better sitting in the kitchen with Fred and Gina, now that I was alone for a few minutes, both my forehead and tongue ached. I splashed cool water over my face. Then I stood in front of the mirror and stared at my tongue. Six inches of dust. Fred was right, and he was kind not mentioning the possibility of gangrene. I tried wriggling my tongue, but it hurt. I took my temperature: 101.5. Reluctantly I put the thermometer back in its case and

opened the bathroom door. Fred and Gina had pulled two chairs to my bedside and sat tickling one another shamelessly.

Fred lurched at Gina for one last tickle and then turned to me. "What were you doing in there? Shampooing your tongue?"

I grinned weakly as Gina tucked in her blouse, shook herself, and for a moment sat primly in her chair. Fred pulled his chair closer to hers and took her hand.

"Now you almos ook ike mommy an ad-ee," I said.

"That's right, like mommy an ad-ee," said Gina. "Here, let mommy Gina take off your robe, ease you into beddy-bye, and tuck you in real good. Okay, Davey?"

"Oh-ay."

After she tucked me in and fixed my pillow, Fred opened a book to past the middle. "It was just like mom and dad to take the family sailing," he said in a storytelling voice. "The weather forecast was good all weekend, and mom and dad and the two children, Dean, who was thirteen, and Andrea, who was eight, planned to sail across the bay to Sterling Island on Saturday morning. Once ashore, they'd spend a whole day exploring the wilderness. Sunday afternoon they'd sail home, arriving dockside Sunday evening at sunset.

"The weekend went according to plan until the last half of the trip home. Then the winds rose and the waters grew choppy. Despite taking down the sails and starting the small motor, the craft made no headway in the sudden squall. As the dad kept pointing the boat toward the dock, the waves swelled higher, then higher still, swamping the deck. With each big wave, the boat rolled and bucked before sinking a little lower. The family huddled closer in the small cabin as the dad attempted to make radio contact with the Coast Guard.

"Then Dean asked if he could stand on the deck for a few minutes to see what the storm was like. His parents said absolutely not. He asked again. They refused. The winds blew harder. Dean said he had to see what it was like on deck, he had to, and when his mom hugged him tighter, Dean pushed himself away and ran up the steps, his dad in pursuit. On deck,

Dean slipped and fell overboard, belly flopping awkwardly into the water before straightening, as if in a delayed jackknife. Despite the pressure from the water, he descended, a liquid juggernaut, body stretched, boring through the depths. Accelerating, he broke through some debris—the rotting spokes of a ships' wheel—and then split the ocean floor, cracking it like a plate.

"On the other side there was nothing but water. Everywhere fat, slow fish lazily flapped tails, their iridescent reds, blues, yellows, greens a sparkling fantasia. Dean laid his belly on pink coral, his hands reaching for a piece of brown sponge shaped like a giant thumb. Then he swam a few feet toward the surface and could feel himself float back down. Grabbing hold of seaweed, he pulled, stuck it in his mouth, and chewed. He breathed in the liquid. Lying on the watery floor, he slept, dreaming of air.

"When he woke, a big black fish circled him. Dean swam to a rock, picked it up, and threw. The fish swam away; the rock sank. Dean swam to the same rock, picked it up, and threw it again. It kept sinking. Then he picked up a shell and put it to his ear. Hearing nothing, he let it go and it sank. In the distance, he saw a sea wall. As he swam closer, the wall receded. Fatigued, he ate more seaweed and rested. He slept, dreaming of land.

"He woke lying atop a giant sea turtle, its shell the size of a dining room table. He gripped both sides of the shell and peered ahead. When the turtle rose, briefly breaking the surface to gulp air, Dean held his breath, afraid. When the turtle dived, Dean let go of one hand and snatched at codfish, rockfish, or mullets. Failing to catch meat, he'd suck on plankton. When the turtle surfaced to deposit her eggs on a beach, Dean swam with the current, kicking with his legs, stroking with his arms, breathing air between strokes. Instead of sleeping on the coral reef, he'd float suspended just below the surface, every so often jumping like a salmon. His eyes grew accustomed to sunlight. In the distance he saw greenery and swam to it.

"As Dean drew closer, the water slickened, covered by a

dark, greasy sheen. His skin grew oily. The green trees were further back, behind a blacktop shoreline. The air smelled of tar. Dean swam clockwise away from this landing, and the further he swam, the thicker the vegetation: first palmettos, then a forest of cedar. Then he came to a rocky inlet where the trees rose atop cliffs, the stony shore broken by a fringe of sand. Dean swam in, and at high tide pulled himself out of the water. He slept on the shoreline and dreamed the sun had spoken to him.

"The next day Dean woke amidst wind and clouds. The air blew cold and he dived under the waves to catch several small fish which he ate as he stood waist-high in the water. He spent the day swimming, the night on shore, and slept on the beach in the rain. He woke to discover that at a nearby rocky point there was a ledge that led to a small cavern, its entrance a yawning mouth of stalactites and stalagmites. He took shelter there through the duration of the night. Everyday, then, he swam and caught fish. Every evening he returned to his cavern where he ate the fish, drank from pools of turquoise water, and slept.

"Once, as he climbed the cliff and explored the surroundings, he hid behind a cedar tree and watched two women gather mulberries in a bucket and then creep toward a family of kestrels feeding on dragonflies. Then the women made a funny cry, and when the birds flew to them, the women unsheathed their knives, grabbed the two plumpest, decapitated them, and stuck them in a bulging bag. After watching this, unable to take his eyes off the women's breasts, Dean stepped from behind the tree and tried imitating the cry that had lured the birds. The women turned and raised their knives at him. Dean raised a fist. Looking at his genitals, the women stepped closer and closer, still threatening. When Dean rushed them, one of the women nicked Dean on the forehead with her knife, stunning him, allowing them to capture him. They walked together, one woman carrying the basket of mulberries, one with the sack of birds slung over her shoulder, both clasping Dean at the wrists.

"The women lived far from Dean's cave, in a camp on the edge of a lemon grove. Several other women lived there also, and when they saw Dean brought in, they spoke to the two women who held him. The two women made sounds Dean didn't understand and pointed at his genitals. All the women smiled. That night Dean feasted, eating a grilled kestrel, a salad, and drinking a sweet liquor. In the darkness, the women made him lie down with them in their huts, one after another.

"The longer Dean remained with the women, the more they grew used to one another. They taught him how to use weapons, to plant a garden, to build huts and beds, to talk, to love. Dean taught them about the water, and showed them the best ways to swim and catch fish. When he showed them the cave he used to live in, they showed him the canyon that the earthquake had made and that separated them from the others.

"One morning four of the women surprised a sea turtle coming on shore to lay eggs. Quickly they sliced off its head, and with much work managed to haul both the head and the body back to camp. While the turtle shell was a favored trophy, the meat was the greatest delicacy, and all day they prepared dinner. After finding over three hundred eggs in its belly, the women cut steaks, saved the blood, and took pains to separate and preserve the liver, kidney, heart, tongue, and eyeballs. That night the camp feasted on turtle meat and turtle eggs and drank turtle blood. Because the women considered both the tongue and the eyeballs an aphrodisiac, they let Dean eat the full portions while sharing the other organ meats among themselves.

"As Dean finished the meal, he coughed several times, spitting blood. The women put him to bed. A few hours later, he woke, feeling sick. He felt strange, too, for there was no woman in bed with him for the first time since he'd come here. As he listened to the noises outside, he coughed lightly. Blood and turtle meat dripped out of his mouth. He got out of bed, gathered his flint, his knife, his hatchet, stole quietly into the darkness, and walked.

"He intended to only go a short way, and lie down until he

felt better, but with each step away from the camp he felt stronger, and he found himself hiking the steep trail toward the canyon. At sunrise he stood there at the edge of the giant ravine, first looking down, then across, then to the sides. As he looked down, he saw there was not even a first foothold, and the fall would kill him. As he looked across, he saw the chasm in front of him was longer than the tallest tree trunk. As he looked to the sides, he saw this was the narrowest spot. Dean sat the edge and slept, dreaming of a boat.

"When he woke, he began chopping the thinnest trees with his hatchet. For several days he worked, stopping only to eat berries, drink from the nearby spring, and sleep. At first, as he chopped, he worried that the women might surprise him and attack. Then he thought of returning to camp, telling them of his plan, and asking for help. But then he stopped thinking of them. If they came, they came. What would happen, would happen.

"All Dean's energy went to this work. By cutting down many thin trees, the wood was light enough to maneuver easily. By tying the cut wood with grape vines, he constructed a kind of mast long enough to reach the other side. By piling many such masts together, he built a span strong enough to support him. Dean made fifteen such masts and laid five of them side-by-side across the chasm so that both ends touched land. Then he laid four more side-by-side so they sat on top of the bottom five, beginning the foundation of a small pyramid. After aligning the final six masts, he straddled the wooden triangle and inched across the chasm. Though the wood sagged from the weight, the span held.

"When he reached the other side, Dean left the bridge standing to allow the women to follow if they wanted to risk the trip. He waited a few days, but no one came. Then he journeyed onward, feeding on apples and prickly pears. The trail circled down, and he continued hiking, reaching a white beach at sunset. Swimming in the bay, a reddening sky ahead of him, he caught a large grouper which he gutted in the water and carried back to the sand. After he cooked the fish and ate it, he slept under the full moon, dreaming of flight.

"The weather remained clear and Dean lived on the beach, spending the days exploring and gathering food, the evenings resting. Often he swam a short way down the coast to a small cove where there was also a lagoon. Early one afternoon, as he waded in the still water and collected mussels, he spotted a woman he had never seen before. She was a good distance away, near the shore of the cove, and she stood thigh-high in water. She was bending over as though she was looking for a shell, or for something she had lost. When he saw her notice him, he waved to her, and she waved to him. When he swam toward her, she swam toward him, and when they met, at the spot where the waters of the lagoon and cove met, they put their tongues in each other's mouths and kissed. They they swam back to his stretch of beach, first she following him, then he following her, then the two of them swimming together. As they touched the sand, they fell into one another and made love, the ebbing tide lapping them.

"They clung for a while, digging like sea turtles making a nest, and afterward, when he looked at her and said his name was Dean, she looked at him and said her name was Candy. Later, as they bathed in the sea, splashing each other and shrieking, a swan landed on the beach. Candy ran out of the water, caught it, and broke its neck. Dean roasted the swan for dinner. After eating the meat, they made love twice more, once in the water, once on the sand, and when they slept, their bodies pressed tight, they dreamed of each other."

I tried listening. Dean and Candy moved inland, built a large hut, had children. Dean built a boat. My eyes closed. Family. The bay. A storm. The son. Cracking. Turtle. Men. Women. Food. Candy. Dean. I fell asleep to a distant humming that sounded like lovemaking.

Tuesday morning I woke past eleven o'clock. An extra blanket had been folded on top of me and all my clothes were on hangers. I got up, put on my robe, and before going to the bathroom I looked in the living room. The vacuumable materials had all been vacuumed; my books had been shelved; my papers were arranged in neat piles. The apartment smelled of chicken soup and bread. I went into the kitchen, cut a slice of rye bread, and chewed on it. I washed it down with a glass of water. Then I called in sick to work, slurring the first *d* in David only slightly.

Then I went to the bathroom. After urinating, I washed my face and examined my tongue, tentatively twisting it this way and that. It hurt less, and looking in the mirror I could see the worst of the splotches were peeling, revealing small pink spots. I kneaded my tongue for a minute, pressing more firmly where there was the soft, spongy pink. I took my temperature: an even 100.

Returning to my bedroom, I found a book on my bedstand. I opened it. The top of the first page was inscribed: *To David, with love from Fred and Gee-ah*. As I thumbed through the book's blank pages, I went to my desk, and picked up a pen. Turning back to the first page, I made my first entry:

Things are starting to happen—I better be ready.

Then I wrote several more sentences, enough for a start. Closing the book, I left it on my desk and got dressed. Then I went to the kitchen and started heating the chicken soup.

I had a lot to do.

Sleep, Dreams, and Snow

He had gone to bed feverish and woken shivering. Earlier he had worked from 11:00 Saturday night to 8:30 Sunday morning, and then come back to this room ready to prove to Sandy Allen that he was a writer.

And he had written, at least for a while, until he had drunk a few beers, smoked a few bowls, written a letter, started feeling lousy, and gone to bed. After he had woken, shivering, he had gone to the bathroom, used the toilet, and washed his hands. There, looking at himself in the mirror, he saw a stranger, and had felt something hard crack inside him. Then he had returned to bed, fallen asleep, and begun dreaming. When the alarm buzzed at 10:00 P.M., he had shut it off, figuring he would lie in bed another fifteen minutes. Then he dreamed more dreams, all of which he had forgotten, all of which he tried to recall as he lay in bed now, thinking.

He glanced toward the window. It was gray outside, not dark. For a few more moments he replayed what he knew, starting again from the beginning. Then he sat up in his bed and twisted to face the clock on his desk. 11:15. 11:15 and gray? He rubbed his eyes, stretched his legs, and quivered: if this was daytime, he had overslept by thirteen hours.

He rose stiffly, put one foot on the Sunday newspaper lying by his bed, and just missed kicking over a can of beer as he swung his other leg around. Then he walked past his desk, stood by the window, and looked outside. It was daytime. Big, heavy snowflakes fell, and he yanked open both the inside window and the storm window so he could stick out his head. Although he couldn't tell for sure, the snow looked shin-high in the alley below. Still leaning out, he thrust his left hand forward, palm up, and caught several flakes. Then he breathed deeply. The air felt still heavy and still. It was so much warmer now, a luxurious warmth, and he guessed it might be twenty-five, even thirty degrees. He took one more deep breath, ducked his head back inside, and lowered the window halfway. He tried to remember the fever he had felt twenty-four hours earlier, but couldn't. It was as if he'd only dreamed it.

He shook his head slowly. Looking around the small room, seeing the unmade bed, the sections of newspaper beside it, the beer cans, the scattered papers and books, the dust, the dirt, he wanted to clean, felt he *needed* to clean. After scrubbing the toilet bowl, the bathtub, and the sink, he swept the bathroom floor, then the floor of his room. Then he packed his books in one box, his papers in another, threw the beer cans and the newspaper in a trash bag, and made his bed. Then he walked to the window. Once again forcing open the glass all the way, he stuck his head out, but this time extending his tongue as far as it would go. He leaned like that, eyes closed, letting the falling snow dissolve, the flakes like watery clouds. When he put his head back inside, he lowered the window halfway, and then sat at his desk.

Quickly he cleared the desktop, first throwing away indecipherable notes, bent paper clips, pens and pencils he didn't like the looks of. After shoving what he wanted to save into the drawer, he arranged the desk: typewriter on the left, notebook on the right, a letter to be mailed in the middle. Then he thumbed through the notebook. The last entry was a letter he had just begun to Samantha, his ex-girlfriend now living in Washington state. She was the one he had moved to Boston with. Samantha had loved him once, but then everything had started happening, and as he reread the half page he had written, he got disgusted and ripped it up. The letter was so obnoxiously sappy he couldn't believe it. He got up, went to his bureau, grabbed his wallet, and found a picture of Samantha. Then he sat back down and wrote a short letter saying that he missed her, that he loved her, that a lot was happening now—what, he didn't know—but that whatever it was, the worst was over. He hoped that she would forgive him because he wanted very much to be her friend. He ended the letter by saying he *would* be good friend from here on out, and he would love it if she wrote back.

He put the letter in an envelope, addressed it, and placed it on the middle of his desk. This one was better, but there was still so much to say, and he still sounded phony. But at least it wasn't sappy. Then he decided he better reread the other letter, the one he had written Crazy Dick the previous morning. He slit the envelope, unfolded the five pages, and cringed as he read. The mentality was teen-aged at best. Why had he needed to call Sandy Allen an icy cunt, a rich bitch, a brainless whore masquerading as a law student? What had he been thinking of, sending this to Crazy Dick? True, the stuff about Sandy's sidekick, Denise, looking as friendly as a dead battery was moderately funny. But, still, there were limits, and he had overstepped them.

He crumpled the letter and the envelope, and tossed them in the trash bag. Then he began sifting through the notebook. On nearly every page was a draft of his story: the same curlicue copied and recopied, followed by variations of the same dead-end departures. What was wrong with him? After skimming the notebook once more, he dumped it in the trash bag. Then he put his head to his hands, and for an instant he wanted to light a match and burn everything down. Then he gasped, and the tears came, harder and harder. All he could think of was he wanted Samantha, a mother, somebody.

After a while, as he stopped weeping, he looked around the room, corner to corner, ceiling to ceiling, making sure he hadn't missed anything. He lingered on the picture of Samantha that still faced him on his desk. He had loved her—he finally knew it—and now she was living with someone else in Seattle. He picked up the picture and held it for a minute, running his fingers over her tan forehead, her blue eyes, her lips. This was his favorite picture of her, taken on the beach at Nantucket. He brought her lips to his lips for a kiss, but then, instead, suddenly rushed to the bathroom, found a match, lit it, and put it to the photograph. Samantha's image smoked, curled, blackened, the small flame shooting orange. Just when he would have burnt himself if he had held on, he dropped the charred snapshot into the toilet. Sobbing and choking, he flushed the toilet and then cleaned the bowl one more time, trying, but not succeeding, in getting rid of the carbon smell.

Still crying, but not as heavily, he got dressed, putting on corduroy pants, a heavy sweater, a light coat, a wool cap, a scarf, gloves, and boots. In one of the coat pockets he stashed the letter to Samantha. Then he grabbed the trash bag, which he'd haul downstairs and around back to the dumpster. From there he'd walk to Charles Street to mail the letter and check the store. Peter would be mad, especially if he had to shut the place for the night, which was probably what happened. For an alibi, he'd tell the truth: that although he had been sick and had slept twenty-four hours straight, he was better now and could work this evening. He hoped that would satisfy him. He dabbed the last of the tears with a glove tip. Work would not be so bad. Monday nights were slow. He'd have time to think. He looked at the clock. It was past 1:15. Opening the door, he slung the black plastic trash bag over his shoulder like a sailor's duffel.

In the hallway, as he shut the door, he noticed the messages tacked from one doorjamb to the other. He put the trash bag down, took off his gloves, and removed the notes. Four were from work. Phillips had called twice, and Peter had called twice this morning. Each message was identical: *Call the store – Urgent.* He quickly stuffed them in his right pocket. There was also one more, from Sandy Allen. She had called midday Sunday, and the message was cryptic: *Dinner date? – Call her back.* After rereading it, he stuffed it in his left pocket. Bo, who lived next to the phone on the first floor, had taken the messages. He stood on the landing for a moment, thinking. He would have to remember to thank Bo later for not waking him. Then he put back on his gloves, hoisted the trash bag, and descended the five flights of stairs.

Outside, the wet snow was piling up. He guessed ten inches, minimum, as he ran his free hand down the handrail, knocking off the snow. Flakes landed on his eyelashes, and he blinked. Small mounds drifted against the steps and the curb. A light wind swirled. He slid on a slick spot as he rounded the corner into the alley, then tossed the trash bag into the dumpster. It felt even warmer than he expected, so he unbuttoned his coat and loosened his scarf. Then, out of the alley, hands in pockets, he lost his balance, and almost fell. He walked down the hill on Pinckney Street, part of the way on the slippery sidewalk, part of the way in ruts made by tire tracks, part of the way sinking in the drifts by the curb.

At the corner of Charles Street, he stuck the letter to Samantha in a mailbox. If he crossed the street and went the one block left, he could stop by the store and explain to Peter what had happened. He crossed Charles, took a step in that direction, and changed his mind. The 7-Eleven would depress him. He knew it. Shuffling on the glazed sidewalk, he hurried the opposite way past a couple of fancy restaurants, the auction gallery, the used book and record shop. Then he crossed Charles at Revere, trying to decide whether he wanted to backtrack and walk along the river toward the band shell, or continue wandering.

He decided to wander. At Cambridge Street he took a right, all the while contemplating work, Sandy Allen, writing, Samantha. He wondered what he was going to do with himself. Realizing he hadn't eaten in over a day, he ducked into a pizzeria for a slice of mushroom pizza, then into an ice cream shop for a bowl of vanilla and chocolate ice cream, then into a natural foods store for a few carrots and oranges. Sticking this last purchase in his coat pocket to save for a later snack, he realized, except for the snow, the walk was reminding him of the walks he used to take when he had first moved to Boston with Samantha.

They had come almost a year before, arriving on a warm April day. Within a week they had found a place on Beacon Hill, and almost as quickly Samantha landed her job selling clothes in a fashionable Newbury Street boutique. One thing led to another. Soon, in addition to her regular job, she was making great money taking free-lance modeling assignments on her off days. With Samantha's support, he hadn't tried to find work, but instead spent his days taking the subway to Harvard Square and meandering, stopping here and there for a cup of coffee, a browse through a book or magazine, a glass of beer. As walked for hours along Mass Ave., or else along the river, he had come closer to figuring out not only his feelings for Samantha, but also for his father, who was just then getting sick, and was now dying of colon cancer. And in doing this figuring, he had come closer to figuring that what he most wanted to do was to write.

Every night he would arrive home just before Samantha and start dinner. Then, after she changed clothes, stretched, exercised, showered, and changed clothes again, they would eat, and he would entertain her, telling her all that he saw and thought about that day. She loved him for the way he told his stories, he knew it, and he wanted nothing more than to write them down for her. But when he took the time to try to write what he had envisioned on his walks, the words wouldn't come, not even close. That had been what had started it. And then he had gotten jealous
. Without realizing it, he had turned up Joy Street, where they had once lived. He brushed the snow off his shoulders, looked at their old apartment building, and kept going. In late September she had come home from a modeling assignment raving about this photographer, Jerry, who wanted her to go to New York the next weekend and model. According to Samantha, he had a show in a Soho gallery, so he wasn't just a commercial photographer, and, besides, she didn't even think he was particularly attractive. When he told her he didn't want her to to go, they argued for the first time. She ended up inviting him along. He accepted, but the weekend didn't go smoothly. During the days, she worked, and he aimlessly browsed bookstores. Both nights they went to parties which she loved and where he felt out of place.

After they returned to Boston, she began acting strangely, and he knew. Or at least he thought he knew. The following week, even though she pleaded and then argued, he started working the odd jobs. He spent two weeks in Tufts Medical Center earning five-hundred dollars for taking part in a drug experiment led by a monkey-faced doctor named Ruth. For three weeks he worked on a survey team for the transit system, counting riders and clocking routes on subways and buses all over the city, sometimes riding from 6 A.M. to 2 A.M. The week after Thanksgiving, he started washing dishes, the all-night shift in a diner near the theater district. And when he wasn't working, he was desperately trying to write in order to impress Samantha he could write stories that were worthy.

Through the fall, they rarely ate together. After he took the dishwashing job, they rarely slept together. Most days they barely saw each other. Once, when she mentioned Jerry's name, he flippantly said he wanted to kill him.

In response, she had called him the biggest idiot she had ever known, the biggest, and packed her bags. Although he apologized profusely, said he'd been joking, had been so tired and mixed-up from his wacky schedule he didn't know what he was saying, that wasn't going to be enough. He hoped they were reconciled when that same evening he called in sick to his job, and she let him hug her and make love to her, and they fell asleep clutching one another. But he was wrong. She moved out the next day. By the first of the year she was on her way west, not with Jerry, but with another photographer, Joe, who was starting graduate school in Urban Design.

It had all been so sudden. Since then, he had moved to Pinckney Street, gotten a job at the 7-Eleven, and stumbled along. His writing was going nowhere. He was broke and practically friendless. He needed to prepare himself for his father's death, which was imminent. He didn't know what to do. In fact, he didn't know anything, and as he realized this, the tears came, this time a long, steady, silent flow.

For a while he stood looking down at the snow falling on his boot tops as his tears abated. He wished he could go somewhere else, be somebody else. He looked around, sniffling, and saw he was on the corner of Joy and Mt. Vernon, the top of

Beacon Hill, across the street from the State House. Finishing his cry, he gazed up at the State House dome, usually a sparkling gold, now white like everything else, a rabbit's tail against a gray afternoon sky. Then he continued walking, crossing Mt. Vernon, passing a mansion, reaching the sidewalk of Beacon Street.

Ahead of him stretched the Commons, today a wide, white field. To the right, on the Frog Pond, the snow had been swept aside and kids were playing hockey. Close by, smaller children were sledding down a small hill that had been packed down for speed. Near the Park Street subway entrance, a big snowball fight was going on. In front of him, a few cars proceeded carefully on Beacon, their headlights shining, windshield wipers beating. Waiting for the vehicles to pass, letting the southeasterly wind blow through him, he bent over, formed a snowball, and aimed it high over the street into the Commons. The ball fell apart mid flight. Taking off his gloves, he made one more ball, packing it as tight as a baseball before throwing. When he released this one, it sailed past the benches, and he saw it bury itself in the white. Then he put on his gloves and crossed the street diagonally, in the direction of the hockey game.

As he stood in the snow, watching the boys skate four against four, he remembered a snippet of a dream he had had earlier in the month. A woman he didn't know had invited him skating and given him a pair of skates. After trying them on and discovering they fit, he had laced them and made his way on the ice. At first he had been worried that his ankles would wobble, but he had done almost as well as she had, following her as she skated backwards, raced forward, then stopped and made the ice chips fly. Recalling the dream and now watching the boys play, he wanted to learn to skate. There was something important in knowing how to stay balanced with blades on your feet as you propelled yourself quickly over ice. The insight made him wish Samantha was beside him so he could share it. Since that couldn't be, he walked on, circling the pond, leaving it behind.

He walked southeast into the wind, which seemed stronger and warmer in the openness of the Commons. The snow blew its fat flakes. With each step his boots sunk to their tops. A hundred yards from the boys on the pond, nowhere near anyone else, he idly scraped up snow, made a snowball, and threw it into the wind. Then he threw another, then another, with each snow packing more and more snow to make the balls bigger and bigger. Then he began packing the balls and throwing them straight up, trying to catch them as they fell. Next, he stood there for a while, trying to juggle two balls in one hand, three balls in two hands, then four balls at once.

Then he threw all the balls in the snow and gathered enough new snow for a snowball the size of a bowling ball. He bent over and pressed this new, wet snow so it felt like clay, and then he picked it up, dropped it to the ground, and rolled it back and forth, continually adding more snow to the mass, molding it so it would stay circular and hard as it grew to boulder size. When the ball was almost waist-high, he left it, draped his coat over it, and started again, packing enough fresh, wet snow for another bowling ball, which he picked up, hefted, then dropped into the snow.

Pushing this second ball, rolling it, making it grow, he looked toward Boylston, its row of theaters, its lights, and wondered whether he would call Sandy Allen or whether he would go to work tonight. Did one preclude the other? He had Wednesday and Thursday nights off, but he missed work last night. Did he even want to see her? Why should he? Why should he go to work anyhow? What did it matter? What was this about a "dinner date?" He rolled the ball in a circle, plowing the snow with it, and when it was nearly the size of the first ball, he left it, and began another.

Taking two handfuls of snow, he packed them tight and added two more. To the east the sky was darkening. He dropped the ball in the snow, took off his gloves and wiped the sweat above his eyes. Directly overhead, the color was still gray. West, the color was gray. North and south, everywhere was gray. But the east was blackening. And the earth was white.

Boylston Street, Tremont Street, Park Street, Beacon Street, Charles Street: surrounding the Commons the city lights shone, illuminating the grayness, the color of the city.

He put on his gloves. Placing his hands back around the third ball, he rolled it around and around. Why was he working at the 7-Eleven? What would he do once his father died? How was Sandy Allen figuring in on this? Was he a writer? Did he want to be? What was he going to do with his life? What did he have to prove? He continued until the ball was a little bigger than a basketball. Then he stepped back to study the three big snowballs sitting like a father ball, a mother ball, and a baby ball. And then he felt a raindrop mixed with the snow, then another.

First he took back his coat from the biggest ball, and put it on. Then, squatting in front of the second ball, he lifted its base, carried it to the first ball, and placed it on top, twisting and pushing to make a stable fit. Then he quickly raised the third ball and jammed it securely on top of the second. Then he backed off and circled, looking closely from every angle, like a photographer, trying to make sense of this snowman without ears, eyes, nose, mouth, buttons, or hat. He studied him some more in the darkening twilight. What this snowman needed was not only a face, but also arms and legs, and a snowwoman and snowchildren. But he didn't have time. He stood there in front of him, looking for twigs or branches, something makeshift.

Then he remembered the carrots. Quickly, he took out his penknife, dug his glove into his pocket, came up with the carrots and began slicing, slivering, and chopping. With the ground snow swirling, the southeast wind blowing, a rain beginning, he gave the snowman orange eyebrows and orange eyes, an orange nose and orange mouth, a thin orange moustache, two orange ears, ten tiny orange fingers and ten tiny orange toes, a long orange penis and two carrot tops for testicles. That would do it, he thought. That would have to do it. The arms and legs would come soon enough. So would the snowwoman and snowchildren. He took one of the oranges out of his pocket, sliced it into quarters, and began to eat, savoring the juiciness, tearing into every last bit of pulp.

Who was he, he asked himself as he sucked all but the rind out of the last quarter. Who was Daniel Bart Pearson? He didn't know, but he knew that he was learning, and that was good. What should he do now? Call Sandy Allen? Call work? He stood behind the snowman, closed his eyes, breathed deeply, and put his hands to the snowman's head. Then he waited. In a minute, some lyrics of a folk song came to him, the beginning of a ballad Samantha used to sing:

> Two lovely sisters were a walking side by side
> Oh the wind and rain
> One pushed the other in the waters so deep
> And she cried a dreadful wind and rain
>
> She floated on down to the miller's mill pond
> Oh the wind and rain
> Father oh father there swims a swan
> And she cried a dreadful wind and rain

He tried remembering the rest of the words, but couldn't. It was Samantha's song. Samantha. He opened his eyes. It was getting dark. Only in the west was there the heavy gray. In the Commons it was raining, the wind was blowing, night was falling. He took off his cap, scarf, and coat, and dressed the snowman. He dug into the snowman's coat pocket, found an orange, and sliced it in half. He gave the snowman his half, setting it in his mouth. Then he began walking away, eating his half of the orange. The direction was southeast, toward Tremont Street, Boston Harbor, the nighttime darkness, the source of this changing weather.

More Decisions

The man and woman sit in the movie theater until the screen blackens, the soundtrack dies, the curtain closes, the overhead lights brighten. Most of the moviegoers have left. The rest, the ones who always linger until the final credit, are shuffling up the aisles. The man and woman are the last ones still sitting. The man is yawning, the woman stretching. Two boys in orange and blue vests are pushing up seats and collecting popcorn tubs.

"So," the man says.
"So," the woman says.
The man glances at his watch.
"What time is it?" she asks.
"Time? Time for one of these," he says, leaning to peck her cheek. Then, exaggerating a supreme effort, he struggles up. "And soon it'll be time for a drink. Maybe we can pick something up for dinner." He makes a clucking sound. "I was just thinking. That Greek restaurant's right down the road. We could do take-out. You know, a salad and one of those garlic pizzas. And maybe pick up a bottle of wine." He claps his hands. "Let's go. Get up. We gotta get moving."
"We need to talk," she says.
"In here? They got another show starting." He smiles. "I mean it was good, different, sure, a little weird, but you don't want to sit through it again, do you?"
She gives him a look. "You know what I mean."
"Do I?"
Shaking her head, she pushes out of her chair, then hurries up the aisle, across the lobby, and pulls open the glass. He is rushing behind her. As she strides down the sidewalk, off the curb, and to the car, he still follows a step and a half behind.

"Okay, you want to talk," he says.
"I'm driving," she says. "Get in."
"Goddamn sun," he says, lowering the flap over the windshield. "I can't see a thing." The first mile stretch has a number of traffic lights, and every other one is red. So much for synchronization, he thinks after the third red light. "There goes Leo's," he says out loud a minute later, pointing, as they speed through a green light. "Guess you didn't want to talk over Greek food." He coughs. "Or *about* Greek food." He coughs again, then clears his throat.
"So, honey, what's up?"
"Don't you 'honey' me?"
"Honey," he says.
"I said we need to talk," she says, flipping the turn signal up, then spinning the steering wheel right.
"About what? The movie? I already told you back there it was pretty good. It was different, okay? I'm glad we went. Does that say it? What else do you want to talk about it? Or do you want me to ask *you* how you liked the movie?" He waits a minute. "Well?"
"Ha."
"Could you repeat that?"
"Ha."
"Is that 'ha' as in funny? Or 'ha' as in funny I asked? Or are you getting at *how* I asked? You know, honey, you're getting to be a little difficult to read these days. Look, I may not be some super-genius film critic like that last boyfriend of yours, but I'm no idiot. If you want to say something, say it. I'm listening. Do you hear me?"
She flips the turn signal, this time as she switches lanes to enter the freeway ramp. The next minute she's yielding. Then she's merging all the way left.
"Honey," he says gently. "Are you feeling okay? Home's back there, the other way."
"Don't you patronize me."
He snaps his fingers. "Oh, I get it. You're thinking the barbecue place that's way out this side of town. Why are you al-

ways making me guess? I have nothing against the barbecue place. It just seems like such a funny night for it."
"Barbecue place?" she says. "What barbecue place? What are you talking about, goddamnit? I'm driving to Utah."
"Utah? You're driving to Utah? It's Sunday night. You can't be driving to Utah."
"You want to bet?"
"Utah's nine hundred miles from here."
"I know. We need to talk." She turns to look at him, then touches him lightly on the shoulder. "Take a quick nap. Or read me something from the paper." She brushes his neck with her fingertips. "Don't worry. I'm wide-awake. Just let me drive. We'll talk all night."
"Honey."
"Shhhhhhhhh, baby. Just look at that sunset."
And into the orange-red light, she aims toward the hay fields that rise from the Plains. Hundreds of miles further west, Utah, the dreamscape.

The Ice Age

The sun was gone and the moon cried tears that froze the ocean. The sun was gone and the moon cried tears that froze the wind. The sun was gone and the moon cried tears that froze the moonlight. For a long, long time ice laced the sky. On earth, all was ice and everything was still but for a red mountain that grew and grew. As the mountain grew taller, it cracked the sky's ice—and what didn't crack, melted. Growing even taller, the red mountain touched the crying moon.
    Don't cry, the mountain said. Don't cry.
    But the moon couldn't stop.
    I've come all this way because I love you, the mountain said. Please marry me, pretty moon. Please marry me.
    It was cold where the moon lived and her tears numbed the mountain's top.
    Please marry me, pretty moon. Please marry me.
    I'm married to winter, the moon said then.
    I love you, said the mountain.
    Winter loves me, said the moon.
    Marry me, said the mountain.
    Why should I? said the moon.
    If you don't, I'll have to kill you, said the mountain.
    Then kill me, said the moon.
    It will be painful, said the mountain. As I grow, I'll dig into your belly. My point is sharp. And I'll dig into you deeper and deeper until my tip will be in your heart.
    Everything is painful, said the moon.
    I don't want you to die, said the mountain.
    Then go somewhere else, said the moon.
    I can't, said the mountain. I'm already here. I love *you*. I want to marry *you*. Please marry me, pretty moon. Please marry me.

I can't, said the moon. I'm married to winter.
You can marry me, said the mountain. If you do, I promise miracles. We will grow tall together.
I can't marry you, said the moon.
Yes, you can, said the mountain. Open your mouth and bite off my top. Inside me's a star.
The moon turned.
A star, said the mountain. I'm going to give birth to a star. And I want you for my mate.
I'm married to winter, said the moon. And if you're ready to give birth, you must be married to winter too.
But I don't know winter, said the mountain.
Winter is everywhere, said the moon.
But I don't see winter, said the mountain.
Winter is everything, said the moon.
Open your mouth and bite, said the mountain.
Winter will kill us, said the moon.
My star is ready, said the mountain. Now bite.

Afterword

I'm writing this Afterword in spring 2025. The stories themselves feel both old and new though I "finished" this collection back in January 1990, a year I was living and teaching in Sitka, Alaska. That's more than 35 years ago! Back then this book was made up of 33 stories, so was a good bit longer. But the publisher, M. L. Lieber, and I have culled what we perceived as the weaker ones. Good for us.

I like how the stories link as a frame within a frame within a frame—an opening myth and closing myth, then a couple going into a movie theater for an indie movie about getting into some writer's head and leaving the theater afterward, then the stories themselves, which are "the movie," which begins with a troubled young man who wishes to write, and who falls asleep one night, and ends with the troubled young man waking and feeling something had "changed," the change being the dreams within, the stories he might someday write if he was indeed writing, was indeed a writer.

I still like the concept, and like how the "dream" stories mirror the young man's concerns, and especially like how the pair of stories with second-person point of view, "Swampland" and "Whitemarsh," are tied to one another, so there are further connections within the dream stories.

Maybe all this trickery is because I wrote most of these while in a graduate school creative writing program where I was writing papers on writers as diverse as Mario Vargas Llosa, Julio Cortazar, Milan Kundera, Raymond Carver, Ken Kesey, Henry Miller, Walt Whitman, and was just starting to read and write poems. I wrote the last of these stories a year and a half after I graduated. Three of these I wrote before entering the program. There's a copy of my MFA thesis somewhere in the University of Alaska Fairbanks library. It's on my list to go track it down and reread it one of my next times back in

Fairbanks. After all, I dedicated this to my younger self. Half of the stories have been published in reasonable journals. I stopped sending out the individual stories more than twenty years ago, except in rare circumstance. Still, every once in a while I'd go into the collection, decide whether another of the stories needed eliminating, and make small changes to the ones that remained. Every year or two I'd submit the collection to a contest or a small press—I always felt this manuscript had merit.

I'm so happy it's finally out in the world, approximately thirty-five years after "finishing." Like my *Now Entering Alaska Time* novel, it's from a pre-internet and pre-cell phone era.

I thank the publisher, Ridgeway Press, and thank all of you who have somehow found your way to this.

BIO

Ken Waldman has drawn on 40 years as an Alaska resident to produce poems, stories, and fiddle tunes that combine into a performance uniquely his. 12 CDs mix Appalachian-style string-band music with original poetry. 24 books include 17 full-length poetry collections, a memoir, 3 children's poetry books, a creative writing manual, a novel, and this short story collection. Since 1995 he's toured full-time, performing at leading festivals, concert series, arts centers, and clubs, including the Kennedy Center Millennium Stage, Dodge Poetry Festival, and Woodford Folk Festival (Queensland, Australia). For more about Ken Waldman, www.kenwaldman.com and www.trumpsonnets.com. And for more about Ridgeway Press, www.ridgewaypress.org.

Ken Waldman's Books

Modern Acrostics
Modern Acrostic for Adventurous Teens
Modern Acrostics for Younger Readers
Now Entering Alaska Time
The Writing Party
Sports Page
Trump Sonnets, Volume 8
Leftovers and Gravy
Trump Sonnets, Volume 7
Trump Sonnets, Volume 6
Trump Sonnets, Volume 5
Trump Sonnets, Volume 4
Trump Sonnets, Volume 3
Trump Sonnets, Volume 2
Trump Sonnets, Volume 1
D is For Dog Team
Are You Famous?
As the World Burns
Conditions and Cures
And Shadow Remained
The Secret Visitor's Guide
To Live on this Earth
Nome Poems